TREAD SOFTLY

BRIAN FLYNN was born in 1885 in Leyton, Essex. He won a scholarship to the City Of London School, and from there went into the civil service. In World War I he served as Special Constable on the Home Front, also teaching "Accountancy, Languages, Maths and Elocution to men, women, boys and girls" in the evenings, and acting in his spare time.

It was a seaside family holiday that inspired Brian Flynn to turn his hand to writing in the mid-twenties. Finding most mystery novels of the time "mediocre in the extreme", he decided to compose his own. Edith, the author's wife, encouraged its completion, and after a protracted period finding a publisher, it was eventually released in 1927 by John Hamilton in the UK and Macrae Smith in the U.S. as *The Billiard-Room Mystery*.

The author died in 1958. In all, he wrote and published 57 mysteries, the vast majority featuring the super-sleuth Antony Bathurst.

BRIAN FLYNN

TREAD SOFTLY

With an introduction by
Steve Barge

DEAN STREET PRESS

Published by Dean Street Press 2020

Copyright © 1937 Brian Flynn

Introduction © 2020 Steve Barge

All Rights Reserved

The right of Brian Flynn to be identified as the Author of the Work has been asserted by his estate in accordance with the Copyright, Designs and Patents Act 1988.

First published in 1937 by John Long

Cover by DSP

ISBN 978 1 913527 57 0

www.deanstreetpress.co.uk

INTRODUCTION

"I believe that the primary function of the mystery story is to entertain; to stimulate the imagination and even, at times, to supply humour. But it pleases the connoisseur most when it presents – and reveals – genuine mystery. To reach its full height, it has to offer an intellectual problem for the reader to consider, measure and solve."

BRIAN Flynn began his writing career with *The Billiard Room Mystery* in 1927, primarily at the prompting of his wife Edith who had grown tired of hearing him say he could write a better mystery novel than the ones he had been reading. Four more books followed under his original publisher, John Hamilton, before he moved to John Long, who would go on to publish the remaining forty-eight of his Anthony Bathurst mysteries, along with his three Sebastian Stole titles, released under the pseudonym Charles Wogan. Some of the early books were released in the US, and there were also a small number of translations of his mysteries into Swedish and German. In the article from which the above quote is taken, Brian also claims that there were French and Danish translations but to date, I have not found a single piece of evidence for their existence. Tracking down all of his books written in the original English has been challenging enough!

Reprints of Brian's books were rare. Four titles were released as paperbacks as part of John Long's Four Square Thriller range in the late 1930s, four more re-appeared during the war from Cherry Tree Books and Mellifont Press, albeit abridged by at least a third, and two others that I am aware of, *Such Bright Disguises* (1941) and *Reverse The Charges* (1943), received a paperback release as part of John Long's Pocket Edition range in the early 1950s – these were also possibly abridged, but only by about 10%. These were the exceptions, rather than the rule, however, and it was not until 2019, when Dean Street Press released his first ten titles, that his work was generally available again.

The question still persists as to why his work disappeared from the awareness of all but the most ardent collectors. As you may expect, when a title was only released once, back in the early 1930s, finding copies of the original text is not a straightforward matter – not even Brian's estate has a copy of every title. We are particularly grateful to one particular collector for providing *The Edge Of Terror*, Brian's first serial killer tale, in order for this next set of ten books to be republished without an obvious gap!

By the time Brian Flynn's eleventh novel, *The Padded Door* (1932), was published, he was producing a steady output of Anthony Bathurst mysteries, averaging about two books a year. While this may seem to be a rapid output, it is actually fairly average for a crime writer of the time. Some writers vastly exceeded this – in the same period of time that it took Brian to have ten books published, John Street, under his pseudonyms John Rhode and Miles Burton published twenty-eight!

In this period, in 1934 to be precise, an additional book was published, *Tragedy At Trinket*. It is a schoolboy mystery, set at Trinket, "one of the two finest schools in England – in the world!" combining the tale of Trinket's attempts to redeem itself in the field of schoolboy cricket alongside the apparently accidental death by drowning of one of the masters. It was published by Thomas Nelson and Sons, rather than John Long, and was the only title published under his own name not to feature Bathurst. It is unlikely, however, that this was an attempt to break away from his sleuth, given that the hero of this tale is Maurice Otho Folliott, a schoolboy who just happens to be Bathurst's nephew and is desperate to emulate his uncle! It is an odd book, with a significant proportion of the tale dedicated to the tribulations of the cricket team, but Brian does an admirable job of weaving an actual death into a genre that was generally concerned with misunderstandings and schoolboy pranks.

Not being in the top tier of writers, at least in terms of public awareness, reviews of Brian's work seem to have been rare, but when they did occur, there were mostly positive. A reviewer in the Sunday Times enthused over *The Edge Of Terror* (1932), describing it as "an enjoyable thriller in Mr. Flynn's best manner" and Torquemada in the *Observer* says that *Fear and Trembling* (1936) "gripped my interest on a sleepless night and held it to the end". Even Dorothy L. Sayers, a fairly unforgiving reviewer at times, had positive things to say in the *Sunday Times* about *The Case For The Purple Calf* (1934) ("contains some ingenuities") and *The Horn* (1934) ("good old-fashioned melodrama . . . not without movement") although she did take exception to Brian's writing style. Milward Kennedy was similarly disdainful, although Kennedy, a crime writer himself, criticising a style of writing might well be considered the pot calling the kettle black. He was impressed, however, with the originality of *Tread Softly* (1937).

It is quite possible that Brian's harshest critic, though, was himself. In *The Crime Book Magazine* he wrote about the current output of detective fiction: "I delight in the dazzling erudition that has come to grace and decorate the craft of the 'roman policier'. He then goes on to say: "At the same time, however, I feel my own comparative unworthiness for the fire and burden of the competition." Such a feeling may well be the reason why he never made significant inroads into the social side of crime-writing, such as the Detection Club or the Crime Writers' Association. Thankfully, he uses this sense of unworthiness as inspiration, concluding: "The stars, though, have always been the most desired of all goals, so I allow exultation and determination to take the place of that but temporary dismay."

Reviews, both external and internal, thankfully had no noticeable effect on Brian's writing. What is noticeable about his work is how he shifts from style to style from each book. While all the books from this period remain classic whodunits, the style shifts from courtroom drama to gothic darkness, from plotting serial killers to events that spiral out of control, with Anthony Bathurst the constant thread tying everything together.

We find some books narrated by a Watson-esque character, although a different character each time. Occasionally Bathurst himself will provide a chapter or two to explain things either that the narrator wasn't present for or just didn't understand. Bathurst doesn't always have a Watson character to tell his stories, however, so other books are in the third person – as some of Bathurst's adventures are not tied to a single location, this is often the case in these tales.

One element that does become more common throughout books eleven to twenty is the presence of Chief Detective Inspector Andrew MacMorran. While MacMorran gets a name check from as early as *The Mystery Of The Peacock's Eye* (1928), his actual appearances in the early books are few and far between, with others such as Inspector Baddeley (*The Billiard Room Mystery* (1927), *The Creeping Jenny Mystery* (1929)) providing the necessary police presence. As the series progresses, the author settled more and more on a regular showing from the police. It still isn't always the case – in some books, Bathurst is investigating undercover and hence by himself, and in a few others, various police Inspectors appear, notably the return of the aforementioned Baddeley in *The Fortescue Candle* (1936). As the series progresses from *The Padded Door* (1932), Inspector MacMorran becomes more and more of a fixture at Scotland Yard for Bathurst.

One particular trait of the Bathurst series is the continuity therein. While the series can be read out of order, there is a sense of what has gone before. While not to the extent of, say, E.R. Punshon's Bobby Owen books, or Christopher Bush's Ludovic Travers mysteries, there is a clear sense of what has gone before. Side characters from books reappear, either by name or in physical appearances – Bathurst is often engaged on a case by people he has helped previously. Bathurst's friendship with MacMorran develops over the books from a respectful partnership to the point where MacMorran can express his exasperation with Bathurst's annoying habits rather vocally. Other characters appear and develop too, for example Helen Repton, but she is, alas, a story for another day.

The other sign of continuity is Bathurst's habit of name-dropping previous cases, names that were given to them by Bathurst's "chronicler". *Fear and Trembling* mentions no less than five separate cases, with one, *The Sussex Cuckoo* (1935), getting two mentions. These may seem like little more than adverts for those titles, old-time product placement if you will – "you've handled this affair about as brainily as I handled 'The Fortescue Candle'", for example – but they do actually make sense in regard to what has gone before, given how long it took Bathurst to see the light in each particular case. Contrast this to the reference to Christie's *Murder On The Orient Express* in *Cards On The Table*, which not only gives away the ending but contradicts Poirot's actions at the dénouement.

> "For my own detective, Anthony Lotherington Bathurst, I have endeavoured to place him in the true Holmes tradition. It is not for me to say whether my efforts have failed or whether I have been successful."

Brian Flynn seemed determined to keep Bathurst's background devoid of detail – I set out in the last set of introductions the minimal facts that we are provided with: primarily that he went to public school and Oxford University, can play virtually every sport under the sun and had a bad first relationship and has seemingly sworn off women since. Of course, the detective's history is something not often bothered with by crime fiction writers, but this usually occurs with older sleuths who have lived life, so to speak. *Cold Evil* (1938), the twenty-first Bathurst mystery, finally pins down Bathurst's age, and we find that in *The Billiard Room Mystery*, his first outing, he was a fresh-faced Bright Young Thing of twenty-two. So how he can survive with his own rooms, at least two servants, and no noticeable source of income remains a mystery. One can also ask at what point in his life he travelled the world, as he has, at least, been to Bangkok at some point. It is, perhaps, best not to analyse Bathurst's past too carefully . . .

> "Judging from the correspondence my books have excited it seems I have managed to achieve some measure of success for my faithful readers comprise a circle in which high dignitaries of the Church rub shoulders with their brothers and sisters of the common touch."

For someone who wrote to entertain, such correspondence would have delighted Brian, and I wish he were around to see how many people enjoyed the first set of reprints of his work. His family are delighted with the reactions that people have passed on, and I hope that this set of books will delight just as much.

Tread Softly (1937)

"Had I the heavens' embroidered cloths,
Enwrought with golden and silver light,
The blue and the dim and the dark cloths
Of night and light and the half-light,
I would spread the cloths under your feet:
But I, being poor, have only my dreams;
I have spread my dreams under your feet;
Tread softly because you tread on my dreams."

Aedh Wishes For The Cloth Of Heaven, W.B. Yeats

IT IS rare that a murder mystery can be considered to have a unique plot. There are certain books that have a unique idea in them, such as the rationale for the murder weapon in Ellery Queen's *The Tragedy of Y*, but such books are few and far between. There are books that are ground-breaking, certainly, such as Agatha Christie's *And Then There Were None*, but these have spawned a number of imitations. But due to its obscurity, *Tread Softly* (1937), the twentieth Anthony Bathurst mystery, has to the best of my knowledge, never been imitated and, again as far as I am aware, has a truly unique plot.

The less said about the plot the better, so the reader may enjoy it unspoiled, but it centres on a courtroom drama concerning the murder of Claude Merivale's wife. Merivale turned himself in, claiming that he was dreaming of fighting off a group of people and, in his semi-conscious state, turned to his wife sleeping next to her and strangled her. The legal situation is simple – if he is lying, he is guilty of murder; if he is telling the truth, he is innocent, as committing a crime requires some element of intent to cause harm. Inspector MacMorran is convinced Merivale is a murderer and asks Anthony Bathurst to help send him to the gallows.

Brian Flynn's primary writing strength is in his plotting and humour, but *Tread Softly* demonstrates a real skill in crafting characters. In the build-up to the trial, we see a number of letters revealing the inner thoughts of characters related to the plot, and a fair amount of insight into Merivale's mind without ever tipping the reader off about what is going on. The highlight is a chapter that details the thoughts of the jury as we move from juror to juror as the verdict approaches, an utterly charming section that nicely ratchets up the tension in a crucial point in the tale.

If you will forgive a personal indulgence, *Tread Softly* is the book that you have to thank for this series of reprints of Brian Flynn's works. It was *The Mystery Of The Peacock's Eye* (1928) that first convinced me that Brian Flynn was worth keeping an eye on, but it was *Tread Softly*, the third or fourth of his books that I tracked down, that truly began the obsession that led to finding all the other books, ultimately for them to be reprinted. I believe that this is the masterpiece that Brian should be remembered for, and I do hope you enjoy it too.

Steve Barge

CHAPTER I
Mr. Bathurst Didactic

Chief Inspector MacMorran thrust his hands into his pockets and shook his head dubiously. Anthony Bathurst smiled. MacMorran went on with what he had been saying.

"But the defence that he's putting up is so extraordinary. You admitted as much yourself just now. I've been in the force for over twenty years—twenty-two to be exact—and I've never heard of such a thing before." MacMorran tossed his head impatiently.

"That may be," said Anthony, "but you can't dismiss it solely on those grounds. Think of all the other things of which you've never heard. Good Lord, Andrew, have a heart."

Again MacMorran shook his head.

"That's all very well, Mr. Bathurst, but let's get down to brass tacks. This man Merivale, *admits* that he killed his wife. Makes no bones about it whatever. Confesses that he strangled her. But he says that he was fast asleep at the time that he was doing it. That all he did, he did in a dream."

Anthony bit at the stem of his pipe.

"H'm. Something novel here, I agree. Does he amplify his story in any way?"

"Yes. That's the devil of it. Merivale says that he can remember almost the whole of his dream. Says that he dreamt he was being attacked by a number of people. They fought him. He defended himself by fighting them. All very natural. In the struggle he turned to the sleeping woman at his side, seized her by the throat and strangled her! In a state of what he describes as semi-conscious unconsciousness. There you are—that's the defence! And when the man came to us in the first place I'd have sworn that he hadn't a leg to stand on."

Anthony lit his pipe and spoke through the flame.

"I don't want to put the wind up you, Mac, knowing your nervous and sensitive disposition as I do, but if you ask me, you're properly up against it."

MacMorran's face was set and immovable. Although to a certain extent he had been prepared for what Anthony had just said.

Anthony went on:

"If that defence is going to be fortified by a strong medical testimony, and you can bet your bottom dollar that it *will* be, I question whether the Crown has little more than a dog's chance of getting a verdict."

MacMorran nodded gloomily at Mr. Bathurst's prognostication.

"I know. That's really the reason why I came here to talk things over with you. They're putting up Campbell Patrick."

"Worse than ever. You're like that celluloid cat in Hades. You haven't an earthly. Patrick's hot. You don't need me to tell you that. Irish brain and Irish tongue. That's a combination, Andrew, that takes a deal of beating. I bet he jumped at the brief. If you ask me, Master Claude Merivale will leave the New Bailey a free man."

"Aye. To marry again, I suppose, and have more wives and more dreams! If you ask me, that's an attractive proposition for a civilized country to contemplate. Well I'm blessed. I could almost say that I'm surprised at you."

Anthony shrugged his shoulders. "Can't help it, Mac. Don't blame me. I'm simply telling you what I think is going to happen. At the same time, though—" he paused.

"What?" demanded MacMorran suspiciously. Anthony replied slowly and deliberately.

"At the same time, there is just the odd chance that Merivale's story may be the truth. It would be wrong of us to shut our eyes to the possibility." He walked to his bookcase.

"If he does get away with it, Mr. Bathurst, think what it means. Do you understand my meaning?"

"Only too well. You mean that only about two and a half per cent of married women will be safe o' nights. Isn't that the idea?"

"Aye. That's just what I do mean. It'll become the new fashion. Man—it's a terrible thought!"

"Don't see why you need worry. You aren't in any danger. But let's have a look here. I want to refresh my mind about something."

Mr. Bathurst turned the pages of his "Black."

"Here we are. I'll read it to you. 'A wakeful memory and imagination may be associated with wakefulness of the motor portion of the brain, as when the person dreams that he is making desperate efforts to achieve some object or to escape pursuit, and his limbs go through movements associated with the ideas projected in his dream. Dreaming is really a form of partial insomnia and is to be similarly treated.'"

Anthony replaced the book in the bookcase and turned again to MacMorran.

"Suffering cats, MacMorran, but I can hear Campbell Patrick for the defence already. What jam for him! You are most certainly up against it."

MacMorran made a sign of doleful acquiescence. Anthony repeated words. "'His limbs go through movements associated with the ideas presented in his dream.' Have you taken all that in? It's pretty comprehensive, you know. Take a deuce of a lot of shifting—that will. Still, let's have a look at the case from the other points of view. What I'll call the *usual* points of view. Motive! What can you tell me about motive, Andrew? Is there anything to work on there?"

Anthony smoked steadily as MacMorran marshalled his facts.

"Well, it's a rare case, Mr. Bathurst, all the way through, as you verra well know. In the first place, this man Merivale gave himself up. Came down to the Yard and volunteered the full story to us—that he'd strangled his wife. Which, I'm afraid, is Point No. 1 in his favour," concluded MacMorran lugubriously.

"Hold there a minute. Don't know that I agree with you," returned Anthony Bathurst. "Seems to me that *that* action *might* all be part of a carefully calculated plan. For instance, as I see things, if this man, Claude Merivale, *did* murder his wife from deliberate intention, and thought things out very carefully beforehand, this 'dream defence' business and so on, the giving himself up voluntarily, together with the telling of a frank story, would also be a part of his plan." Anthony nodded as though reassuring himself of the soundness of his own theory. "Yes—I think that that is most certainly indicated and that your contention is destroyed. You *can't* put it down as Point No. 1 in his favour. No, sir! It's as much against him, to my mind, as it is for him. Go on, though, I can bear to hear a great deal more."

"Well, his story was investigated. Naturally. It was found to be true. The facts of the case which we could check up were exactly as he had stated. Mrs. Merivale was found dead in bed. Strangled! Merivale had come to the Yard as soon as day had broken. We found that the bedroom door was locked. He had locked it, he told us, when he had come out to walk to the Yard. He handed in the key and we used it to open the door when we went down to look at things. Everything that we found in the house confirmed the man's story."

"And you accepted it?"

"Of course we accepted it. What do you mean by that? Why should we have done anything else?"

"Did he tell the 'dream' story at once? When he first reported that his wife was dead? Tell me—I'm interested."

"Almost at once. Let me put it like this. Then you'll understand me clearly. He finished up his statement with regard to the murder with this yarn about his dream."

"There was no appreciable interval between the first statement that he had killed his wife and the putting up of the 'dream' defence? As though, for instance, the latter might have been an afterthought?"

"Oh—no. Nothing like that."

Anthony nodded. "Now I'll tell you something."

"I've no doubt you will," replied the Inspector drily. "I never knew you when you couldn't."

Anthony grinned.

"Listen, you ancient ruin. I'm going to tell you something that you aren't going to like. I'll detail for you the things you haven't done that you ought to have done. The stones you have left unturned that you should have turned. The avenues you have left unexplored that you ought to have explored."

MacMorran wrinkled his face.

"Oh—I dare say. But, man, look here—" Anthony waved a deprecating hand.

"Wait. Otherwise—patience. I'm helping—not hindering. Here they are."

Anthony ticked the points off on the fingers of his left hand with the stem of his pipe.

"One—you didn't trouble to ask the police doctor how long the woman had been dead. Reason—he told you that she had died of strangulation just as Merivale had said and for which crime he had surrendered himself to you, and you were content with the statement. In other words, the exact time of her death didn't arise. Two—you took no particularly careful steps to find out what Merivale had done *after* murdering his wife and *before* coming along to the Yard. Reason—the same—it didn't arise. It wasn't an ordinary murder investigation. Your work had been done for you—the murderer was in your hands. There was no problem upon which your brains were required to work. Three—you didn't realize the strength of the defence until some time had elapsed. Reason—it was psychological, not of the 'earth—earthy'—and therefore away from the ordinary routine matters of the Yard. Now, Andrew, I asked you something a few moments ago. And you haven't yet answered. Motive! How do you go with regard to motive? Because it's going to count a lot, see?"

MacMorran took his time over replying.

"The motive that the Crown will use will be one of the oldest of all motives. The triangle."

"Neither isosceles nor scalene, I presume?"

"Neither. The Crown will try to show that Mrs. Merivale had a lover. That Claude Merivale discovered her infidelity and as a result took this means of adjusting matters."

"Where's the house?"

"St. John's Wood. Enthoven Terrace. Not over far from Lord's Cricket Ground."

"What is Claude Merivale?"

"Profession?"

"Yes."

"Stage and screen. Does a bit on each of 'em. Been fairly successful on the whole. Not actually dependent on either for a living. Which has probably helped him. Private income left him by his mother. Father's money in the first place, but both mother and father dead. Well-educated bloke. Forest School and Keble College, Oxford."

"Good-looker, I suppose?"

"Very," returned MacMorran emphatically. "Tall, dark and handsome."

"Your chance of hanging him grows less and less, Andrew. Think what an attractive personality he'll make in the dock. His looks, added to the novelty of his defence. All the young women on the jury will be for an acquittal right from the beginning of the trial."

"Seems to me, then, that we might as well go along now and let him out," remarked the Inspector with a touch of asperity. "Judging by the way that you're talking."

"When's the trial?"

"Three weeks to-morrow."

"Who's the doctor? The man that Campbell Patrick will call for the defence on the dream question."

"Gaskell. Quinton Gaskell."

"Is he, by Jove? The neurologist? I can see what's coming. You'll have to rub up your Freud, Andrew. Tie a towel round your head and get right down to it. Otherwise you'll be in for a sultry passage."

"I'm rubbin' up nothing. Why should I? After all, it's not as though I'd arrested the man on suspicion. He asked for accommodation in a cell—and he got it. Who could have foreseen that he'd scream a defence of this kind?"

Anthony smiled at MacMorran's discomfiture. "Only Freud himself, probably. And it's lucky for you that they can't call him as a witness."

The Inspector looked a little scared. Anthony Bathurst put the results of his further meditation into words.

"You see, Andrew, you've no accumulative evidence that you can put before the jury to help you. None at all."

"How do you mean, exactly?"

"Why, in this way. Take the case of George Joseph Smith. Of 'Brides in the Bath' ill-fame! Do you think that any jury would have found him guilty if he had been tried for the murder of Margaret Lofty without any reference to the deaths of Bessie Mundy and Alice Burnham? No, Andrew! It was the treble that did it. Three wives. Three baths. Three insurance policies. Three illnesses. Three visits to the three doctors. Three faints in the bath. Three relishes for supper for George Joseph to purchase when he waited for the water to run over. Three *Nearer my Gods to Thee* on the harmonium before he betrayed his anxiety. Three of everything. See what I mean? You've nothing of that, you know. Merivale hasn't had three strangling dreams. He's only had one. Which is going to make all the difference to the case, sonny boy."

MacMorran rubbed his nose. Then Anthony continued:

"Remember the words of W.B. Yeats: 'But I, being poor, have only my dreams. I had spread my dreams under your feet. Tread softly because you tread on my dreams.' And that's what you have to do if you want to convict Merivale. Tread softly! Not only on Claude Merivale's dream but all the way through your case. I'll give you that piece of advice, Andrew, free, gratis, and for nothing."

The inspector grunted non-committally. Anthony had another question. "What was Mrs. Merivale like? Attractive?"

Again the Inspector nodded assent.

"An unusually beautiful woman, I should say. Merivale met her when he was playing at Oxford. She was a professional."

Anthony whistled.

"O.U.D.S., eh? Well, I can understand that. I met a girl there once in similar circumstances. Glad I didn't marry her because I'm inclined to dream myself on alternative Mondays. A man never knows his luck, does he, Andrew?"

"No, never, Mr. Bathurst. You've been pretty destructive all the way through—do you think you could put in a little bit of constructive criticism? If you were in my shoes, now, what would you do yourself?"

Anthony parried the question. By the simple method of asking another of the Inspector.

"Tell me, Andrew. Do you want to hang Merivale for the murder of Mrs. Merivale or will another body do for you?"

"Another? How do you mean? There are times when you talk—"

Anthony grinned again.

"I know. I agree with you entirely. Worse than that, even. But think again over the question that I asked you."

"I want to hang the woman's murderer." MacMorran spoke doggedly. "Merivale's the man. Therefore to me they're one and the same. Claude Merivale's confessed that he did it. The 'dream' business is all poppycock. And it's up to the Crown to prove as much. That's how I see things."

"Men have confessed before to crimes that they haven't committed. I could quote you a dozen cases. You know that as well as I do."

"Not like this one," defended MacMorran sturdily.

"This is a cut-and-dried case, if ever I saw one. And if you won't help me—well, then, I shall have to take steps to help myself."

Chief-Inspector Andrew MacMorran seemed a trifle disgruntled. Anthony reassured him.

"I'll help you, Mac, all right. That is to say, I'll look into one or two things for you. But not necessarily, mind you, from the point of view of hanging Merivale. I'm not starting with that object definitely in view. As I said, there may be more truth in his 'dream' stunt than meets the eye. That's all! Once again, Andrew, take my advice—tread softly!" Anthony knocked out the dottle from his pipe. Then he continued—as MacMorran seemed inclined to silence. He quoted Havelock Ellis in his essay on St. Francis: " 'Our feet cling to the earth, and it is well that we should learn to grip it closely and nakedly. But the earth beneath us is not all of nature; there are instincts within us that lead elsewhere, and it is part of the art of living, to use naturally all those instincts.' Is there any essential difference between a dream, using the word to convey the ordinarily accepted meaning, that is to say something which comes to us in our nightly sleep, and a day dream? A dream need not be a nightmare. And if there are good dreams—then also we must envisage the possibility of there being bad dreams. Now where are we, Inspector?" MacMorran shook his head.

"Don't know. Couldn't say. When you talk in that strain you travel too far for me. What do you want me to do? If you let me know, I'll arrange matters and the necessary steps that you desire to be taken. But remember, you've only got three weeks in which to do the job."

Anthony smiled at him.

"Twenty-two days, Andrew. Why rob me of one, you cheeseparing Scot? Don't make matters worse than they are. Tell me. More questions. Has Merivale any children?"

"Yes. A boy and a girl. Too young to have anything to do with the case. About nine and eight respectively. Each at boarding-school. The girl in Sussex—the boy in Hampshire."

"His parents are not living, you said, didn't you?"

"Both dead. Years ago."

"What servants are there in the house in Enthoven Terrace?"

"One, a maid. Eva Lamb. Been with the Merivale's some years."

"She would be the only person, I take it, living in the house with the Merivales. Is that correct?"

"That is."

"Spoken to her. About the case?"

MacMorran shifted uneasily in his seat.

"Er . . . yes . . . I've had words with the girl."

"What did she have to tell you? I'm interested." Anthony eyed the Inspector with some curiosity. "Nothing much. Of any importance, that is."

"You say that the Crown's case is a lover and Mrs. Merivale's infidelity. Did you sound this girl, Lamb, in that direction?"

"Aye." Anthony noted the curtness of the reply. He followed up. "Any luck?"

"No. At any rate, the girl knew nothing definite. Unless, of course, and I'm quite prepared to believe it, she was shielding her mistress. Keeping something up her sleeve. She's been with her a long time, remember."

Anthony pulled at his top lip.

"Still, you got nowhere with her. That's what happened, isn't it? Come on, Andrew, own up."

MacMorran argued.

"Well . . . as a matter of fact, I was handicapped."

"Why? How were you handicapped? You interest me still more, Mac. Tell me more of this little Lamb."

"Oh . . . it was nothing . . . much . . . don't get all hot and bothered about it. An excessively simple matter. Just this. Eva Lamb couldn't tell me anything of her mistress's movements on the night of the murder. That's where I ran up against a bit of a barrier. Nothing in it. It was just a piece of rank bad luck. You see—it was Eva's evening out and sometimes when Eva had an evening out, as a special concession to her, she used to sleep at her mother's house in Poplar."

Anthony stared at him as though at a temporary loss for words. Eventually he found them.

"So it was little Eva's evening out, was it? Oh . . . Andrew MacMorran . . . I wonder! I most certainly wonder! What happened while little Eva was out to make Claude Merivale dream so terribly?" His grey eyes looked into the distance. MacMorran watched him, and then, slowly shook his head.

"There you go again! Imagining things!"

Anthony Lotherington Bathurst made no reply.

CHAPTER II
Eva Lamb Epistolary

The following is the substance of a letter written by Eva Lamb to her mother, Mrs. Clara Lamb, of 18 Bath St., Poplar. It was the longest letter that she had ever penned, or, for that matter, is ever likely to pen.

22 Enthoven Terrace,
St. John's Wood.

Dear Mums,

Oh, Mums dear, I hardly know how to start this letter to you. I don't really. I'm not sure whether I'm standing on my head or my heels, as the saying is. Now don't you go and get worried, dear, and bring on your neuritis because it's nothing to do with me or Rose or even young Albert. Now you can set your mind at rest more comfortable like and read on. Oh, Mums, the Pictures ain't in it—really they ain't. Not even the most horrable ones. Well, you know how I left you yesterday morning to get back here in time for my morning's work after my evening out, all merry and bright, and pleased about young Albert having had the shilling a week rise from the firm before the year was up, well when I got to the address as above, my heart went as cold as a stone and my flesh all goosey—because when I got to the door a copper was standing there, as large as life, and I could see at once from his face that something was up! Oh, Mums, I can't tell you how I felt. Not if I live to be as old as that man in the Bible, Mepistofelees. It was as though something had twisted inside me all of a sudden. Awful! He came up to me—the copper I mean—and I told him who I was and what I wanted there, and then I heard the dreadful news. And what do you think it was? The master, Mr. Merivale, had strangled the mistress during the night! With his own hands. At least that was the story what was told to me by this copper. Strangled her dead. "Gertcher," I says to the copper—"tell me another one, 'oo's leg are you pulling? Mr. Merivale is a gentleman, well-dressed and well-spoken and without a false tooth in his head, and his wife's a lady. Both of 'em right out of the top drawer, and no mistake. I tell you—at once—I don't believe it, not for a single blessed instant." "Well, my gal," he says saucy-like, "whether you believe it or not, it's true. Mrs. Merivale's corpse has just gone down to the morchary and your guv'nor, Mr. Merivale, is in our hands." "Coo," I says, "fancy your little self, don't you? Your hands indeed. If that's so, I reckon he must have give himself up! That's a cert if ever there was one."

You should have seen the look on his face when I cracked that at him. Anyhow, Mums dear, although I just can't believe it, it's as true as true can be, and here I am all alone in a house of death. Every half-hour I come over all creepy and gooseflesh. Other police have been here poking their noses round the place, as you may well guess, but they haven't made Eva Lamb open her mouth too wide. They don't know poor Dad was a hairdresser. Oh, no? I'm loyall. Right through. Especially to the hands what have fed me! And I don't believe he killed her! No—not if old Musserlini hisself flew over here and swore to it! The master and the missus was not of the bickering sort. Leastways, I never heard nothing going on between them, and if I didn't, who could have done? And no girl could have had a better place. I'll say so! When I think—of the things that I have heard from other girls about other places—and what they have to put up with—well, Mr. and Mrs. Merivale was two of the best. I couldn't say better than that for anybody could I, not even if they was my own flesh and blood? When I think of them two poor little mites away at school all them miles away in the country, not knowing a blind word of what's happened to their Dad and Mum it gets me right down, and I could fair howl my eyes out. Not that that would do 'em any good, of course. I only mention it to show how my feelings are. As you know, I've always been a girl to feel for others. No uncles, no aunts, no grandparents, who knows what will become of the poor dears with their mum lying dead and cold and their father to be hanged by the neck until he is dead and his body buried within the presinks of the prison, whatever they may be, as I've often wondered when having heard the frase used, or read it on Sunday in the "News of the World." Isn't it too awful when you think of how things work out in this world, with no rhyme or reason as you might say, as I can show you when I say that it was my evening out, as you know yourself, and that if I had been in and not out perhaps what worked up to the tragedy would never have transpired, but you never know. Mrs. Merivale was ever so keen on me always having the evenings as they became due to me, and on this occasion she wouldn't hear of fur not having it because she hadn't been too well in herself the last few days, and I'd offered to fourgo it on that account, and have it some time later on, when she was better. But "no, Eva," she said, "you go. You've worked hard while I've been poorly and haven't complained at a bit more to do—and the time's rightly yours and dew to you. So you take it and don't mind me, because I shall be all right." Funny they should be the last words that I should ever hear her say with her own lips, ain't it, Mum? Who knows, perhaps if I'd stopped in the house that evening, and hadn't come to you, I might have prevented whatever it was what caused all the trouble and she might be alive and well as we are today. Because you never know, do you? But there you are, you can't foursee these things, and God don't mean you to, if you could people wouldn't go nowhere or do nothing, and now she's dead, and all the talking in the world won't bring her back, will it? Oh— something I forgot to tell you, Mums, my pictures been took for some of the daily papers. A nice young fellow came down the other day and asked for me, and took it for the Aggalmated Press, I fancy he said it was. Anyway, his name was Horace, which was good enough for me, and for anybody else, I should think. You never thought as how you'd see your Eva's picture in the daily papers, now, did you? It'll be either next Friday or Saturday, so the young chap told me, so you'd better order half a dozen copies in advance from old Matterface, and tell the old rat the reason why you want them, and send one to Uncle Will in Canada and another one to Aunt Mary Ann down in Sussex. It ought to be a bit of a leg up for them being relations of mine whose got mixed up in a famous case like this, because I don't suppose it's ever happened to one of the family before. Maybe Uncle Will wont have his nose in the air quite so much now, which he never ought to have had by right, seeing he was only the boy at Hagmire's the pork butchers when he started out in life and before he got into the iron-mongery, as I've heard Dad tell him many a time when they was talking man to man like. Well, Mums dear, I must close now as it's nearly time for the post to go at the piller-box round the corner, give my love to

Rose and young Albert and tell him to be a good boy and not spend the bit of money he'll get extra of a week on fags and pictures but put some by for a rainy day, which comes to us all sooner or later when God wills, and heaps of love for yourself, dear Mums, as well. Hoping you're all well as it leaves me at present, your loving daughter, Eva xxxxxxxx Will write again direckly I have more news to send you xxxx, Eva.

The following is a copy of a second letter written by Eva Lamb to her mother, Mrs. Lamb, some time subsequently to the writing of the first letter. It will be seen therefrom that Eva has by this time attracted some little attention in other directions than the official Police and Press photographers. As, of course, might well have been expected. Here is the letter.

22 Enthoven Terrace,
St. John's Wood.

Dear Mums,

Thank you ever so much for your letter, Mums, in reply to mine and I can't say how welcome it was and all, seeing all that's taken place since I last wrote you. As you know no doubt from the "News of the World" on Sundays poor Mr Merivale comes up for his trial in less than three weeks time, and I hope and pray that if only for the sake of them two little kids down there in the country that he ain't brought in guilty. Because if he is it'll be too awful for words and I can't bear to think of it and I haven't slept for nights, it's been on my mind so. But I've one ray of hope, as you might say, like a little candle shining in the night, as you used to teach me to say when I was a little girl going to bed, and that's because another gentleman's been here making all sorts of inquiries about the master and mistress and me and my being out that evening when the dreadful thing happened. When I told him how poor Mrs. Merivale what's dead and buried now, but of course no stone up yet, and perhaps never will be, seeing what's likely to follow in the near future, which I think's a crying shame about the stone, I mean, had insisted upon my having my evening off although she hadn't been well herself just before that, he was most considerate to me. Most—and said what a good kind lady he could see she was and what a lot she must have thought of me. His name's Bathurst—or something like that—and oh—such a gentleman, you wouldn't beleeve, in every way you could think of. And such perfect manners. *Really beautiful. As good as Ronald Colman and Herbert Marshall themselves. Well, this gentleman had several little chats with me while he was looking round the place, and between you and I and the gatepost, Mums, he isn't altogether satisfied with things as they are and has hinted more than once to me, darkly—like, that there's a good deal more in the case than meets the eye. Fancy that. And* what *do you think he arsked me? Mums, you'd never guess not if you kept on guessing till next August Bank Holiday. Honestly you wouldn't. He asked me if Mrs. Merivale had a lover. It fair took my breath away. The police had hinted it but this gentleman acktewally said as much in plain words. I said no she hadn't, she wasn't that kind of lady, the idea, and that she loved her husband far too much to go in for anything of that kind, and then he said did any gentleman ever come to the house when I was there, and I said that the police had already cast asturtians in this way and I had said "nothing of the kind" to them and I still said "nothing of the kind" to him as he asked me at that moment. He was all smiles and affable like and said as how he didn't mind in the least what I said as long as it was true and all above board, which was all he wanted me to tell him. Well, Mums, to cut a long story short and to get to the 'osses, as Dad used to say, this gentleman had showed the policeman what was on duty here a card with something written on it, and the policeman let him go all over the house and see everything that he wanted to see, so that proves he must be somebody high up in the Cabinet or on the County Council or something like that, otherwise he would never have been aloud to have gone on as he did, now would he? espechally when you think how careful the police are when a murder's been done as I know from seeing them on the pictures at least half a dozen times. When nothing whatever must be touched in case of finger-prince, or things like that. This Mr. Bathurst or whatever his name was asked me some more questions about a snapshot of the master and mistress which he found in one of her drawers of the dressing-table in the bedroom which must have been taken on their honeymoon, I should think from looking at it since they're both sitting by the sea in deck chairs and both looking as happy as happy can be, and the master must have been gorgeous looking when he was younger even better than he is now, which is saying a lot. Mrs. Merivale must have treasured it ever so because she'd never shown it to me and she used to show me most things of hers as I can tell you, and as you know full well. Well, Mums, everything comes to an end, both good and bad, as the tin-can said when the boys tied it on to the dog's tail, and once again I must close this letter to you because if I don't hurry up and get a move on I shan't catch the post and if I miss this one there isn't another until to-morrow morning, and you won't get it until to-morrow night and I know you'll be expecting it first post to-morrow morning. Give my love to them all, Mums dear. Rose and young Albert and Mrs. Cupper at the ham and beef shop in Chrisp St. and take a whole heap for yourself, hoping that you are well as it leaves me at present, your loving daughter, Eva xxxxxxxx*

P.S. If the worst happens at the Trial, which God forbid, I shall of course come home for good until I can get another place. Miss Merivale, that's poor Mr. Merivale's sister—she's lovely she is—has promised to do her best for me with splendid references, because she says she knows a good and reliable girl when she sees one meaning me your Eva, which is very nice of her, isn't it? Good night, Mums. Keep your pecker up and don't worry and don't trouble trouble till trouble troubles you.

CHAPTER III
Mr. Bathurst Progressive

"So you reckon you've got something, eh? Trust you! I might have known that would happen when I suggested you should take a look at things." Inspector MacMorran's eyes glinted humorously, but with a shade of admiration.

"Don't smother yourself with optimism, Andrew. And don't forget, also, that I'm not in the case for the one purpose of hanging Claude Merivale. I think that you're inclined to overlook the fact. I'm in for Justice, St. Denis, and the King of France and as for rebellious Burgundy—"

"Eh? Hold on! I haven't a lot of time to waste. When you're in that mood of yours and try to put over that play-actin' stuff there's never any knowing when you'll stop. Pack it up and tell me what it is that you've fastened on to."

Anthony lit a cigarette. He blew out the match before he answered the Inspector's question.

"Three things. Three things at the moment. One—the question of the marks on Mrs. Merivale's throat. She was strangled, you know. Two—a photograph that I discovered in Mrs. Merivale's bedroom, and three—Claude Merivale's tie. The tie that he wore when he surrendered to the police, and the tie, the same tie, my dear Inspector, that I presume he is still wearing in the cold comfort of his prison cell. There may be one or two other matters to which I shall give some little attention before long but these three top the bill for the nonce. Notice the expression, Andrew, genuine old English meaning 'for the nonce,' that is to say, for that time only. All the same, do you know my greatest regret?"

MacMorran shook his head in hopeless resignation.

"I know a good many of 'em. I'm not sure of the greatest. Tell me and I'll tell the missus to-night at supper. She'll always listen to gossip about the famous."

Anthony grinned at the sally.

"That I wasn't in the room with your people when Merivale came in and gave himself up as a lamb to the slaughter. If I had been, I could tell you for certain now whether his story were true or not. At least I think I could."

"Go on! Now that's a pity! Next time I get a case like it I'll ring you up and invite you down for the initiation ceremony. Then all the problems that come to us will be stone-gingers."

"Don't try to be funny. It doesn't suit you. Listen. Come back to those three matters that I mentioned to you just now. For the time being, I'm going to deal with only one of 'em. That of the marks on Mrs. Merivale's throat. I'll deal with the other two later. By the way, it's clearly indicated that I must see Claude Merivale himself with regard to his tie and the colour of that tie and I'm seeing a Miss Jill Merivale, that's Claude Merivale's sister, of whose existence, let me tell you, Andrew, you didn't inform me—concerning the photograph. The photograph has two deck chairs showing in it. The chairs are by the sea. You know—threepence a time. But I'm not sure at which of our appalling, rain-infested watering places (happy word, that, Mac.) the snap was taken. I am inclined to consider this photograph important—but 'nous verrons.' That brings us back to the marks on Mrs. Merivale's throat. I want you to read this. I got it yesterday." Anthony foraged in his pocket for a letter. The letter found, he took it from its envelope and tossed it to the Inspector for his perusal. It read as follows:

88 Harpole St.,
London, W.1.

My dear Bathurst,

Salaam! At the request of Sir Austin Kemble, the Commissioner of Police, supported, I believe, by your own august request, I have examined the body of the late Mrs. Merivale. I have seen also the report of Doctor Moxom, the police doctor who performed the autopsy in the first instance. I may as well tell you that I asked to see it. The following are my observations. The skin of the throat showed considerable signs of bruising (external) round the trachea. So much so, that I would give it as my opinion that the woman was strangled by the pressure of two thumbs, one pressed hard against each side of the trachea. Your suggestion that identification of the finger-marks round the throat might be possible is, I regret to say, untenable. The bruises and marks generally are much too indistinct and blurred for anything of this kind to be considered as a practicable possibility. I should say from the condition of the body token I saw it, that Mrs. Merivale died not very long after midnight. I am sorry that I have not been able to be of greater assistance to you and feel like weeping scalding tears on that account.

If it is likely to be of any use to you, however, I will pass on two more pieces of information that I was able to pick up as the result of my examination. Perhaps information isn't the best word for me to use, because strictly speaking it applies to only one of my points. Which is this. There isn't the slightest doubt that Mrs. Merivale, before retiring that night had applied a face-cream to her face and neck. I am able to make this statement with absolute certainty. That it was one of the better known cosmetics, I should assert quite confidently. Very likely "Ponds." There you have the piece of information which I promised to you. Point No. 2 is this. In my opinion—opinion merely, mark you—the person who strangled Mrs. Merivale wore gloves when he did the job. Had you considered the idea yourself? If you put this up to Scotland Yard I'm very much afraid that you will be laughed at for your pains. I'll tell you why. On the left hand side of Mrs. Merivale's throat was a long scratch. In the circumstances, obviously, nine people out of ten would say "caused by a finger or thumb nail." I suppose, too,—I may as well admit it frankly—that those nine people would be right. Nevertheless from the condition of the other marks on the throat and the condition of the flesh generally I think that the murderer wore gloves. You see, despite the scratch, I still think so! Reads a bit Irish, doesn't it? But it's none the worse for being that. Kind regards to yourself and Mrs. Folliott (it's years since I saw her) and always yours, my dear chap, Robert Doyle.

Inspector MacMorran read the letter from Dr. Doyle in the way that he read everything, carefully, slowly and deliberately. When he had finished he looked across at Anthony Bathurst. The later spoke first.

"That pleases you, doesn't it? Should do, considering all that you've said to me on the case. Your wish has always been father to your thought."

MacMorran wrinkled his nose.

"How do you mean exactly? Seems to me that it gets me nowhere at all. Nowhere definite, that is. Sort of contradictory—and when I meet plain contradiction in a problem of this kind, I'm far from being pleased—let me tell you. You should know that."

"Think, Andrew, think. You should sometimes, you know. Accept for the moment that Dr. Doyle's theory of the murderer's gloves is a sound one. Never mind for the time being whether you agree with him or not. As a layman, whatever opinion you may have on that particular point can't be worth over much against his. Now where are we?"

MacMorran shook his head. Anthony helped him out.

"You want to upset Claude Merivale's 'dream' defence, don't you, and put the rope round his neck? I'm not blaming you. You do so, because, rightly or wrongly, you are convinced in your own mind that Merivale murdered his wife in a fit of jealousy and hatched up this defence as an afterthought. That's true of you, isn't it? Own up, Mac!"

"Yes, I suppose you can put it that way."

"Well, then, a man who dreams he is being attacked, and, in his dream, tries to save himself from his enemies, doesn't walk in his sleep, go downstairs and put his gloves on, does he?"

MacMorran rubbed his hands as he took in Anthony's point.

"I should say not."

"Well, there you are then. On a plate for you with oyster sauce as a garnish."

"Yes—that's all against Master Merivale. I can see that. If we can prove this glove business. It depends on that."

"Dreams, Andrew, are supposed to come through one of two gates—the Ivory Gate or the Gate of Horn. Those which delude us and trick our senses, pass through the Ivory Gate. Those which come true, come through the Gate of Horn. Sir Thomas Browne wrote: 'Sick men's dreams. Dreams out of the Ivory Gate and visions before midnight.' Remember how Anchises, 'the *old* Anchises,' Andrew, dismissed Aeneas through the ivory gate, when quitting the infernal regions, as an indication of the unreality of his vision, or have you completely forgotten your Virgil?"

MacMorran grinned. Secretly, he enjoyed Anthony pulling his leg.

"I reckon I've forgotten it. That'll do, anyway. You got a fat lot of Virgil at the school in Glasgow where I went."

Anthony went back to business.

"Dr. Doyle again. And let me tell you that Bob Doyle's the goods. Don't have two ideas on that. I'd take his opinion before almost anybody's. Bob Doyle's mistakes—that I've ever come across—could be counted on the fingers of one hand."

The Inspector stroked his chin and murmured suitably. Anthony came at him again.

"How does Dr. Moxom's report compare generally with what Dr. Doyle says in this letter to me?"

MacMorran considered the question.

"Well . . . barring the gloves . . . he agrees pretty well with your doctor chap. Especially about the thumb marks."

"Did he mention the fact of the cream on Mrs. Merivale's face. If he did, you didn't tell me about it."

MacMorran looked at Anthony impatiently.

"Lord, man, what was there about a woman mucking her face up when she went to bed that needed talking about? He would have more like mentioned it if she hadn't. Thank God, my missus doesn't do such a thing. She *dare* not."

Anthony smiled.

"I am not the man to come between husband and wife. It's against the great Bathurst tradition. Far from it, and heaven forbid. So Moxom did mention it, eh?"

"Yes. It's all there in his report."

"Good. That strengthens Doyle's position, then. If you can prove that Merivale wore gloves, if you can *find* that pair of murdering gloves, you've got him in the hollow of your MacMorran hand. From which no criminal ever escapes. I'm telling you, Andrew."

"You're tellin' me!" The Inspector radiated indignation and disgust. "When are you seeing this other woman that you mentioned? This Miss Merivale? About the photograph that you've found?"

"Tomorrow, I hope. She lives at Kingston-on-Thames. As the Western Brothers would say, 'Up the Casuals.' I hope to hear from her by to-morrow morning fixing an appointment with me. I'm afraid that there's a lot of work to be done before we see the last of this case." Anthony's eyes twinkled. "And, as usual, I expect you'll leave me to do the greater part of it."

MacMorran's face twisted. "That's good organizin' and don't you forget it. Puttin' the work out and all that. That's what they made me a Chief Inspector for."

"Thanks for letting me know. Because, to tell you the truth, I've often wondered."

"If you didn't wonder about that you'd have been wondering about something else. So it makes no odds. But just a minute." Anthony saw that MacMorran was thinking hard.

"What's the matter with you now, Andrew?"

"There's something I ought to tell you. Your reading that letter from that doctor friend of yours has brought it to my mind."

"What's this you've got for me now? More important information that you've kept up your sleeve? You're incorrigible. You don't mean giving me an even break. Come on. Out with it, Andrew."

"It's to do with that nail-scratch we were talking about. On the left-hand side of the woman's throat."

Anthony immediately showed interest.

"Oh—what about it? Did Doctor Moxom make any special reference to it?"

MacMorran shook his head.

"Not that exactly. That isn't what I meant. He saw it, of course, and commented on it. You couldn't help seeing it. Nobody could very well have missed it. No. My remarks are concerning Claude Merivale himself."

Anthony's interest increased. He knew from MacMorran's tone that the Inspector was feeling pleased with himself.

"Come on, Andrew. Spill it."

"Well, I've been thinking—Merivale not only drew our attention to the scratch but he showed us also how it had been caused. I don't know quite what to make of it."

Anthony looked at him curiously.

"What's that? Oh, Mac, this gets better and better! So Merivale showed you the scratch, did he?"

"From your point of view, perhaps it does improve. But yours isn't the only one. What I'm going to say's this. Claude Merivale had a torn finger-nail and he showed us how he had come to scratch his wife's throat. Nothing much in it, I suppose."

"Which hand?"

"The right hand, of course."

"Which finger?"

MacMorran thought over the question.

"That wants a bit of thinkin' about. Now let me see. The second finger. The longest finger. Yes—that's right. I remember now that he held it out for us to look at. The second finger-nail was jagged and broken."

Anthony looked puzzled. He walked over to the Inspector and eyed him whimsically.

"Let me experiment with you for a second, Andrew. I don't get this at all."

He stretched out his hands and pressed a thumb either side of MacMorran's wind-pipe.

"Some job to scratch the throat with the nail of the second finger. Isn't it? The nails of each hand are near the cheek. Look here." He suited the action to the words. "No. I don't get the idea at all."

He released his hands and walked away thoughtfully. MacMorran made his collar more comfortable with his finger and straightened his tie.

"That's only based on your Doctor Doyle's theory," he said with unusual meekness. Anthony turned on him in a flash.

"No. You can't have that. Your Moxom said the same thing as my Doyle. You admitted as much just now. Thumbs, Andrew, thumbs."

MacMorran looked uncomfortable under Anthony's criticism.

"Yes. So he did. I remember now. My mind went astray for the minute."

"Well, then, that's my point in a nutshell. Where does the scratch come in? I've just demonstrated to you that it doesn't fit in properly."

MacMorran rose.

"Well, the days are going by, one by one, and we don't seem to be making a lot of progress. Either for proving our man guilty or not guilty." He walked right up to Anthony Bathurst. "Tell me," he said, looking at him resolutely, "do you believe that there's any truth in this dream business. Candidly now?"

"Candidly, Andrew," returned Mr. Bathurst—"I don't! You see—I can't forget two things. Dr. Doyle's gloves . . . and the strange way death may come to any one of us. Aeschylus, for instance, was killed by the fall of a tortoise from the claws of an eagle in the air, on to his bald head. See Valerius Maximus, Andrew, for verification, and also our old friend Pliny."

MacMorran shook his head. "I shan't. I'll take your word for it."

CHAPTER IV
Jill Merivale Perturbed

The following letter was written by Jill Merivale, sister of the accused Claude Merivale, to an old school-fellow of hers now married and living with her husband at Helston in Cornwall, a Mrs. Grace Onslow, affectionately termed from the beginning of her school days as "Taddie."

8 Broderick Avenue,
Kingston-on-Thames, Surrey.

Dear Taddie,
I cannot thank you enough for your sweet letter. It was ever so appreciated by me. If, and when, this dreadful trouble

passes, I most certainly shall come down to the West Country, take advantage of your so generous invitation and stay with you. Thank George for me, too. But before that can happen, there is much to be faced and gone through. How one's personal horizon can change in the twinkling of an eye, as it were! Last week—and now this! I won't weary you, Taddie, with vague opinions of my own as to what may, or may not happen to Claude. Or will I attempt to conjecture what may, or may not have happened on the dreadful evening when the ghastly business started. It would be a shame to spoil all the charm and beauty of your home in the West Country, "the first and the best country," by stories of wretchedness and evil or by mere suggestions as to the causes of Vera's death and my poor brother's brainstorm. For brainstorm it must have been, I feel absolutely certain. A lot of the things that you wrote to me in your letter were lovely and I can't tell you how much I appreciate them but I expect that you put them in to cheer me up and comfort me. It's just the sort of thing you would do because it's just the sort of thing that you've always done—ever since I've known you. Do you remember how we sat in the dormitory at Ravenswood the first night we ever met, and you confided all your hopes and fears to me and I whispered to you of all my ambitions and desires. Just two silly things together dreaming of the future. Happy days, Taddie, and days that will never come again! To me, that is, at least. Ah well, it's not a bit of good "reminiscing" and being sentimental over what's gone and will never come back. Life, as it's lived now, has no time for these things. It's relentless towards them, and we are all, I suppose, made to toe the line, one by one, even though the lines may be different. The gods seem to keep us, I think, on a chain, and it's only the length of the chain that differs. Some are longer than others. You ask me in your letter if I have any more news—and you obviously mean have I any more good— or shall we say—"better" news. You mean about poor Claude. It's a funny answer to give you, Taddie, but I don't know. I'm just clinging to a hope of a sort. A hope that has appeared absolutely "out of the blue." Now—listen! Who do you think called here yesterday? Oh—I was expecting him all right, so it wasn't anything in the way of a surprise for me. Because he had written to me and asked for an appointment. Anthony Bathurst! Yes, the Anthony Bathurst of the famous crime investigations. Until I heard from him, asking me to make the appointment with him, I hadn't the slightest idea that he was interested in my brother's case. It has seemed so horribly clear and all such plain sailing that one hasn't imagined that anybody would take the trouble to investigate it. There seemed no real reason why anybody should. But it appears that Anthony Bathurst has been round to poor Claude's place, at the request of the police or something, and had what they call a look round there. There's nothing in that, of course—it might be just routine—but while he was there, he happened to come across a photo of Vera and Claude taken at the seaside somewhere. Not a real photo—just one of those silly seaside snaps that you see about everywhere. Claude and Vera are sitting in deck-chairs looking at the sea. The chairs are close to the sea. It's awfully good of Vera and you can see it's Claude all right. There's no mistaking the line of his jaw and that profile of his. I mention these points with a reason, as you'll see later on. Well, it appears that Anthony Bathurst's chief point in bringing it here to me was to ask me how long ago it had been taken and to ask me, too, if I could tell him where the place was. He said he had half a theory lurking at the back of his brain and thought perhaps if I could answer these two questions, the answers that I gave might really help him. You know what these seaside snaps are—the places all look alike—sea and shore and sand and pier and deck-chairs and promenade, and all the "seasidey" things that we know so well. Well, I looked carefully and thought things over and I said that I thought it must have been taken three summers ago at Worthing. They were at Brighton, you know, about a fortnight before you and George were married—in the July—and it looked to me like Worthing—where they could have easily spent a day from Brighton—shingle beach and solitary pier and the parade close to the water and that elephant shaped dome at the beginning of the pier where the concerts are held and where all the people run when it rains. I told Anthony Bathurst this, as I said, and he thanked me. "Worthing—three summers ago," he said. "I see. Thank you, Miss Merivale." He's a perfectly charming man, let me tell you, Taddie, and I'd love you to meet him. Now for my surprise. A surprise to him, to me, myself, and I know it will be to you when you hear it. I looked at the snap again, more curiously than anything else, I think, to see what Vera was wearing. I recognized the dress immediately. It was the one she bought in Paris when she and Claude went over there for that French picture he was in. You remember it—you liked it, and said how well it suited her. But that's not the point I'm after. I looked at Claude just casually. I looked at the chair in which he was sitting. Remember—for no real reason! I looked at these things. And, do you know, Taddie, a most curious idea struck me! . . . An idea that wouldn't have struck anybody else in the world, now that Vera's gone. She and I would be the only two people who would have known and understood the point—that was interesting me so. You see—I've sat with Claude hundreds of times in deck-chairs. Right from the days when we went to the seaside together as kids with Daddy and Mother. And I've never sat with him unless he had his deck-chair right down to the very last groove at the back. You know what I mean. The seating part of the chair as near to the ground as possible, so that he was able to lie right back. I've been with him, as I said, hundreds of times and I've always— without exception—seen him lower his chair in this way. I've heard him say, too, every time that he sat down in one, that he positively couldn't sit in a deck-chair for a second unless it were lowered like this. I knew this trait in him so well that I regarded it as almost an obsession. Used to tease him about it sometimes. When I tell you, Taddie, that my brother Claude, in this snapshot that Mr. Bathurst showed me, was sitting in a deck-chair, arranged in the top groove, I could hardly believe my eyes. I simply stared and stared and stared. Then the fun started, of course. Anthony Bathurst saw me staring at the photograph, and I suppose that he saw something in my eyes, too, that looked like incredulity. So he pounced on me. With-

out mercy. "What's the point, Miss Merivale? What have you seen here that puzzles you? For I can see that there's something." What could I say to him, Taddie, that wouldn't sound incredibly foolish? Imagine it for yourself. I looked like a silly owl, and stuttered—"the chair. The chair. The deck-chair." His reply almost staggered me. "Miss Merivale," he said ever so quietly, "do you remember that case of the master Holmes, which figures in his adventures under the title of The Speckled Band? *A bad case—sinister and bizarre. But I believe I am right in saying that the first clue came to the great detective from a terror-stricken girl who cried out to him these strange words, 'the band, the band, the speckled-band.' Your recent remark about the chair reminded me very forcibly of that."*

"Did it?" I replied weakly. "Yes," he returned, "and I'm wondering whether it will prove as valuable a clue to me as it did to him." I gasped, Taddie. Why? Well, I hardly know. I think, only think, mind you, *that it flashed into my mind that the clue on which he appeared to be hopeful of "building so much" was after all so very fragile and insignificant that to almost anybody except me, it would have been too ridiculous to mention. "Well," he said, half-smiling at me, "aren't you going to tell me all about it."*

Well, Taddie, the long and the short of it was, of course, that I told him all that had just passed through my mind—feeling all sorts of a fool as I did so. What else could I do? To my utter surprise, my statement seemed to make a tremendous impression on him. Really it did! As I made the various points to him, one by one, he would say "yes, yes," or "I agree with you," and when I finished the yarn he said: "Miss Merivale, I can't tell you how much you have interested me, and also how much you have helped me. I regard it as a most important and significant factor in the case. It's the little, apparently trivial personal matters that always count in cases of this kind, and this that you have told me about, is most certainly one of that sort." Then he went across to where I had placed it and looked at the photograph again most carefully. Took it to the light where he could see all the points of it, most clearly. Then,

Taddie, he brought it back to me. "Is the man sitting in this deck-chair absolutely like your brother, Miss Merivale? I mean is the likeness to him unmistakable?" "Mr. Bathurst," I replied, "I feel certain that it is my brother. Beyond the shadow of a doubt. I know that what I've told you about the deck-chair has made you doubtful and sent your mind running about in other directions—but you must forget about it, if it's going to make you believe that this is not Claude who's sitting here but somebody else. You can't mistake that jaw. And that nose. It's the Sanders's nose. From mother it comes—you should have seen Grandma Sanders. You'd never have forgotten her. And the profile generally. I know his face far too well to harbour any doubt about it. You see—I can't have you deceiving yourself all because of that deck-chair incident. Claude's my only brother, you know!" He smiled at my eagerness. How shall I describe it! A really charming sort of pitying, sympathetic smile. As though nobody could feel more deeply for me in my trouble or could be more desirous to help me. "I won't deceive myself," he said. "Don't worry about that. Even though I may be deceived. Even though you may be deceived. Sometimes when the solution of a dark difficulty seems farthest away from us there it is all the time to our hands, ready for us to see it and to take it to ourselves in comfort. It may be so in this instance, Miss Merivale. One never can tell. What puzzles you now and doesn't puzzle me, may, ere long, be plain to you but dark and obscure to me. The scene changes and the conditions with it. But, out of the reactions of the two of us, the truth may suddenly come and be understood by the two of us."

Soon after that he left me. I think that he left me chiefly wondering. Comforted, though, as well. He said before he went that he would probably come to see me again. When he comes, he will, I expect, find me still wondering.

Well, Taddie, dear, I've written you a dreadfully long letter and I do hope that you have had the patience to wade through it all and that it hasn't actually bored you. The outlook for us is terrible at the moment and I dare not dwell for a minute on what the immediate future may have in store for me. If it be true that the darkest hour is the one which precedes the dawn, well then, the dawn must be very close at hand; for I can't remember an hour in all my life which was quite as black as the one through which I am now living—or better still—trying to live.

Give my kindest regards to your adoring George, and with heaps of love to yourself, my dear loyal Taddie,

I remain, yours affectionately,

Jill.

P.S. Write soon! Your letters do more towards cheering me up than anything else in the world. This isn't flattery—it's the sheerest truth. Also, I need your prayers.

Mrs. Onslow received the letter, read it carefully twice and then took it to her husband who read it less carefully but with a great deal of interest.

"Funny thing, that," he commented, "about the deck-chair business. Don't quite know what to make of it. 'Straordinary thing!"

Mr. Onslow handed the letter back. He thought for a moment or so, scratched his head, and then repeated his previous statement.

"'Straordinary thing."

His wife shook her pretty head. She was without the power of dismissing such a momentous letter with such a brief opinion. She watched her husband rise from the breakfast-table and make his way into the garden. As far as he was concerned the cloud that hung over Jill Merivale was non-existent. He filled his pipe and proceeded to his vegetable garden. The damned black fly were getting at his beloved broad beans. Blast the black fly!

CHAPTER V
Claude Merivale Defensive

Sir Austin Kemble, Commissioner of Police, held consultations and conferences with Chief-Inspector Andrew MacMorran. The

Inspector put certain aspects of the Merivale case to him. The Commissioner was rather more impatient than usual.

"Surely the case is cut-and-dried, MacMorran," he said testily, "if ever a case were. I don't see why I should do any of the things that you suggest."

The Inspector proceeded to make his position more clear to the Commissioner. To his credit, let it be said, Sir Austin Kemble listened with a greater grace.

"You went along to Bathurst, you say?"

"Yes, Sir Austin. I wanted to talk matters over with him. I felt that I should. As you know, sir, this defence that the prisoner has put up has rather taken the wind out of our sails. It's off the beaten track. As Mr. Bathurst pointed out to me, the position resolves itself into this."

MacMorran, greatly daring, recapitulated Anthony's views, as they had been expressed to him. As he listened, the Commissioner frowned more than once.

"Well, MacMorran, look here," he said at length, "if it's your wish, I'll fall in with the idea. I see your point, and also the force of what Bathurst has said to you. It certainly would be better from the Yard's point of view to dig out the truth of the case, rather than go hot and strong for Merivale's conviction, if there's just a shade of a chance that he's not the man. I don't want the Crown to lose another case. I'll get permission for you and Bathurst to see him tomorrow. I can arrange that almost at once, I've no doubt. Get me put through to Major Gregory, will you?"

MacMorran obeyed silently. For once at least he had had his way.

When Anthony Bathurst and the Inspector were shown into a bare-looking room of uninviting aspect they were accompanied by Major Gregory himself. The last named briefly outlined the situation as it had been presented to him by Sir Austin Kemble. A few minutes later and the accused man was seated in the same apartment, the length of a table between him and his visitors. Anthony saw that MacMorran's estimate of his comeliness had by no means been exaggerated. His hair was very dark, his features clear cut, his eyes expressive and his whole appearance both pleasing and distinguished. Anthony noted the nose inherited, as he had so recently been informed, from Grandma Sanders. Immediately Merivale expressed himself as entirely willing to answer any questions that his visitors might desire to put to him.

"I suppose that I am allowed to have my solicitor present, but I'm quite willing to waive that. I have nothing whatever to hide. It makes an enormous difference to a man when he can feel that."

Anthony watched him as he spoke and he quickly formed the opinion that Merivale had recently passed, despite any protestations that he might make to the contrary, through the stress of a terrific and devastating emotion. Claude Merivale rattled on. But his voice was high-pitched, and there was an edge to it that was disturbing. The man's nerves were frayed—beyond the shadow of a doubt.

"I find your visit surprising, but extremely welcome. When Major Gregory asked me if I would talk to you, I consented at once. Cell life is monotonous beyond words. One has so little to do, other than thinking and writing. For myself, I fear that I shall soon become a victim of 'Scrivener's Palsy.' My hand and fingers ache more, I think, on each succeeding day."

MacMorran spoke to Major Gregory. The latter listened and then nodded. Anthony was given a free hand. If Claude Merivale had been anticipating a series of questions concerning the science, or otherwise, of dreams, Mr. Bathurst's first question must have come in the nature of a decided shock to him.

"How many years ago is it, Mr. Merivale, since you were at Worthing with your wife? Can you remember?"

Claude Merivale stared at him as though he had taken leave of his senses. There was a long pause. The silence was intense. Anthony waited patiently for Merivale's reply. Nobody within the room made a sign. The engine of a train whistled at no great distance away. Merivale at length came to the point of answering.

"I don't think that I understand you. The question surprised me. I have never been to Worthing with my . . . with Mrs. Merivale."

Anthony questioned him again immediately.

"Never? You're positive on the point."

Merivale's lip curled.

"Why, naturally I am! A man doesn't forget the places he's visited, does he?" A spot of colour showed in Merivale's cheeks, and his eyes flashed with a hint of anger.

"I had a reason for asking you. An excellent reason. You will see what I mean if you look at this." Anthony's hand went to his pocket and he produced the photograph which he had previously shown to Merivale's sister. He handed it down the table to Claude Merivale and again watched the man with the closest of scrutinies. Merivale took the photograph almost fearfully. The spot of colour that had shown, disappeared and his face took on an ashen pallor, as he looked at the photograph. His lips parted twice as though speech were coming before words actually were ready.

"Oh . . . this," he laughed almost hysterically. "You've made a mistake, and your mistake has caused me, perhaps, to give you a wrong impression. This isn't Worthing, you know. That's how you had me wondering. Although I admit it's like it very much from the view. No. This is a little place on the Belgian coast. Near Heyst. We went there for a day some years ago. Mrs. Merivale and I. Charming little spot. I forget the name. Something like Frenkel. It isn't too well known to the ordinary tourist crowds. You can find it on some maps."

He stopped suddenly as though he had made an effort which had seriously taxed his strength.

"Thank you," returned Anthony Bathurst. "That information will assist me materially to clear up a little matter that has rather puzzled me. Frenkel, you say, on the Belgian coast? I must remember that. Now I wonder whether you would be good enough to answer me another question."

"I don't mind in the least. As I said, I have nothing to conceal. I am simply the victim of a most terrible misfortune. A scurvy trick of Fate. Ask me whatever you like."

"After you woke on the night of your tragedy, Mr. Merivale, what did you do? I mean when you came out of your dream. First of all?"

The answer came, prompt and controlled. "I tried to revive my wife. Clumsily, perhaps, but in the best way that I could think of in the circumstances. I was almost beside myself. Frantic. I tried to give her as much air as I could. Loosened the neck of her pyjama jacket. I did all these things until I realized that they were all no good. Then I stopped."

"It didn't occur to you to send for a doctor, I suppose?"

"It did. Of course it did. That was one of the first things that I thought of. But, to me, as I saw things then, with my wife lying there either dead or unconscious, *haste* and *immediate action* were indicated. I mean that I felt I couldn't risk the delay which trying to get a doctor to come along, would have inevitably meant. I'm afraid that it sounds unconvincing now, and that it's difficult for you to understand, but I'm telling you the absolute truth."

"What happened after that? When you realized that your wife was dead? Past help."

"I sat on the edge of the bed with my head in my hands. I was beaten. Done. I felt dreadful. As though all my life had been drained from me and that I was on the point of fainting. I don't know how long I sat there like that but it seemed an age. Then I decided to dress myself and give myself up to the police. Tell them the whole story. Not to the first dunderheaded policeman whom I might chance to meet, but to go to Scotland Yard as soon as it was light, and make a clean breast of everything. I couldn't stand the idea of making my ghastly announcement to an open-mouthed bobby in the open street. Felt that when I did do it, I must do it in private and under cover."

"Did you have any breakfast before you went out?" Anthony put the question quite simply.

"Good Lord—no! You don't think that I felt like eating, do you?"

"I can well understand that you didn't—if you tell me so." Anthony half-smiled sympathetically. "But tell me this, Mr.

Merivale—I'm trying to reconstruct the situation as you say it was—did you shave?"

"No, of course not. I didn't think of doing such a thing. I can honestly say that it never entered my mind."

"Did you wash yourself? Did you have a bath?"

Merivale stared down the table at him—almost wonderingly. On this occasion, as with the query about the deck-chair photograph, there seemed to be a slight hesitation accompanying his answer. Anthony felt certain, as he waited for him, that the man was deliberating in his mind as to the exact terms of the reply which he was about to give. Eventually that reply came.

"No. I didn't even remember to do such an essential thing as either of those. But don't you see—it all goes to show what my state of mind was like. I suppose that I didn't really know what I was doing. All I could think of at the time was that I had had a dreadful dream and killed my wife. Until a person has been in my position he has no idea of the terrible emotions through which he passes. That's all I can say in defence of, or to explain, these apparently peculiar actions of mine."

Merivale stopped abruptly and his jaw set.

"I see." Anthony looked at Inspector MacMorran. The latter nodded. Anthony took his cue.

"This is a strange case. Very different from the ordinary. It may be said to fall into a category that is entirely its own. I question whether there has ever been one like it before. When you came in that evening, Mr. Merivale, did you take your gloves up to the bedroom?"

Merivale stared. But he paled again.

"Certainly not. What on earth gives you the idea that I did?"

Anthony ignored the counter question.

"When you dressed yourself, you put on, I take it, the very same clothes that you had taken off when you retired to bed on the previous evening."

"Yes. Of course I did. It was my easiest course. They were all, more or less, ready to hand. I had not been out to dinner anywhere specially that previous evening. I'd dined at my club. I often do. I had worn this lounge suit that you see me wearing now. It was there in the bedroom where I had taken it off when I went to bed. Conveniently to hand. I put it on again. Don't think from what I have just said that I *considered* the question of what I should wear. I didn't. Again—it never entered my head. The suit and the other things were close at hand. I dressed myself in them because they were there. That's all that there was to it."

"Are you inclined to have violent dreams? Habitually?"

"I dream a lot. I always have—ever since I can remember. Habit, I suppose. Not bad dreams—in, the sense of nightmares, that is. I think dreams have helped me in my career. I think that they're a sort of guard against despair. You know what I mean. Inspirers of a quality that is akin to hope. Isn't there a prayer or a hymn somewhere with a line, 'Holy dreams and hopes attend us.' I seem to remember having heard it somewhere. Dreams give us a peep behind the scenes, giving us an assurance that though *here* we may see as through a glass darkly, *there* we shall see face to face."

Anthony was impressed by Merivale's voice, and also by the expression in his eyes. It seemed to him, as he looked, that Merivale had drawn aside a veil and shown him something behind that veil that was deeply spiritual. That he had fled incontinently from the area of ordinary obligations that beset him and steadfastly climbed the Hill Beautiful, the picture of which was eternally mirrored in his soul. But Anthony resolved, to put a further question to him. He *must* come back to the commonplace.

"When you left your house in Enthoven Terrace that morning, to go down to Scotland Yard, I understand that you locked the bedroom door behind you and took the key away with you. Is that right?"

"Yes. Quite right."

"What was the reason for your doing that? Would you mind telling me?"

"So that nobody should go into the room and see my wife . . . lying there dead. I felt that I *must* keep the sight of it all, away from everybody. Just for a few minutes I felt panicky. Came near to losing my head completely."

"But who could possibly have entered the house and seen it?" Mr. Bathurst pressed him quietly. Merivale gave no answer. Anthony thereupon came in with a further question. "Who *could* have got into the house? Who could have *admitted* anybody to the house? There was nobody on the premises." A look of annoyance passed over Merivale's handsome face. "The maid had had the previous evening off. She might have returned during my absence and gone to my wife's bedroom."

"But I understand that you surrendered yourself to the police in the early hours of the morning. Was it the practice of this maid of yours to return to your house as early as that?"

"The time of her return varied. You could never tell when she would come in. I have known her come back very early in the morning."

"As early as your going out on this particular morning?"

"Well—no, perhaps . . . not quite as early as this was. But, remember, I wasn't in the mood to work everything out to an exactitude. I thought of her being out and possibly returning."

"Yes. I can understand that. Now one last question, Mr. Merivale, and then I won't trouble you any more. What time was it when you came in on the previous evening?"

Merivale shook his head. "I don't see what that has to do with the case at all. It hasn't the slightest bearing on it as far as I can see."

"My dear sir," returned Anthony Bathurst gently, "who can tell the texture of the stuff that dreams are made on? Who of us knows the real cause of the dream which you say came to you during the night? *Any* fact may be of assistance to us in our efforts to reach the truth and to promote the cause of justice. I am here to help you . . . if I possibly can."

"Very well, then," conceded Merivale, with a shrug of the shoulders, "have it your way. I left the Catena Club at eleven o'clock. I arrived home about half-past eleven. A little before that, if anything—let me think—say about eleven-twenty-two. That ought to be fairly exact."

Anthony made a note of the time in his note-book. "Thank you. I don't think that I want to ask you anything more. Thank you for answering my questions. Allow me to express my sympathy with you." He turned to the others. "And thank you, gentlemen, for your infinite courtesy and patience."

Some moments afterwards, Anthony spoke to Major Gregory in his private room.

"One of the most remarkable cases, sir, with which I have ever come in contact. I fancy, that before we see the back of it, we shall run against a good many obstacles. What has his behaviour been like since he's been here?"

"Oh—very *good*! Exemplary. I've nothing to complain about in that respect. I should say that the man's passed through a terrible experience. If you know what I mean—I think that he's still a bit dazed or 'muzzy' on account of what he's gone through. You can detect it in many little ways and mannerisms. No doubt he murdered the woman in a fit of temper, or jealousy, saw red just for a fatal second or so—and, ever since it happened has shrivelled in Hades over it. I guess that's about the size of it."

When Anthony and Inspector MacMorran left the prison the former was silent for a long time. When he eventually broke his silence, there was the gleam in his grey eyes which betokened to the Inspector the fact that Mr. Bathurst was well satisfied with things as they had turned out.

"Andrew," he said whimsically, "here's something that I counsel you never to forget. That The Now is an atom of sand, and the Near is a perishing clod. But afar is a Faery land. And Beyond is the bosom of God.'"

"As though I'd ever be likely to be forgettin' it," returned MacMorran. "I tell ye I've lived a godly, righteous and sober life, I have, ever since I left my mother's knee. Even though it's pleased the Almighty to set me down beside crime and criminals."

"Present company excepted, I presume," quoth Anthony.

CHAPTER VI
Peter Hesketh Sympathetic

The following is a copy of the letter written by Peter Hesketh, screen actor and scenario writer to the Britannia Picture Production Company, resident at 228 Virga Vale, West, and friend and associate, by reason of his daily work, of Claude Merivale, then awaiting trial for the murder of his wife, Vera Merivale. The letter is important, as the latter realized when he read it.

228 Virga Vale, W.

My dear old Claude,

You know as well as I do, laddie, that this letter's going to he damned hard to put together. It would be for Junius, or was it Juvenal, let alone for yours truly. I felt, my dear old chap, that I simply must drop you a line, if only to say how frightfully sorry I am at the lousy break you've had and to wish you all the best in the near future. You know what I mean by that. Everybody down at the studio is with you to the last ditch and most of us sufficiently broadminded to understand that any one of us may have the bad luck to get into a jam the same as you have and need all the smiles of Dame Fortune that are going, to get out of it, once we're in it. And those that don't *think in this way and see matters in this light, don't damn well* count*—and that's that! Most of us in the "flicks" game knew Vera almost as well as we knew you and we know, too, that* whatever *happened, must have been something just too ghastly for words and just— well, an accident—that shouldn't have happened—and would never have happened again, if the old Universe could be put back and the gods gave you yesterday again. You know what I mean!*

Am afraid that this is a foul letter—but I'm doing my best, so don't shoot, as the notices read which were hung round the pianist in the Alaskan dancing-saloon. By the way, while I'm on the question of what all the boys and girls think, if there's anything that you want—*either sent to you, or done for you— just drop me a line and say the word and I'll give it the O.K.*

like a shot. You're in a jam—that's all there is to it, as far as your pals are concerned—and you need all the help that you can get from them, so don't forget! And if you like, shout the roof off. Just let me *know what it is and it'll be done. When you say the word they won't see my backside for dust, believe me, Claude old chap! If it's a spot of cash—just whisper how much. If it's a whip-round to get the best man in the world to do the chin-wagging for you—say the word again—and he's yours. Leo Meux, Hugh Assheton, Les Vining and Bradley Cole, together with Vicky Garland and Trix Belmont all wish me to remember them to you specially, and they all join with me in wishing you the very best of luck. In fact, tears have been in little Vicky's eyes pretty nearly all the time you've been away from us, and Hugh seems to have lost his zest for everything. Also—before I forget to tell you—the great A.J.C. himself actually unbent and spoke to me the other day. Just before we went on to the set. Asked me if I would be writing to you, and if so, to associate him with all our expressions of sympathy and good-will. That shows you how you're thought of even in the highest places. There's one thing about a spot of dirt, Claude, old wallah, it shows you conclusively always, who and where your real old chinas are. It does, doesn't it?*

Now, here's something else I want to say to you. I want to get it off my chest as soon as possible. I suppose the authorities will let you reply to this screed of mine (well-censored and duly thumbed, no doubt) and you can let me know how you feel about the idea, when I've spilt it to you. Which is this! If you would like me to come to see you any time, don't hesitate to say so. Or anybody else, come to that. If there's anybody you'd like to see particularly, name him—or her—and I'll fix matters up down here at this end. I suppose you can *have visitors at odd times, can't you? If, on the other hand, you'd rather* not *see any of the boys or girls, just forget all about it, don't breathe a word, and we'll take it as read. Re. the new picture. They've transferred various members of the cast and things just for the finish up, on the whole, I suppose, have been going pretty well in the circumstances and all things considered. But A.J.C. has insisted on the proviso that if things go well with you, you will return to us, and the closing scenes re-shot. Hugh Assheton has moved over to do extra work and Dickie Winston has slipped into his stuff. Each is putting up a good show but, of course, Hugh isn't you and he jolly well knows it. But not quite as well as all the rest of us know it! A.J.C. had to do something, the end of the show couldn't be hung up indefinitely, and perhaps on the whole he's made the best of a rotten job. But Vicky doesn't team up with Dickie in the way that she always did with Hugh, and the inevitable result is that the final big emotional scenes aren't getting over as they were when you were under the lights with us. Leo's all right, I know, but his sob-stuff isn't quite convincing and nobody knows what that means to a picture better than yourself. Hugh and Trixie as the supports are O.K. and in point of fact I think, there is only one part of the show where I prefer Leo to Hugh. That's just before the last scrap. Not a lot in it, perhaps, but I give the balance there, such as it is, to Leo. The big scene that he has—in Trixie's bedroom—you know the one I mean—with me—is thundering good, though I ses it wot shouldn't. One of the best things I've ever done. The day before last, A.J.C. came down to the set as "livery" as a Mayfair footman and looking like a thundercloud in the Adirondacks, but Trixie, Hugh and I made it our business to be very sweet to him and pulled him round. When he saw the scene that I just mentioned we soon had him cackling like Mother Siegel herself. Or should it be Mother Carey? Or even Shipton? I know—I'll take a chance—make it Joanna Southcott and we'll open the notorious box together.*

You told Jill, I understand, when she saw you last, that you had had a visit from Anthony Bathurst. Get it into your head, old man, that this is a good sign. I don't think that there's the least doubt of it. Thumbs up, old son. If Bathurst came to see you where you are, you can bet your bottom dollar that the Scotland Yard blokes have got their own doubts about something, otherwise Bathurst wouldn't have troubled to interview you. Take it from me, everything in the Yard garden can't be lovely! I've often wondered about him. Is he any relation to the notorious Benjamin Bathurst who disappeared on the Continent somewhere, donkeys years ago? Haven't I a remembrance that he was the son of a Bishop or something? I seem to remember reading about the case in Stanley Weyman's "Traveller in the Fur Cloak." Thumping good yarn that, believe me. I've often thought of writing a scenario for it.

How are you spending your time? Finding it pretty slow, I bet. Don't worry! *I know it's easy to preach on these matters, but keep your pecker up and don't let* anything *get you down. It's the darkest hour always before the dawn, remember (how I revel in clichés), so keep your old head up, your fists clenched, and your jolly old shoulders squared. What little things turn a man's destiny, to be sure! I've been thinking over things generally and how that fact has come home to me! If you had gone down to Brighton that evening to see Max Zinstein, as had been arranged for you and had been your definite intention, you would not have returned to Enthoven Terrace at all that night and all this misery would have been sidetracked. What a pity it was that Woolf, too, changed his mind the week before! He had been angling for you for weeks, fixes things up to suit all parties concerned, and then, when the stage is all set for the doings, he takes fright, takes fright at nothing at all, runs away, stashes things up—and does his little bit thereby to land you in this ghastly mess. I hope all this isn't wearying you. Forgive me, if it is, and credit a silly ass like myself with the best intentions. Oh—I forgot to tell you. My pen keeps running away with me so—A.J.C. has at last decided upon the title for the new show. You know how he turned down about a dozen suggestions. Well, he's got one that satisfies him at last. S'right! See my finger wet! "The Painter of Ferrara." Not too bad, I suppose, though I preferred "The Dark Canvas." Think that it suggested more than the other. Tickled the imagination a bit, which is what you want. Definitely! Once you start making the public* think *about a picture—you're half-way towards big box-office; suggestion by title does count so. I've been long enough in the "flick" game to know the truth of that. A.J.C. asked me my opinion on the matter and I told him straight to his face that I considered "The Painter of Ferrara" miles behind the other. Thought I might as well be positive about it and start a damned good argument. Assheton agreed with me but Dickie Winston and Leo Meux played the "please, teacher" card and came down on A.J.C.'s side. All, of course, according to the book of form. I don't think that it made any difference as A.J.C. had made his mind up before he asked for opinions. Can't see him waiving an idea of his own just because somebody else was in disagreement. Especially considering D.W. and L.M. No, sir— not A.J.C.! He wrinkled his fat nose and rubbed that long line of jaw and said "really now, Hesketh! Miles behind the other— eh? Well—there's nothing like knowing your own mind. Well, we've had 'Dark Angels' and 'Dark Houses' and 'Dark Forests,' and 'Dark Horses' are always with us! So I don't think we'll worry about any 'Dark Canvas,' even though it's partly your picture." Then he screwed up those little eyes of his and looked at Trixie and Vicky Garland like the satyr that he undoubtedly was before he became what he is. So "The Painter of Ferrara" it is and "The Painter of Ferrara" it will remain. Well, my dear old chap, I suppose that I must close this up before long. I hope I haven't bored you stiff with all my old tripe, and if I get time, I'll write you again in the very near future. Look here, Claude, I'll make time, I promise you.*

Once again wishing you all the very best—we'll have a beer together at some local "Cow and Coffee Pot" far from the madding crowd when this is all over, because the past's the past, it's gone and nothing can alter it, no matter how and what you may think about it and the present's the present, that is to say "Life" which has got to be lived, whether we feel like living it or not! See, old scout?

Ever thine, to the proverbial cinder, and cheero,

Peter Hesketh.

It is to be recorded here, that, upon receipt of this letter from his professional associate, Peter Hesketh, Claude Merivale tore it deliberately into tiny pieces. He was fully conscious why he did this. But that knowledge he was disinclined to share with any other living person. More than disinclined—determined! As has been previously stated, this action of Merivale's was important. Let there be an attempt at explanation. We will suppose a certain situation. That Anthony Bathurst, to take one person in the world for whom the case held intense interest, had been present in Merivale's cell when the letter from Hesketh had been first received by him and that Bathurst, peculiarly privileged in this one respect, had leant over Claude Merivale's shoulder during the latter's reading of it. Continuing the visualization of this imaginary yet intriguing situation, that Bathurst had also been present to observe the deliberate tearing of the letter into the tiny pieces that have been already mentioned. It is possible, more than that, highly *probable*, that this action would have presented a significance to Anthony Bathurst when he saw it, the help of which would have proved invaluable to him in his initial attempts to understand thoroughly the psychology of the case.

And, let it also be remarked, once the psychology of a case is understood by an investigator, he is at once, perforce, on the way to a satisfactory solution. But Merivale was alone and that isolation made all the difference. After Claude Merivale had destroyed this letter, he began to pace his cell. An activity from which, so far during his imprisonment, considering that he had been something of an athlete and in excellent physical condition, he had kept singularly free. Several times he paused in his pacing as though he were considering a decision on a question of paramount importance. But evidently he came to none, for he invariably resumed his pacing and kept at it until the mood of deliberation returned again to him and he once more paused. Apart from his only sister Jill and his two children and . . . but why, he thought bitterly, dwell on the sadness of what would be? His thoughts tangented then to the recent visit of Anthony Bathurst and the series of strange questions that Bathurst had asked him. What had been the real point in Bathurst's mind behind all that questioning? What, in the name of all creation, had his dream and its tragic sequel, to do with dressing himself, with washing and shaving, with locking the bedroom door behind him and taking the key, when he had gone down to the

Yard to surrender himself and then to seek possible sanctuary behind the ingenious theory of his defence? He reflected carefully and methodically upon all the various details of the story that he had told the police. Had he made the vital error that so many murderers had made in the past, and would, no doubt, make in the future, of overlooking some trivial point that by reason of the overlooking, might become fatal to his story, to his plans, and ultimately to himself? It was usually a point of excessive simplicity. He deliberately brought his mind back to all the incidents of that tragic night after the trouble had started. He went over each one of them in the order and sequence of his remembrance of them happening. He checked up on each one of them with meticulous care. The pillow. The curtains. The bed-clothes. The gloves. The gloves! He stopped abruptly. He had taken the gloves downstairs to the garden and burned them. The buttons—the two buttons—there were only two—he had cut off before committing the gloves to the fire . . . he remembered doing that quite clearly . . . and . . . now what the devil had he done with those two buttons? He remembered that he had used a small pair of nail-scissors with which to sever the threads and he knew that after taking the buttons downstairs he had replaced the scissors in Vera's bedroom. Yes . . . he was absolutely sure of that . . . he could recall with certainty that he had laid them on a corner of the dressing-table . . . the right hand corner, as you faced it. In his mind's eye he could see them lying there now just as he had placed them. But those two buttons . . . what the blazes had he done with those buttons? He remembered putting them on a ledge in the outhouse. Yes, that was it. Cutting them off the gloves, putting them on the palm of his hand, taking them downstairs, and then laying them carefully on the ledge. What had he done with them after that? Claude Merivale thought hard, and the perspiration beads broke out on his forehead. Had he done anything with them? Had he just left them on the ledge? Try as he would and ransack his brain as he might, he could recall nothing to do with the two buttons that had occurred *after* he had placed them on the outhouse ledge. A clammy sweat now covered his brow. If, by any chance, those two buttons had been found, then a clever detective might well see the real reason for their being cut from the gloves and lying there on the ledge. Merivale frowned at the reflection and his face twisted with annoyance. From cut buttons to the gloves from which they had been cut, would be but a simple step for a man like Anthony Bathurst. What a clumsy fool he had been! And he had thought himself clever and that he had effectively covered everything! Claude Merivale finished his nervous pacing and sat down on the edge of his straight bed. He pressed his hand wearily across his forehead. How difficult it was, to be sure, to *remember* the performance of mechanical actions. Had he disposed of the buttons after he had burned the gloves, as had been his original intention? Again he strove furiously to think. His original intention had been to throw one as far as he could in one direction and the other similarly, in the opposite direction. Everybody in the vicinity was sleeping, and the buttons would have been well lost. Buttons don't burn well, and he had come to the conclusion that to rid himself of them in the manner described was a sounder proposition than trying to dispose of them by fire. But, for the life of him, he could recapture no certain memory of what he had finally done with them. Two wretched glove buttons. And those gloves that he had burned were of no pattern with his dream. Claude Merivale cursed softly under his breath, and put his head between his hands. Peter Hesketh could go to hell! With his letter!

CHAPTER VII
Vera Merivale Pleasure-Seeking

Anthony Bathurst's second visit to the house in Enthoven Terrace, now under the benevolent eye of Eva Lamb, whom Jill Merivale had asked to stay on for a time at least, yielded him one more line of inquiry. From an unexpected source—at that. In a silver flower-vase he found two tickets of admission, part of which tickets had been torn away, for a dance and dinner at a fashionable night club in Maidenhead. Mr. Bathurst flourished the two tickets before the eyes (by no means benevolent now) of Eva.

Mr. Bathurst fell to questioning.

"Did Mr. Merivale dance a lot? Or was it Mrs. Merivale that was the devotee?"

Eva shook her head woodenly.

"Not the master, sir. Never 'im. He always said as 'ow he was too tired after a hard day's work on a picksher to go out dancing. I've 'eard 'im say it many a time, sir, when poor Mrs. Merivale had sort of 'inted that she'd like 'im to take 'er to a 'op."

Anthony nodded wisely, as though Miss Lamb had made a statement to which the gods themselves had been all ears.

"What about this dance, then, shown on these tickets here?" He gave her a closer view of the two tickets. "It's less than a month ago. Look at the date on them. That is what interests me, chiefly. Did she get him to accompany her there, do you know?"

Eva Lamb (somehow the name irresistibly reminded Anthony of the Salvation Army) screwed her head round so that she could see the two tickets better. She noted the place where the dance had been held.

"Maidenhead!" she exclaimed. "I've never heard tell of that place. I never recall that name ever being mentioned here!" She shook her head. "No, sir. I never heard Mrs. Merivale ask about this."

"Or even talk about it afterwards? After she had been there, I mean. For she obviously *did* go. Look where the tickets have been torn." Anthony brandished the tickets in front of her.

"Looks as though she did," conceded Eva, "don't it? Funny she didn't say anything about it. Not as I heard."

"Did she usually?"

"Usually what?" responded Miss Lamb.

Anthony smiled patiently.

"Did she usually talk to you afterwards about the places to which she had been? That's what I meant—nothing more than that."

Eva Lamb immediately became pop-eyed.

"Did she? The missus! Did she *not*," she replied enigmatically.

Anthony, knowing her class, took the meaning that she intended.

"I wonder why she didn't talk to you about this Maidenhead affair, then, if she always made a point of discussing such matters with you afterwards. Perhaps on this occasion she didn't want *you* to talk about it afterwards," he concluded insidiously.

"Oh—and what makes you think that?" demanded an indignant Eva with a toss of the head. "Oo should I be likely to talk it over with?"

"Perhaps she didn't want Mr. Merivale to know that she had been to Maidenhead. You never know! Perhaps he didn't approve of night-clubs."

"Very likely, I should think," said Miss Lamb with heavy sarcasm, "and that's why she brought the tickets back home with her and left 'em on such a private place as the mantelpiece. It all points that way, don't it? Call yourself a detective?" Anthony grinned at the overwhelming censure. "Just a minute," he said. "You're too devastating by far. Let me defend myself. Don't be so ruthless. *You* say that she brought the tickets home and put them on the mantelpiece. I beg to differ. She put them in a vase on the mantelpiece. A very different proposition. If you like, I'll go even further. I'll say that she actually *hid* them in a vase on the mantelpiece."

Eva grumbled at him. "Hid 'em! Hid 'em, did she? Ses you! You found 'em fast enough, chance it. So they couldn't 'ave been very well 'id."

"On the other hand, *you* had never found them," retorted Anthony Bathurst, "and you have been in the room two or three times every day, I suppose, since they were placed there. Why—you actually dust the place. And the vase. Or at any rate, you're supposed to."

Eva, however, nothing daunted, had the last fling. "I don't pry into things. That's the point. You do. It's your job. You're a Nosey Parker. And as for saying I don't dust properly—you can't prove it—and you never will be able to prove it—so there."

"All right, Eva," said Anthony. "I won't give you away, so don't worry unduly. Don't lose any sleep over it. Miss Merivale will never hear of it from me, I promise you."

"Miss Merivale indeed! I like your style. She's got a very high opinion of me, let me tell you! She wouldn't listen to no stories from you running me down. And when I leave 'ere, she'll see me properly placed. She's promised me as much."

Anthony left it at that and after a few minutes' meditation, decided upon a journey to Maidenhead. He couldn't lose anything by it and it was well on the cards that he might gain. On his way, he telephoned to, and, as a result, picked up Inspector MacMorran. The latter regarded him questioningly.

"Joy-riding—at your age?"

Anthony smiled at him happily.

"Not exactly, Andrew, although it's always a joy to travel with you. Remember our last jaunt together? When we visited the local undertaker at Mill End when we were at work on the Somerset problem? By Jove, Andrew, how you revelled in that coffin shop. I shall never forget it. What's the name of your new bungalow? 'Tombstones,' isn't it?"

MacMorran wagged his head.

"Now tell me where you're proposin' to take me today. Because that information is of far'r greater'r importance."

"I propose to take you to Maidenhead, Andrew, that riverside resort of undoubted beauty. Well, Andrew, are you on? Or are you letting me travel alone?"

"What's the idea behind it? I'll guarantee you aren't going there for the contemplation of the scenery."

"For once you're right. I congratulate you. Our visit to Maidenhead, note the plural pronoun, is *not* unconnected with the case of Claude Merivale. Now what do you say about it?"

MacMorran nodded sapiently.

"Aye—I guessed it was that when you first rang me. And what is it that's doing with the Merivale case down at Maidenhead?" As he spoke the Inspector got in the car. Anthony quickly gathered pace with it.

"I'm curious," he said eventually, "to discover how the late and ill-fated Mrs. Merivale spent some of her last leisure time. Here you are—have a squint at these, Mac." He handed over the two torn night-club tickets which he had previously discussed with Eva Lamb at the house in Enthoven Terrace. The Inspector took them gingerly and turned them over but made no remark until he had finished looking at them.

"Two of 'em," he said.

"Marvellous deduction, Andrew. Again. Heartiest congratulations. You observe, according to the date, that 'then' was the time for dancing. See what I mean?"

Anthony nodded towards the tickets that MacMorran held in his hand.

The Inspector permitted himself the luxury of a smile.

"Coming my way, then, after all, aren't you?"

Anthony failed to understand.

"How do you mean, Andrew?"

"Looking for the lover in the shadows, aren't you? Just as I thought the case would turn out when we first got to grips with it. What did I tell you? Didn't I forecast as much, right at the start?"

"Don't be *too* sure. But I shouldn't be surprised, all the same. I'll give you that much. I've had a chat with the maid at the Merivale establishment, and I gather that when Mrs. Merivale went dancing, it wasn't always Mr. Merivale who accompanied her. And as it was the habit of Mrs. Merivale to talk to her maid about the various places she visited, a habit which was honoured in the breach rather than in the. observance as far as this Maidenhead occasion was concerned, I shall be interested to know who her companion was that time, and why she was so unusually reticent thereon."

"I see."

"And now, Andrew, you know all that there is to know . . . so far. You know as much as I do myself. Lucky man."

MacMorran glanced at his wrist-watch. The car was travelling fast.

"You're doin' very well," he said.

"I know I am. You don't have to tell me. She's running beautifully. Sit back and enjoy yourself and I'll talk to you some more."

The Inspector obeyed the injunction.

Anthony continued.

"You remember the interview we had the other day with Claude Merivale, Andrew?"

"Very well. And I'm afraid it didn't get us very far. I was vastly disappointed at the result. Still—what about it?"

"I showed Merivale that photograph that I found in his wife's bedroom. Remember? A photograph, which I am *assured* by people who should know, was taken at Worthing in Sussex. Usually known as 'Sunny' Worthing, Andrew, though I've never been able to discover why. I've often argued about it with Worthing's prettiest girl."

Anthony waved his hand and acknowledged a car that he had just passed.

"Go on," said the Inspector.

"Well—it's this that I wanted to say. You listen and don't interrupt so much. One can't get a word in edgeways with you, you garrulous old blighter."

"You should talk! Why I—"

"Shut up, can't you? Now listen. Merivale, when he first heard me ask about Worthing, declared that he had never been there with his wife. But when he saw the photograph which I handed to him, you remember, he shifted his ground, denied that the place *was* Worthing and stated, on the other hand, that it was somewhere in Belgium. Can you remember all that? Or is your brain too puddeny?"

"Yes. I can. And I know what you're goin' to say next."

"That's right—rob a man of his triumphs! What I was going to say is this. That the place *was* Worthing, the woman was Mrs. Merivale, *but the man wasn't Claude Merivale*, as we know him! Now why the hell, Mac, did Merivale say that it *was* he himself? When we know that, we shall know a hatful, Andrew! Unless it was to . . ."

Mr. Bathurst paused. The Inspector came in.

"It looked like Claude Merivale."

"Now—did it? I'm beginning to wonder. Are you absolutely convinced of that. Look at it again for yourself. I've got it here." Anthony took one hand from the steering-wheel and fished in his pocket. He handed the photograph to the Inspector. Anthony then reiterated his previous statement.

"Now *does* it look like Claude Merivale? That's the point I'm after. When you look closely into it, I mean. Tremendously like him? Keep looking at it, Mac. Soak yourself with it before you answer me. Make absolutely sure. In the meantime, I'll suggest certain things. Amongst others, I'll suggest *this*, with which to start. That the man in the photograph is wearing a hat. Notice same. A brimmed hat. Which means that *inevitably part* of the face or part of the *appearance* of the face is hidden from the person who looks at it. That's point number one. Secondly—the man's face is taken in profile, and moreover, it's partly on the turn. Sort of half-way business. Part has been turned away from the camera and towards his companion. Do you get that, Mac? Have a look."

MacMorran nodded and grunted with the nod. "Right! I'll keep on keeping on then. Why did Jill Merivale (that's Claude's only sister, let me tell you), think that the man in the photograph was her brother? Shall I give you the reasons which, in my opinion, swayed her? *(a)* The woman was Vera Merivale—ergo, Jill *expected* the man to be Claude, her brother. It was the natural corollary of companionship, as it were. *(b)* The man is *like* Claude Merivale, in build and general make-up, and *(c)* the line of his jaw, which is the most prominent feature of the face in the photograph, is extraordinarily like Claude Merivale's. Or, in other words, she *imagined* an idea and what she *saw* didn't contradict this effort of imagination, so she accepted it without demur. Do you follow me, Mac?"

"Aye—and which is more—I agree with you, which is a *great deal* more, Mr. Bathurst. Also, I'll take my hat off to you, once again. You've got the knack of expressin' things that aren't too clear to the ordinary mind." He paused and then uttered something as an after-thought: "But even now, assuming that we're all O.K. and on the right track, it doesn't explain why Merivale himself should lie about it."

"Surely it *does*," returned Anthony, with quiet insistence, "if you look at it properly. Let me show you what I mean. You *prove* that Mrs. Merivale had a lover, then as a natural consequence you at once saddle Claude Merivale with the motive for her murder. At the same time, I'll agree to go part of the way with you, Mac, and admit that the procedure is, to say the least of it, unusual."

"The case is full of 'ifs' and 'buts,' Mr. Bathurst. I don't like it because of that. Doubts about everything everywhere. No—I don't like it." The Inspector shook his head gloomily as he made the announcement.

The car ran imperiously into Maidenhead. Anthony looked at the portions of the tickets he had brought with him.

"Reveres," he said "that's the place we want—ask the policeman on the point there which is the quickest way from here. Talk to him in your best Yard manner."

MacMorran spoke to the policeman through the window. The uniformed man pointed towards the Thames. "Straight down towards the river—and you can't miss it." The Inspector thanked him, withdrew his head and the car proceeded. A run of three minutes brought them to Reveres. Anthony swung out of the driving seat. MacMorran followed him. They entered what was evidently the restaurant portion of the establishment. A waiter attired in evening dress came to meet them.

"This is a place," said Anthony, "unless I'm very much mistaken, where an eighteen-penny lunch costs a man twenty-five bob. I've been had in the past like this myself, so I know what I'm talking about. Look out—here's the waiter bloke."

The waiter came right up to them. He gave the semblance of a bow. His voice matched his appearance.

"Will you be wanting lunch, gentlemen? If so, will you please come this way?"

MacMorran shook his head. It must be admitted that Anthony Bathurst's statement concerning the relationship between eighteen pence and twenty-five bob, as calculated by

Reveres, had caused him intense suffering. His religious views, he felt, had been sorely assailed. He continued to subtract one and a half from twenty-five and each successive result gave him more pain. Out of his ancestry came a wave of hostility and aggression. He eyed the waiter stormily and at the same time produced his official card. The man took it and looked at it furtively. There is nothing quite so furtive, let it be said, as a furtive waiter, of uncertain nationality. MacMorran, by now impatient, put the man's thoughts into his own words.

"Inspector MacMorran, Scotland Yard. That's me. I want to speak to the proprietor here, if you please." He scowled comprehensively round the restaurant.

"Yes, sir," returned the waiter. "I will tell Mr. Revere to come at once." He sidled away, something as an amateur anarchist at a dress rehearsal of an assassination would have, towards the interior of the establishment.

"He's gone for Paul," quipped Anthony to the Inspector, "and maybe he's out riding."

The allusion was wasted. Within a few minutes the man in the boiled shirt and black bow returned with a tall man of heavy exterior who was wearing a suit of plus fours. As he came nearer to them Anthony could see that the man was unusually tall. He calculated, from a rapid comparison with his own height, that this man who approached must stand nearly six feet four inches. He was dark with a neatly trimmed military moustache.

"I am Major Revere," he said curtly, "and the proprietor here. Now, gentlemen, what is it that you wish to see me about?"

The Inspector looked at Anthony Bathurst. The latter nodded his understanding. He assumed his most pleasing manner.

"Good afternoon, Major Revere. We are extremely sorry to trouble you like this. This is Chief Inspector MacMorran of Scotland Yard, as you've seen from his card. My name is Bathurst. We want you to be good enough, if you will, to give us a little information."

Revere ostentatiously fingered his moustache. Anthony produced the torn portions of the two tickets from the vase on the mantelpiece of the house in Enthoven Terrace.

"The dinner-dance to which these refer was, I take it, held here?"

Revere looked at the tickets and nodded.

"It was. One of our most successful evenings for some time."

"I see. Were you acquainted with a Mrs. Vera Merivale, may I ask?"

Revere pursed his lips. The name evidently had its significance and had struck home. Anthony continued:

"I won't disguise my intentions. I refer to the lady who was recently found dead in bed. But no doubt you will recall the case immediately?"

He waited for Revere's reply. It came sooner, perhaps, than he had anticipated.

"Yes. I was. There's no reason that I know of why I should conceal the information. As a matter of fact, Mrs. Merivale was a fairly frequent visitor here."

"Thank you. And she was here on the evening of which I speak?"

"Yes. She used these tickets that you have here. I can tell you that with absolute certainty. I saw her here dancing during the evening." Revere stopped.

"She had an escort, of course?"

"Oh . . . yes . . . naturally. The same man always accompanied her when she came here. To my knowledge, that is. I never saw her down here with anybody but him."

Anthony heard the answer, noted its significance, and eyed Major Revere shrewdly.

"That information of yours fits in with the line of our inquiry. It was not Mr. Merivale, I presume?"

Revere was again curt.

"It was not."

"From your reply, then, I take it that you know Claude Merivale?"

"Very well indeed. In appearance that is. I've seen him in more than one of his recent pictures. The man who habitually accompanied Mrs. Merivale here was certainly not her husband."

MacMorran and Anthony exchanged glances.

"How long has she been coming here with this man?" The question came from the Inspector. Revere considered the question.

"Some months, I should say, at least. She was a very charming and attractive woman, you know, and we were always extremely pleased to see her down here. On second thoughts, I'll place it at nearly a year."

Anthony produced the snapshot of the man and woman in the deck-chairs. He handed it to Major Revere.

"Is that the man?"

Revere gave the photograph a quick and almost uninterested glance.

"That? Oh—no! Certainly not! Nothing like him! Not a bit like him."

It is true to say that both Anthony and Andrew MacMorran were surprised at Revere's answer.

"No?" queried the Inspector, too surprised to add to his question.

"Oh, no," repeated Major Revere, emphatically. "This man in the photograph, as I should say from what I can see of him, is a tall, slender, well-built fellow. The man who accompanied Mrs. Merivale here was a short, stout, plump sort of chap. With a pleasant, laughing face. Nothing like this man here." He tapped the back of the photograph with his finger-nail. Anthony Bathurst at once joined issue with him. He realized that he must follow up at once.

"Do you mean that the short, stout man whom you describe is the man who habitually accompanied Mrs. Merivale when she came here?"

Revere looked somewhat astonished at the question.

"Oh—yes—of course. I thought that I must have already made that clear."

"I suppose that you had really," conceded Anthony, "but I was just assuring myself of the fact. Pardon me for the seeming insistence."

"Do you happen to know the man's name?" asked the Inspector.

"No," returned Major Revere. "As it happens I don't. I have never had occasion to bother about it. I have always dealt with Mrs. Merivale from the point of view of correspondence with regard to the tickets and so on. I used to send her, at her request of course, notices for most of our bigger affairs and as a matter of fact, but for this sad business that has just taken place, she would have taken a prominent part in our big fancy dress carnival night. We run one once a year, and she had promised us her support. This year's show comes off in about a fortnight's time." Revere gave his big shoulders a heave as though everything about the interview was distasteful to him. Then he suddenly added something to what he had previously said, evidently as an after thought on his part.

"Mrs. Merivale had invited several well-known people to our social circle down here from time to time, and we welcomed all of them. Many of them showed signs of becoming 'regulars' here with us. In that way Mrs. Merivale was valuable to us. She was a tremendous personality. People like Mrs. Merivale always are. They have a wide circle of acquaintances. Much more extensive than the average person. It's the snowball effect over again."

MacMorran seemed dissatisfied with what he was hearing.

"Didn't you ever hear Mrs. Merivale address this man by name? Surely you *must* have, if they came here as many times as you say they did."

Revere looked superior.

"Mrs. Merivale always addressed her companion as 'Tollie,'" he stated severely. "Beyond that, gentlemen, I'm afraid that I can tell you nothing." He turned away as though desirous of ending the interview. Anthony took the hint from him and shortly afterwards he and MacMorran withdrew from the establishment.

"Well, Mr. Bathurst," remarked the latter, as the car made its way out of the town. "Do you call that interview a profitable investment or otherwise? Bearing in mind, of course, that it was your bloomin' idea in the first place."

Anthony smiled. The remark was so typically MacMorran.

"Profitable, of course, you old sinner. Why not? How else can we look at it, if we're sensible. How many times have I told you that *all* information is valuable? You and I are endeavouring to discover why Mrs. Merivale was strangled in the night, aren't we? Not so much 'who' this time, as 'why.' The more that we discover about her, therefore, the nearer we are likely to get to the truth."

"Who is 'Tollie'? Light or dark?" grunted MacMorran.

"Exactly," said Anthony. "That's just it. And I'll leave you to get to work on it. You might have a worse field of inquiry."

CHAPTER VIII
P.C. PIKE HOLLOWAY OBSERVANT

POLICE Constable Pike Holloway was in plain clothes when Inspector MacMorran brought him to Anthony Bathurst's flat.

The visit was entirely unexpected.

"Hallo," said Anthony, "what's this? Re 'Tollie' or merely a bolt from the blue?"

"Sit down, Holloway," said MacMorran, "Mr. Bathurst won't eat you. He's convalescent and therefore off slops. Sit down over there."

The Inspector indicated a chair and the policeman who had entered heaved his burly form into it. Anthony pushed over his tobacco. Pike Holloway felt better.

"Smoke, Constable? It's a mixture of my own. I think you'll like it. Not quite as bad as most. Fill your pipe, if you've brought it with you. What will you drink? I'm out of cocoa, I'm sorry to say. All I have is beer. Sorry. Try to forgive me."

Pike Holloway chuckled noisily. He was a heavily built man with the policeman's proverbial big feet. His hobby was gardening and twice he had won the Division Cup for the best-kept allotment. He could see that this Mr. Bathurst whom the Inspector had brought him to see, was a lad. Not 'arf he wasn't!

"I'll make do with a glass o' wallop, sir, if it's all the same to you. Don't worry about having no cocoa. I'll drink your health, sir, if it's not takin' a liberty."

"Tankard suit you?"

"Prefer it, sir—not so 'pansy-like' as a glass, if I may say so."

Anthony grinned at him and poured amber beer into a tankard.

"That was my grandfather's tankard, Constable. You'll find it cool and pleasing."

Pike Holloway raised the tankard reverently. "Your grandfather, eh, sir? A fine man, I've no doubt."

"A magnificent man, Constable. We Bathursts are all proud of him. A fighter—*and* an orator."

Pike Holloway expressed surprise. "You don't say so, sir."

"Yes. On one memorable occasion it took six policemen to get him to the lock-up. And he could kick a front door down with anybody."

Pike Holloway grinned and drew the back of his hand across his mouth.

There would be a tale for him to tell on the morrow.

"While his language when attempting to push a stud into a boiled shirt . . . well . . . Constable as I said . . . an orator. . . ."

"What was his name, sir?"

"William Bath Bathurst. Born in County Cork. He'd have been 122 years old on the 22nd of September this year, were he alive."

"Handy with his fists, I take it, sir?"

"Beautiful, Constable. Packed a tidy wallop in each one of 'em. There was very nearly serious trouble once. He half killed an Italian baked potato-seller in the City on one occasion for selling a little boy bad potatoes on a bitterly cold night in the winter. They were soft, he said. He likened them, I believe, to a certain natural softness."

Pike Holloway drank from the tankard that had been the property of the late W.B. Bathurst and put it down again on the table. MacMorran, practical as ever, endeavoured to check the flow of Bathurst reminiscence.

"I've brought Constable Holloway round here for a purpose. I wasn't anticipatin' that you'd give him your life history right from the kick off. When you're ready we'll get down to business. And it's not about 'Tollie.'"

Anthony nodded.

"All right, Andrew, we will—we will. If you used your eyes you would see that Holloway has already done as you desire. Fill up again, Constable. That's right."

MacMorran shrugged his shoulders and gave up the unequal contest. He resigned himself to the inevitable and waited Anthony's pleasure in the turning to more serious matters. It matured at last.

"Now, Andrew," said Mr. Bathurst, "to what am I indebted for the pleasure of Constable Holloway's company?"

MacMorran sighed and took up the parable.

"I'll tell you, now you've come to your senses. When we had that little interview with Claude Merivale you asked him certain questions, ordinary questions I'll call them, which I should say he was inclined to resent. Remember that, Mr. Bathurst?"

"Resent!" Anthony reflected upon the word questioningly.

"Yes, I think so. That was how it appeared to me."

"I don't know that I altogether agree with your choice of the word, Inspector, but go on with what you were going to say all the same. I think that I can recall the questions to which you refer."

"It was towards the end of the conversation, just before we left the prison."

"Yes. I know. Go on."

"One of the questions that you put to him concerned the time that he arrived home in Enthoven Terrace on the evening of the tragedy. Can you remember that?"

"Perfectly. I had a reason for asking it." MacMorran nodded. "I've no doubt about that." He turned towards P.C. Pike Holloway. "That brings me to the explanation as to why Constable Holloway is here with us now. What was Merivale's answer to that question, Mr. Bathurst? Confirm my own memory, will you?"

"With pleasure. Merivale said that he left the Catena Club at eleven o'clock. Then he said that he arrived home at eleven-thirty. But he knocked eight minutes off that time shortly afterwards and made it eleven-twenty-two, said he was almost certain of it. Go on, Inspector. You're making me much more interested."

MacMorran turned again to Pike Holloway with an air of triumph. Of triumph long delayed.

"Tell Mr. Bathurst, in a few words, what you have told me, Constable Holloway."

P.C. Pike Holloway, moving uneasily, and obviously no disciple of girth control, first cleared his throat and then the tankard from in front of him. He pushed it carefully to one side.

"I will, Inspector. Only too pleased, as you might say. It's like this, sir. On the evening of the murder at Enthoven Terrace, this 'ere Merivale murder, I was on ordinary duty. My beat extended from Baker Street Station as far as Stoddart Road and Warner Crescent, passing down to Enthoven Terrace about two-thirds of the full distance between the two points. Do you follow me, sir?"

"Quite well. Proceed, Constable."

"Well, sir, I want you to understand that I know Mr. Merivale pretty well, see? A lot depends on that—that's why I'm mentioning it to you."

"How do you come to know him? Explain more fully—do you mind, Constable?"

A vast smile spread slowly across the broad face of P.C. Pike Holloway.

"Don't think as how we're old college mates. Nothing of that. I'm one of the old type. I don't mean anything like that. I only went to the Hay Currie School, under old Bob Wilde. Mr. Merivale was 'posh.' What I mean is—I knew him well by sight. Through being on that particular beat and going down Enthoven Terrace pretty regular. And I know his voice, which fact is even more important. A nice warm round sort of voice, I should describe it as. He often used to pass the time of day with me. Got the idea, sir?"

Anthony smiled at the man's effort.

"Absolutely, Constable. You have told me just what I wanted to know."

"Well, sir, it was like this. I was passing the house in Enthoven Terrace where Mr. Merivale lives, and the time I went by would be about half past six in the evening. And as I passed it, I saw Mr. Merivale entering the house."

MacMorran intervened quickly.

"There, Mr. Bathurst! Do you hear that? At half past six in the evening. Note the time. Holloway *saw* him. Yet in Merivale's story to us he puts the time of his going home at nearly five hours later. Why? What was behind all that? That's the reason why I brought the Constable here. I can't understand it at all. This discrepancy in time—it worries me."

Anthony half nodded.

"Half past six, you say. H'm—strange Merivale didn't mention this to me. You are certain that it was he, I suppose?"

"Positive, sir." Holloway moved his head with decision.

"Where was he when you saw him? I mean—where was he exactly? You say 'entering.' What do you mean actually by that?"

"I saw him standing in the porch of his house, and just at the moment as I passed by I saw the front door open and Mr. Merivale go in. See? That's why I feel so certain about it."

Anthony began to examine Pike Holloway's statement.

"In the porch, you say? Well, then, wouldn't that mean that he was standing with his back to you? Think carefully over that, Constable."

Pike Holloway pushed his shoulder-of-mutton hand through his hair.

"Well, sir,"—his usual start to a sentence—"I wouldn't agree to that altogether. No, not at all. I wouldn't say that his back was towards me. I caught sight of him more to the side than from the back, as you might say. Oh, it was Mr. Merivale all right. You can rest assured of that, sir. I know him too well to make any mistake over him. Know his walk and his stand. Know the clothes he wears. And as I said, know his voice. I heard him speak as he went through the front door. It was him all right, sir. I wish I was as sure of a thousand quid as I am of that."

Anthony heard him out. The man was certain enough of the truth of his story. He *should* be sure of his ground, seeing and meeting Merivale constantly as he had stated he did. Anthony thought carefully over the various points that the constable had made in support of the soundness of his identification. What had he meant by the expression "know the *clothes* he wears?"

There was nothing remarkable that he himself could remember with regard to Merivale's lounge suit. He, Anthony Bathurst, had seen him wearing it when he had interviewed him in the prison. It was an entirely ordinary lounge suit from what he could remember of it that certainly wouldn't distinguish a man from other men. What did Pike Holloway really mean by this statement? Anthony addressed him on the point.

"You said, Constable, that you knew 'the clothes' that Merivale wore. Your point was that this assisted you in identifying him. How did the ordinary lounge suit that he was wearing that evening serve to distinguish him so from other men? I don't know that I quite follow you there."

Pike Holloway shook his head decisively.

"Oh, no, sir, begging your pardon, sir, but I must differ with you there. Mr. Merivale was not wearing an everyday lounge suit, when I saw him. He was wearing his suit of white duck, what he's worn for some time now, sir, and which he wore on that evening."

"Eh! What's that? Say that again," said Mr. Bathurst, sitting up suddenly and taking notice.

P.C. Pike Holloway steadily repeated the statement he had just made. Anthony Bathurst swung round in his chair towards Inspector MacMorran.

"Here—were you aware of this fact as well, Inspector?"

MacMorran shook his head.

"No. I wasn't. To tell the truth I hadn't heard of it prior to this. I accepted Constable Holloway's story that he had seen Merivale come home about half-past six and naturally didn't inquire any further. The time was what mattered to me. This news about the suit is as fresh to me as it is to you. Peculiar, isn't it, when you come to think of it? I mean—there doesn't seem any sense in any of it. Different times—different suits—what have they to do with strangling his wife and his dreaming beforehand?"

"Answering you, *(a)* what we don't know, and *(b)* what we have to find out." Anthony's reply was curt.

Mr. Bathurst filled his pipe with deliberation. He sat there for some moments in silence, pressing the tobacco into the bowl.

"Queer," he remarked at length. "Extremely queer." He noticed P.C. Pike Holloway's bewildered expression as he watched. "You're wondering what's puzzling us, I suppose? I'll tell you. It's your statement about Merivale wearing this white duck suit at half-past six in the evening. According to the information that he gave us himself he dressed himself, after the death of his wife, in the same suit that he had worn during the evening. That is to say, identical with the suit that he's still wearing in prison. Which happens to be an ordinary lounge suit—a dark grey one. Certainly nothing in white duck."

P.C. Pike Holloway stared in undisguised amazement at Mr. Bathurst. He then looked from Anthony Bathurst to Chief Inspector MacMorran, and following upon that from the Inspector back to Anthony. He picked up the tankard of the late William Bath Bathurst, saw regretfully that it was empty as he had half guessed, and put it down again. Anthony immediately rose and made good the deficiency. P.C. Pike Holloway at once showed an active gratitude for the gesture. He wiped his lips with the back of his hand.

"Very funny, sir. As you say. Very! I see your point. Does make you wonder, doesn't it? Still, you can take it from me that what I've told you is gospel."

Anthony thought hard for a moment.

"Merivale approached his house, I presume, from the opposite direction to you?"

"Yes, sir. That is so. He must have been just a little distance in front of me. I mean—he got to the house just before I did. Otherwise I should have run slap into him. Usually I'd meet him face to face somewhere in Enthoven Terrace but on this particular evening Mr. Merivale must have been a little earlier than usual. Just a second or so. Enough to turn the corner by Warner Crescent, get into Enthoven Terrace and into the porch of his house before I reached the front gate."

"I see. But you heard and recognized his voice, you say, as he went in?"

"I did that, sir. And as I told you, there was no mistaking it."

"Seems conclusive, Inspector," said Anthony Bathurst, "which ever way you look at it!"

"Does so! I agree." Having spoken thus, MacMorran relapsed into silence. For some minutes Anthony puffed hard at his pipe. "We've got a partial check-up on him, you know, MacMorran. On Merivale. According to the story that he told us when we went to see him, he spent the evening, or part of it, at the Catena Club. Said that he dined there, didn't he? It won't fill up an alibi for the whole evening, I know, but it will help."

"That'll be something," concurred MacMorran.

"The girl's useless," said Anthony. "That's another thing."

"What girl?" MacMorran's tone held the hint of surprise.

"The maid at the Merivale house. Lamb. Eva Lamb. It was her evening out, remember."

"It would be," asserted the Inspector, gloomily.

"More than that," Anthony was decisive.

"More than that?" The query was MacMorran's.

"Yes, more than it would be. It was." MacMorran regarded him pointedly. "Arranged?"

"Convenient, let us say."

"How do you mean?"

"When the Lamb was away—the mice could play."

MacMorran let go a low whistle.

"You think so? Pretty sure of your ground'?"

"Oh, absolutely, Andrew. No doubt at all on the point. I'm coming to the view that the Lamb's absence was a vital point in the whole structure. But beyond that general conjecture, I don't seem to get very far, do I? Inspector, why the hell did you go out of your way to pitch the wretched case under my nose?"

MacMorran shook his head at Anthony accusingly.

"You love it. You know you do. So don't pretend the opposite."

Anthony smiled at the implied censure. P.C. Pike Holloway smiled in unison. His heart was gradually warming to the position in which he now found himself. From the point of view of his professional career this was the biggest and most important thing that had ever happened to him. It had always been his boast that he had prevented crime rather than discovered it. This last episode, too, was all due to his powers of observation. He ached to return to Mrs. Pike Holloway so that the joy of recounting the story to her might be his. Also . . . there was his small son . . . who sang in the choir. . . .

"What manner of place is the Catena Club? I don't know it very well." The question came from Anthony.

"Frequented mostly by film people. And people connected with the film industry, generally. Reputation's all right. As far as I know. Which means that I've never heard a word against it. What do you say, Constable?" MacMorran addressed P.C. Pike Holloway.

"As you say, Inspector. I couldn't have put it better. Never heard a whisper against the Catena. And if there is anything doing in that direction it usually comes our way, sooner or later. It's a certainty. I should say from what I know of the place that it's a well-conducted club. Nothing like 'The Purple Calf,' or 'The Golden Scimitar,' for instance. They're both very 'peas in the pot,' as you probably know without me telling you."

MacMorran frowned at the Constable's effort. But Anthony accepted it without comment.

"I think that we shall have to call at the Catena, Inspector. And before long. I can see that sticking out all right." He turned again to the policeman. "By the way, Constable, you didn't happen to hear what Merivale *said*, did you, when he entered his house that evening?"

Mr. Bathurst's visitor put his hand across his mouth and considered the question.

"No, sir," he said at length. "I can't say that I did. But I think that I heard him mention one word. And I'm trying to remember what that one word was. I've been trying for some time."

Anthony watched while Pike Holloway furrowed his brows. There was a period of silence. A silence that both MacMorran and Anthony Bathurst respected. Suddenly the Constable's face cleared. A light shine in his eyes. He raised his hand in a half-gesture of conquest and achievement.

"I've got it," he declared with gusto. "I know the word that I heard. I heard it just as Mr. Merivale passed through the front door into his house. I heard him say it. 'Painter.'"

Anthony groaned. "Painter?" he queried. "Are you certain that was the word, Constable?"

P.C. Pike Holloway nodded vigorously.

"Absolutely positive, sir. It's all coming back to me now I'm concentrating on it. I can remember thinking it was a funny word for Mr. Merivale to use, as I passed along towards the end of my beat."

Inspector MacMorran and Anthony Bathurst exchanged glances. At length MacMorran shook his head, with a hint of resignation to the inevitable.

"I give it up," he said. "Can't find rhyme or reason in it. All the same, I don't see that it matters to us a great deal. The conversation might very well have something to do with what he was talking about when he went out first thing in the morning. Look at it like this. Mrs. Merivale let him in. We know that, because the girl Lamb was out. Well—work it out for yourself. She might have asked him to do something for her, or to get her something when he had gone out in the morning, and he might have made a remark that had to do with something like that directly he returned in the evening. Commonplace! With no special significance whatever. So that I don't see why we need bother our heads about it. Perhaps the word was paint and Constable Holloway heard it as 'painter.'" MacMorran sat back in his chair with the air of a man who has pulled off a good job of work and is perfectly well aware of the fact.

"I know, Inspector," conceded Anthony quietly. "I realize the sound sense behind everything that you have said. But all the same, I'm disturbed."

"Why? Why should you be? You're bein' ridiculous. Why go out of your way to look for trouble?"

"I'm not. Don't you believe it. On the other hand, though, I don't feel inclined to neglect anything just because of the fear that it may lead us astray. We don't know! We can't be sure! It may not. So far from that—it might even lead us to the truth. All my previous investigations teach me that fact, as you yourself should be the first to admit."

MacMorran gave him a grudging assent.

"Yes . . . I know . . . but this is different. There's nothing in this to catch on to, or get hold of. 'Painter.' Somebody coming in to have a slap at the bathroom, in all probability. Nothing more romantic in it than that."

Anthony smiled at the MacMorran phlegm.

"Are not Abana and Pharpar," he quoted, "greater than all the rivers of Israel? 'Twas ever thus, Inspector. We turn eagerly to the bizarre for the explanation of our problems, and are contemptuous towards the commonplace and the comparatively simple. To you, 'painter' means less than nothing, where as it may be the most pregnant word of the investigation that has so far reached us."

"Well, assuming that it is, what can you do about it? The woman it was addressed to is dead and therefore can tell no tales, and you can bet your life that Merivale himself won't be oratorical if we question him about it."

P.C. Pike Holloway felt that it would not be polite to drink more beer. He put the historic tankard on the table again and looked at his watch.

"It's time I was going, Inspector," he said to MacMorran, "if you'll excuse me, gentlemen. I enjoy the pleasure of your company . . . but . . . there, you see, duty's duty, and the Sergeant won't send a Rolls-Royce for me." He rose and stretched himself. Anthony shook hands with him warmly and spoke to the Inspector.

"Thank you for coming—both of you," he said, and P.C. Pike Holloway felt certain that Mr. Bathurst meant every word he said. Mr. Bathurst went on to say more. "Your visit has been valuable, if only for one thing. You have given me a new idea, Constable. And I find that word 'painter' of yours very intriguing. When you've gone, I'm going to make it at least a one-pipe problem. Goodbye! Any time you feel inclined to drop in to see me, do so by all means. If only in honour of the late W.B. Bathurst." His eyes twinkled. Anthony waved his hand to them as they descended his staircase. Then he returned to his arm-chair and slowly filled his pipe. "Painter," he repeated to himself. "Or, in other words, one who paints. H'm! Or even something we might let go. I wonder."

CHAPTER IX
Montague Jenkins Indignant

The premises of the Catena Club are situated in Piccadilly. Its members, almost all of them, owe allegiance to stage and screen—mostly to the latter. As Montague Jenkins, whose father had been a coal and coke merchant, said of them, "they had been well screened," which statement, as meant by him, was in the nature of a decided compliment. Montague Jenkins, himself, let it be said, was a man who, in most things, took an immense amount of pleasing. While Anthony Bathurst was walking westwards through Leicester Square on his way to the Catena Club, Montague Jenkins was holding an audience in the smoking-room. That is to say, Montague Jenkins was functioning entirely normally. The room was well filled. Montague, as a true artist, had seen to that. That's why, to use a Parliamentary term, he was "up." He himself would probably have used an unparliamentary one. But he made a strict point of never casting his pearls before swine that were few. He liked his swine to be many before they rushed down their own sheer heights into the sea that he cunningly prepared for them.

He was a strongly built, florid man with no lack of personality, however. His neck was fat but hard and strong. There was fire in his reddish-brown eyes, too, and spirit in his countenance. He was neither popular nor unpopular. Women liked him, perhaps, a little better than men. Nobody liked him overmuch. Suddenly Montague Jenkins paused in his harangue and looked out of the window over towards the railings of the Green Park and to the outlines of the trees beyond them. On this occasion he happened to be "up" on the Merivale case. For Montague Jenkins had strong views on most things and as Claude Merivale had been a member of the Catena Club at the time of his arrest and, therefore, well known to him, his views on the case in point were even stronger than usual. There were sundry head-noddings and eyebrow-liftings as Montague Jenkins made his points, one by one and proceeded to elaborate them. More swine came into the room to join in the hunt for the Jenkins pearls. He concluded his first long address:

"I tell you, gentlemen," he said, with the air of one who bestows a tremendous favour on those to whom he speaks, "that I was far from surprised when I first heard of the tragedy." His voice dropped to a half-whisper. "Indeed, I had almost anticipated it. I had seen Merivale. I had heard him. I had almost found myself watching him because I found him interesting me so—psychologically, I mean, of course. I pride myself a little on my gifts in that direction."

His reddish-brown eyes blazed with a self-awarded triumph and his voice at the moment had all the harshness and disagreeableness that the smoke-room of the Catena Club knew so well.

At that critical moment in the Jenkins address, Anthony Bathurst pushed open the swing-doors of the entrance to the Club and walked with long quick strides towards the centre of the entrance hall. If Montague Jenkins had seen him enter, it would have meant nothing to him. As he didn't see him, it still meant nothing. At the foot of the staircase, leading to the smoke-room, Anthony halted and spoke to a tall, languid-looking man who lolled there.

"You will pardon me," said Anthony. "I am not a member of the Catena Club. That probably is more my misfortune than anything else. But I have business with one of your members. I desire some information with regard to a certain matter and I've been recommended to come here to have a few words with the gentleman. His name is Jenkins. A Mr. Montague Jenkins. Can you help me?"

Anthony waited to see what effect his statement would produce upon this tall man who lolled. The latter cocked a codfish eye at Mr. Bathurst.

"Yaas," he said, "yaas—I see. Quaite." Then he nodded benignly to himself and said, "yaas" again.

Anthony waited patiently for the birth of a notion. He was right and his judgment sound. His patience was rewarded. The tall man found more words. This time words of greater significance.

"Jenkins. Montague Jenkins. Yaas. You want to speak to him?"

"Yes. That's the idea. You've seen through it at once. Is he on the premises?"

The tall man nodded as a drunken man will nod. With that suggestion of the sharing of a sinister secret.

"Yaas. Here. Now. Yaas, on the premises. What you said."

Anthony, exercising illimitable patience, projected a request.

"Could you direct me to him, do you think? Would it be troubling you too much?"

A shake of the head from the languid man assured Mr. Bathurst that it would not be a trouble. The man then put his finger between his collar and his throat, in an effort, evidently, to achieve a greater degree of comfort. Anthony found it easy to believe that he was physically uncomfortable. The codfish eye wavered and then met Mr. Bathurst's. It vacillated over his features as a blob searchlight wobbles glutinously and unsteadily across the night sky, before coming to rest on a fixed spot. The eye on this occasion appeared to become fixed on the tip of Mr. Bathurst's nose. The owner of the eye removed his finger from the territory of his Adam's apple and began to speak again.

"I can't take you to him. No. Definitely no! He's upstairs. In the smoke-room. He's always in the smoke-room at this time of the day. I said I can't take you to him. Did you hear me say that? That's because I never, on any account, go to the smoke-room when Mr. Montague Jenkins is there. It's against my principles. I haven't many principles, but what I have I make a point of sticking to. Yaas. Like a limpet. My mother was similar to me in that respect. I trust that I have made myself clear." He threw his head back bibulously and regarded Anthony something as a man regards an earwig which he has hit revengefully with a hammer. Anthony replied to him immediately. He felt that he had already endured enough from the stare of that codfish eye.

"Where is the smoke-room, please? Would you be good enough to direct me?"

The languid man pointed over his shoulder up a staircase that showed behind him.

"Up here. Straight up. Go to the top and then the door is straight in front of you. Yaas. You can't possibly miss it."

"Thank you," returned Mr. Bathurst. He had his foot on the first stair when he felt the languid man's hand descend on his shoulder.

"Just a minute, sir. I want to ask you something. I trust that you will take no offence."

Anthony half-turned on the step. "Yes? What is it?"

"You don't mean to tell me seriously, *seriously*, mind you, that you *want* to speak to Montague Jenkins?"

"I do. That is my sole reason for being here." He raced up the staircase. The languid man watched him disappear and slowly shook his head. "Absolutely amazin' and incredible thing! Running upstairs to speak to Montague Jenkins. The man can't have even met him."

By this time Anthony had reached the top of the staircase and had then come to the smoking-room door. He turned the handle and entered the room. The sound of a voice smote his ears. Then he knew, in an instant, that he had run to earth the redoubtable Montague Jenkins. The man standing in front of the fireplace, with his thumbs in the top of his waistcoat, his voice raised pontifically and his cheeks bulging, must surely be he. There could not be two of this kind. Anthony, ever courageous, advanced towards him. Jenkins had just concluded a most impressive utterance, ex-cathedra. His final words had been:

"I haven't the slightest doubt that my version is the correct one." He never had. There were certain reasons, almost excuses, for this condition that was so inevitably his. His father had been an elementary school teacher and his mother an extremely aggressive health visitor. The sole issue of this iniquitous union had been Montague.

As Anthony approached towards him, several members of the crowd that had been listening to him drew away to various corners of the smoke-room. Anthony caught his bovine eye and contrasted it with that of the man whom he had just left. Certainly the Catena Club had "characters." Montague Jenkins knew instinctively that this stranger had business with him. He half-opened his mouth. Before he could advance a stage Anthony had spoken to him. He closed his mouth.

"Have I the honour of speaking to Mr. Montague Jenkins?"

The mouth had closed with a snap but now it opened again almost instantaneously.

"You have, sir. I am Montague Jenkins. Son of Barham Jenkins of Milton in the county of Hampshire. At the age of ten, sir, my father put before me the exclusive use of his own personal library and study. He was a discerning and far-seeing man and early recognized my academic inclinations."

"You surprise me," murmured Mr. Bathurst.

Montague Jenkins glared at him. He was unused to replies of this kind. Anthony gilded the pill. "The age that you mention is indeed remarkable. Ten! Dear me! Worthy to be ranked with the historic case of the notorious Jack Skinner, who undressed himself and ran upstairs to bed at the tender age of six months."

Jenkins softened somewhat. This was praise indeed.

"I wonder if you could help me," proceeded Anthony. "That is the reason for my being here. I have been recommended to apply to you. My name is Anthony Bathurst. You may have heard of it. I represent, unofficially, the Commissioner of Police, Scotland Yard."

Even the habiliments of Jenkins billowed forth and became truly bombastic in recognition of the supreme favour for which he had been chosen.

"Ah," he said. "Yes. Of course I have heard of you. Now in what way can I serve you? Command me."

Anthony looked round the room significantly.

"My business is of the highest importance. That is why I have come to you. Where can we talk quietly? With just a little more privacy?"

Jenkins beckoned to him.

"Come over here to this table in the corner. You will find that it will serve our purpose admirably. It is away from everybody."

Anthony moved over to the table with him. They seated themselves. Jenkins assumed his best air.

"Now, Mr. Bathurst. You will find that if we sit here we shall not be disturbed. When it is seen that I am engaged with you that will *assure* you absolute exclusiveness. The members accept certain things as traditions."

It was an enigmatic sentence, but Anthony thought that he understood what his companion meant. He therefore leant over the table and spoke to him.

"My business, Mr. Jenkins, concerns the case of Claude Merivale. I expect that you have already guessed as much."

Jenkins wagged his head. Anthony could almost hear the preening of his feathers.

"Yes. I knew it," Jenkins answered with an air of triumph. "Directly you spoke to me I felt certain of it. May I inquire who sent you to me? Is it permitted?"

Anthony leant forward again and whispered a name. Jenkins clucked. Anthony almost found himself looking for the egg.

"Of course! Naturally! I might have known it, if I had stopped one second to consider. Charming fellow. So—er—flamboyantly—er—academic! Don't you think so?"

Anthony, without in the least understanding, lied bravely and said that he did. Jenkins beamed.

"Now, Mr. Bathurst," he said, "tell me *exactly* what it is that you want to know, and I'm your man."

"That suits me," returned Anthony. "I will. I want to go back to the evening of Mrs. Merivale's death."

"Pardon me," said Montague Jenkins, laying a restraining hand upon the Bathurst sleeve, "but I'm a man that faces up to things, and gets right down to them, that hates milk and water—and deals with facts as facts and NOTHING ELSE! You understand me? Well then—call a spade a spade—Mrs. Merivale's MURDER." Jenkins sat back in his chair all prepared for the halo distribution.

Anthony shrugged his shoulders. "Have it your way. Were you here in the Catena Club on that evening in question?"

"I was. And, what's more, my dear sir, I saw Claude Merivale here."

"Excellent. I imagined that you might have. That's going to be a great help."

"That's what you want—help."

"Yes. Did you, by any chance, speak to Claude Merivale?"

"I did. More than once. I think that he, in common with the others—rather liked me to notice him. Let me put it like this—he was apt to be a little hurt if I were busy on any occasion, and, by reason of my being busy and my time thus occupied, compelled to ignore him. Understandable, on his part, I think, don't you?"

The face of Jenkins took on the likeness and circumference of a prize dahlia. It became radiant with pride, and an enterprising earwig would have moved in immediately and joyously taken up possession.

"Can you remember, then, Mr. Jenkins, what suit Merivale was wearing when you spoke to him? And also, if possible, what the time of your encounter would be?"

Montague Jenkins patted his cheeks. Here was opportunity knocking at his door demanding him to prove himself. To demonstrate the difference between himself and the average man. A demand was being made upon both his power of memory and his power of observation.

"As it happens," he said, "I was here in the smoke-room when Claude Merivale arrived on the evening of the tragedy. The time was about half-past seven. I can remember well the suit that he had on . . . it was a white duck suit. He has been wearing it for some little time. He's making a new film, you know. The scenes are just being shot. I fancy that this white suit has been worn for that purpose. I believe that the scene of the picture is laid somewhere in Italy. We've pulled his leg about that suit more than once here, believe me. But, do you know, Bathurst—it's a funny thing—but your question has set me thinking."

A curious expression flitted across his face as he spoke. Anthony wondered what it was that had caused it. He waited patiently for explanation.

"Funny," went on Montague Jenkins immediately and speaking almost to himself, "funny that . . . and it hadn't occurred to me before. H'm." He rubbed the ridge of his jaw with his fingers.

Anthony's facial expression almost spoke the question that was in his mind. Jenkins turned to him again and from the light in his eyes Anthony knew that the explanation of the puzzled expression would be soon forthcoming.

"This is funny. Something I've thought of. Really very funny. I told you when you first tackled me on the subject, that I spoke to Claude Merivale more than once during that evening. Well, from what I can remember, and I fear that it sounds foolish, considering what I have just said, but on the last occasion I spoke to him, I believe that he was wearing an ordinary *dark* lounge suit. What annoys me is that the fact of the two suits being worn on the same evening hadn't struck me before! See what I mean? If you hadn't turned up to question me on the subject, I should probably never have thought of it. Remarkable how we are inclined to accept things with our eyes, isn't it? First impressions as it were?"

Montague Jenkins looked somewhat crestfallen at this semi-confession. He had failed himself! Anthony became severely practical.

"You are telling me that he changed his suit while he was here. That's the explanation, surely?"

"He must . . . er . . . undoubtedly have changed his suit. My point—here—during the evening. On the premises of the Club," Jenkins nodded. "He must have done."

"Is it customary for members of the club to change their clothes here?"

"It's done. Many members avail themselves of the privilege. If they haven't much time, for instance, and desire to dress for dinner somewhere—quickly. Either here or elsewhere."

"I see." Anthony thought over Police Constable Pike Holloway's statement. This story of Jenkins tallied with that all right.

"This isn't quite the same thing, though, is it? Merivale didn't dress for dinner exactly, did he?"

"No-o. But the white duck suit was just... a little... conspicuous, perhaps, had he intended to go somewhere specially. He *may* have been on the way somewhere, to a crush of some kind, and felt that a change of apparel was desirable."

"He would take the suit away with him, of course?"

"Probably, I should imagine. But not certainly. There are facilities for leaving clothes on the premises. I'll settle that point for you with pleasure."

Montague Jenkins rose from the table and pressed the bell. To the steward who answered it, he said in the best Jenkins manner.

"Ask Hill to come to me at once, will you?"

Hill came in due season. Jenkins questioned him severely. Information was given by Hill immediately.

"Yes, sir. That is so, sir. Mr. Merivale did use one of the dressing-rooms on that evening of his trouble. He wanted to change his clothes. He came to me and I at once arranged matters for him. As a matter of fact, the suit he took off is here *now*—on the premises. He hung it up in one of the wardrobes—we often arrange things like that for members—as you know yourself, Mr. Jenkins—and, of course, the suit still remains there. Naturally so... in the circumstances. Would you be the person who 'phoned through about it the other day?" Anthony pricked up his ears and looked at Hill. What was this? Another keen interest in the suit of white duck that Claude Merivale had discarded?

"No," he replied, slowly. "I haven't 'phoned about it. But I'm interested. You've roused my interest all the more, saying that. Tell me all about this telephone inquiry that you say you had. What was the point behind it?"

Hill looked at him doubtfully.

"I don't know that I can rightly say, sir." Anthony was puzzled.

"Why not? What's to stop you?"

"Oh—it's not that, sir, it's just that I'm not sure myself what was behind it all. See my meaning, sir?"

Anthony looked at him steadily.

"I think you'd better tell me all about it, Hill. As I suggested to you just now."

The man looked nervous and flustered under Anthony's scrutiny.

"Well, sir," he replied after a moment's thought, "the suit belonged to Mr. Merivale, didn't it? It was his private property . . ."

"It was."

"And Mr. Merivale's in the dirt, as you might say—under a cloud, isn't he?"

"I'm afraid that he is. What's your point?"

"Well, sir, things aren't normal and ordinary, are they, with Mr. Merivale? His wife's dead and he's in prison and I'd thought I'd better let the suit be left here, stay here, until somebody acting for him claimed it. So I gave orders to the assistant attendants that unless special application came for it from somebody more or less responsible it wasn't to be touched. There it 'ung in the wardrobe. Well, about a couple of days after Mr. Merivale had been arrested, I was told by one of the men 'ere that I was wanted on the 'phone. When I answered it, the inquiry was about the suit. Had it been left here at the Club and, if so, where exactly was it?"

Anthony intervened.

"Who was the inquirer?"

"I understood that it was Mr. Merivale's solicitor, sir."

"Did he ask for you by name?"

"Yes, sir. The man who answered the call in the first place says that that is so. I've asked him that myself—since."

"H'm! Strikes me as significant, that." Anthony looked into space. "Extremely significant."

Hill hesitated to go on. Eventually, however, he spoke again.

"I hope that I didn't do wrong, sir. I should be sorry if I have. I suppose now that I look back on things that I should have referred the matter to Mr. Austin, the secretary. But I gave the information that was required. I just said that the suit was here and mentioned where it was."

Anthony pulled at his top lip.

"H'm. You did—eh? Did the inquirer give any name on the 'phone?"

"Yes, sir. Campbell Patrick."

"That settles it," said Anthony, turning to the magnificent Montague Jenkins with a shrug of the shoulders. "Merivale's solicitors are Chamberlain, Alexander and Rolfe. Campbell Patrick's the barrister who's defending him." He swung round again towards the man Hill. "Are you sure, Hill—listen carefully to what I say—that the word *solicitor* was mentioned in the conversation?"

Hill nodded vigorous corroboration.

"Yes, sir. Absolutely certain on the point, sir." Anthony nodded.

"Thank you, Hill. I'm afraid you've been bamboozled. May I see the suit? Would it be troubling you too much?"

"No, sir. At least I don't think that—" Anthony observed the man's new spirit of reluctance and understood it. He handed him his card.

"It will be all right, Hill. Don't worry about that. If you look at the signature on that card you will see that everything's in order."

Hill glanced at the card that Anthony handed him and was suitably impressed. Anthony spoke to his other companion.

"You will come with me, Mr. Jenkins? I should be extremely gratified if you would."

Montague Jenkins beamed with delight. Really . . . this was . . .

"Certainly. Certainly. Of course. Only too delighted."

Hill turned on his heel and moved towards the door.

"Come this way, then, gentlemen—will you?" He piloted them out of the smoke-room along the thickly carpeted corridor, until they came to a flight of stairs at the end of it. They followed him up these stairs and then along a similar corridor. Hill eventually stopped before a door fronted by an outer portal of green baize. He made explanation. "There are three rooms on this floor, sir, where members of the Club can dress or change if they so choose. The rooms are reserved for that purpose. This is one of them and the room which Mr. Merivale used on that last evening when he was here."

He pulled away the outer protecting door, took a key from his pocket and unlocked the inner door for them. "Will you come in, gentlemen, please?" He pushed open the door of the bedroom and stood aside to allow Anthony and M. Jenkins, Esq. to cross the threshold. Anthony saw at once that the room resembled the bedroom of an ordinary hotel. Hill walked at once to the wardrobe that was ranged against the wall on the left-hand side. He pulled open the doors of the wardrobe.

"Here's the suit that Mr. Merivale took off, sir. It's the only one in here, so that you haven't to look very far for it."

Immediately he had spoken, Hill gave vent to a half-smothered exclamation and his hand went to the side of his face. "It's gone"—that was what Anthony Bathurst understood him to say. Anthony looked into the wardrobe over Hill's shoulder. There could be no argument about the statement that Hill had made. The wardrobe was absolutely empty. Hill turned to the two men behind him with astonishment written on his features.

"This beats me. I'm fair knocked over, sir. It was here the other day when I looked. Hanging on that hook at the side there." He pointed into the wardrobe. "On a hanger really, the coat. Just here. The trousers were folded and put away neatly just there." Hill pointed into the darker recesses of the wardrobe. Anthony smiled at the discomfiture of the attendant.

"Although the wardrobe is empty, Hill, I think that we can truly say on this occasion that there's more in it than meets the eye." His smile broadened. "What do you think about it yourself?"

Hill swore fiercely.

"Exactly," returned Mr. Bathurst. "I don't think that I could have put it better myself. Come on, Mr. Jenkins, you and I must talk this over. Let me listen to you."

Montague Jenkins, taking a deep breath, prepared for action.

CHAPTER X
The Trial

The days went by and the time came for Claude Merivale to be tried before Justice Lamacraft. The trial started on a Tuesday. It was problematical when it would end. The case for the Crown was in the able hands of Sir Percival Keene, supported by Idris Griffith, K.C. Merivale, as MacMorran had informed Anthony Bathurst, when he had first broached the case to him, was defended by the famous Campbell Patrick. Famous indeed—almost notorious—Campbell Patrick was an Irishman from Co. Derry, who had made his name in the celebrated Melaniphy Scandal case, and he didn't accept a brief, no matter how highly it was marked, unless he considered that he had a fighting chance of winning his case. He had been quite content to accept the brief in this case of Rex versus Claude Merivale. His keen black eyes had danced when it was first offered to him. He had studied the points of the case thoroughly and had almost immediately decided to rely implicitly on Merivale's own line of defence—the unconsciousness of the dreaming. He had at once taken steps to obtain Quinton Gaskell, the neurologist, to appear as the expert medical witness for the defence. Quinton Gaskell, from the beginning of his career, had been a thorn in the side of many Crown prosecutions, and a sharp pin-point in the seats of the mighty. The minority, the underdog, and the outcast generally, had always held a greater appeal to him than those whose lot it was to sit in high places and wield potent influence. This case of Claude Merivale, with its extraordinary first line of defence, had attracted him from the moment that it had burst into being, and when Campbell Patrick, K.C., had consulted him on behalf of his client, he had responded to the overtures at once. Also, Sir Percival Keene, appearing for the Crown, was an old opponent of his with whom he always took delight in crossing swords.

Idris Griffith, supporting Keene, was a young Welshman who was beginning to make a name for himself at the Criminal

Bar. His nationality and his political views, carefully selected and, naturally, by no means immutable, had been his most valuable assets. This was as well from his own point of view, as he had little else with which to carve a career. The jury for the Merivale trial consisted of nine men and three women, after two men had been successfully challenged by the Counsel for the defence. The twelve who eventually served and thereby became almost ephemerally famous, were as follows: Foreman, Daniel Vanbrugh, a retired schoolmaster. The remainder of the men in order of their seating were, John Claringbold, builder's architect, Frank Forrest, a Post Office Official (retired), Leonard Stokes, an artist, William Richmond, a florist, George Arnold, commercial traveller, Arthur Vinall, fishmonger and poulterer, Henry Pollard, house agent, and Vincent Cornibeer, a dentist. The women seated together were a Mrs. Annie Adamson, proprietress of what she herself called a café-restaurant, a Mrs. Letitia Bryce, widow of a retired Civil Servant (Ministry of Labour) and a Miss Veronica Burns, assistant librarian at one of the bigger circulating libraries and the eldest daughter of a horse-dealer, who had seen better days and worse nights.

The morning of the trial broke warm and sunny. The court was crowded, every inch of available space being taken. The case had filled the columns of the newspapers for some time and, being distinctly unusual, had attracted much more than ordinary attention. When Mr. Justice Lamacraft took his seat punctually at the appointed hour a nervous buzz went through the Court betokening that feeling of suppressed excitement such as "the house" often feels as the "rag" rises on an important and much-heralded first night. It will be interesting if we record the thoughts of the twelve members of the jury at this precise moment. Mr. Justice Lamacraft has just taken his seat.

Vanbrugh, the schoolmaster, thought that it was a tribute to the intelligence and to the general good sense of people that his companions of the present adventure had elected him to be their foreman. After all, he argued, there was something about, a teacher that the man in the street was usually quick to perceive. Teachers were well informed. They "knew" all about things. That old tag that they were "men amongst boys and boys amongst men" was ridiculous, and utterly unjust. They were respected and looked up to, at any rate. Here was proof of it. Mr. Daniel Vanburgh, an old "Sinjun," had been elected almost unanimously, mind you, to be the foreman, that is to say, the leader of this most important jury. In a case where the foreman *must* be a man of the highest intellectual standard. It would be his lot, when the evidence had been weighed and sifted, to announce the verdict. Again—just as well that it were he and none of the others. His elocution would be perfect. He would see to that. His vowels of true quality and his consonantal attack clear and precise. "The Duke would say . . . let him roar again." Daniel Vanburgh stroked the hair at the back of his head and settled down in his seat to watch the expressions that flitted across the face of Mr. Justice Lamacraft. He would have made a good judge himself. He felt sure of that. Better probably than most of them who had been so honoured.

Claringbold, the builder's merchant, thought that it was a standing disgrace that lead should be so dear, compared with the price that it had been less than a year ago. He was convinced that there *was* "a ring" somewhere. A ring that was conspiring to keep the price of lead inflated. He had told Alderman Plummer the other day—a man who in his time had been Mayor of the Borough—of these suspicions of his, but the worthy Alderman had disagreed with him. In the ring himself, very likely, thought Claringbold, with bitter suspicion. If he thought that he could get away with it . . . he'd . . . What was that the Clerk of the Court was saying? Claringbold listened and his views on lead and Alderman Plummer receded.

Forrest, the retired post-office servant, thought of his early days and of the strange fact that during them, he had known the notorious Henry Wainwright, the murderer who was convicted of the killing of the ill-fated Harriet Lane. Wainwright had been a lecturer and entertainer of no mean ability and, as a small boy living in the same district, Forrest had seen him and heard him more than once. His thoughts went back to the trial of Henry Wainwright and of his brother Thomas, and of how a boy friend of his own, also an employee of the Post Office, had started a foundationless rumour in the district after the two brothers had been sentenced, that the elder brother had been reprieved. That boy friend had later become an immediate colleague of Forrest's and had also . . . Forrest, like Vanbrugh, settled down in his seat and began to watch the expressions on the face of Mr. Justice Lamacraft.

Stokes, the artist, thought on these lines. That, in this place of so-called Justice, there should be, more appropriately, the flash of helmets and the glint of spears and the dim shadowy waving of plumes and banners. That knights in full armour, and lords, and men-at-arms, should be passing to and fro instead of these drab figures of the Courts. That something like the Judgment-Trumpet itself should be blown by an angel, with grim and austere folds down his back, and with the strong west wind blowing his wild gold-hair far out behind him in a straight stream, with the wind rippling the long scarlet pennon of a lance that he carried in his other hand. Then Stokes thought that the angel should look down into the Court from his height in heaven, very sorrowfully, as a man who has just risen from a long illness and who carries with him a dull pain that he knows will be with him until he dies. Stokes caught sight of Mr. Justice Lamacraft and slowly and gradually the vision of the angel with his trumpet and lance faded from his sight. The Clerk of the Court was speaking. The Judge was fidgeting with his sleeves and the corners of his elbows.

The prisoner in the dock was brushing his hair from his forehead with his long white fingers. Leonard Stokes, like Vanbrugh and Forrest, settled himself down to do his duty as a member of the Jury . . . as an intelligent member of the Jury.

This brings us to the contemplation of William Richmond, the florist. Richmond, strange though it may seem in these days of materialism, had gone into business as a florist for the simple reason that he loved flowers. Better than animals, better than his fellow men and women. More than anything else that the earth gave to him. This Court in which he sat, to listen to a sordid unfolding of murder and jealousy and passion (he feared) had nothing of the loveliness that was a flower's. Or even that was a tree's. He thought of willows, by the side of rivers, willows, growing grey-green with the coming of spring. He thought of the topmost twigs of great tree-limbs, of cowslip time in the country. Of brooks that murmured lazily over clean stones. Of the songs of birds ringing through the hedges. Of the soft sweet colours of the sky and of the clouds that floated languorously through the blue of it. Of blooms, of tender fresh grass, of the sweet young shoots of all flowering twigs, of brown stones and of broad-leaved waterflowers. Of lush marsh-marigolds, of the rustling of hard magnolia leaves, of golden daffodils under acacia trees. Of blue and red and yellow flowers, of the black tulips that . . . why didn't the judge keep still and not move restless arms and fingers? Richmond came back to the Court.

Arnold, the commercial traveller, like Gallio, "cared for none of these things" of Richmond's. If it weren't for this wretched murder trial having come along to take up his time, he would have been in his little bus on the road to Colchester just about this time. This was his day for Colchester. Once a week. He would have stopped on the way, too, . . . for lunch at the Red Dragon, Broome. Good lunch at the Red Dragon. They did you well. Nice little barmaid there. Red-haired and saucy. Doris. He liked Doris! What was that old Shuttleworth used to say about red-haired girls . . . damn good it was, he knew, if he could only remember it . . . Yes . . . he had remembered it. . . . "Ever slept with a red-haired girl . . . no . . . not a wink all night." That was it. Damn good, that! Arnold almost chuckled audibly. Yes—he thought again. Good lunch at the Red Dragon. Steak-and-kidney pudding with oysters, tomatoes and mushrooms today. Didn't get that in any sort of pub. And plenty of it. No stinting. "Kate and Sidney" he called it. When he called it that, Doris always knew what he meant. Got a quick come-back—Doris. Goodness knows what sort of a lunch he'd get up here in this hole. Nothing like the one in the pub, at Broome. What was that the old boy in the wig was saying? Doris wouldn't half laugh if she could see the old boy's face. All dolled up and nowhere to go. Lot of tommy-rot all of it! Why couldn't they settle these things without summoning twelve men for jurymen—taking them away from their job and their daily bread, and wasting their time. Time meant money. Crying shame if was. Ought to be looked into, it did! Why didn't *John Bull* do something about it? Good mind to write to them about it. What was the old bloke saying? Silly old blighter!

Vinall, the fishmonger and poulterer, had taken a comparatively long time to adjust himself to the unusual surroundings in which he found himself. He was so unused to it all. Out of his element. When he had entered the Court that morning, his mind had reverted to the Essex village of Torpingham in which he had been born, and brought up with his two brothers and three sisters. The farmhouse that had been so important to his boyhood stood out clearly in his mind's eye. It lay about half a mile behind the village church of Holy Cross. Rector, the Reverend George Grout, M.A. (Oxon). The atmosphere of the Court had reminded Vinall of the atmosphere of that church. The village was within thirty miles of London, but for all that, it had been both primitive and sequestered. It had contained but few houses that held any pretensions to gentility. They were the Hall, the Rectory, and White Lodge. He thought of his mother peeling potatoes and washing lettuces over the sink in the scullery, and he saw himself, as a small child, walking down the long avenue of big elms that led to the Hall where Squire Truelove had lived and died. He remembered as he sat there in the Court, that day in October, it was the third, he remembered it well, when tragedy had come so unexpectedly to the village of Torpingham. When a big elm had crashed in the grounds of White Lodge and killed Reuben Harbottle, a farmer who had been visiting there. He, Arthur Vinall, playing not far away, had heard the crash of the great tree, and the cry of the hurt man, and had raced through the gate of White Lodge to the spot where the elm had fallen. The dead man, he could see him now, as plainly as he had seen him then, lay face downwards, his neck close-pinned by a huge branch. It was the first time that Vinall had looked on death and he had shuddered at its sight. Death . . . His thoughts pivoted . . . the man standing there now in the dock might soon be called upon to face it. If the verdict were "guilty" . . . it meant the condemned cell and the hangman . . . *he* would have a part in the bringing of that verdict . . . he must listen carefully to what was being said. It would not do for his thoughts to wander. You *mustn't* make a mistake over a matter like this!

On Vinall's immediate left sat Pollard, the man who described himself as a house agent. Pollard was a little, hairy man, black-haired and sallow-faced. He had taken to his house agency business but recently. Had had money left him by an equally hairy aunt which had made the venture possible. He was full of nervous anxiety and his fingers twitched uneasily as he looked from one fellow juror to another, awkwardly, and with little sidelong glances. His mother and sisters were in Newcastle on holiday (they were a strange family, the Pollards) and he wished that he were there with them. Also he had slept badly the night before. Nervous dyspepsia. Thoughts of this coming trial had disturbed him, no doubt. He had always been like that, or at any rate ever since boyhood. A nervous wreck on the thought of any unusual testing that lay in front of him. Would come over sick in school just before an examination. Cornibeer, the dentist, was a man of surprisingly little intelligence. He had weak eyes, a straggling mouse-coloured moustache and a receding chin. He was undeniably proud to be a dentist and usually thought in terms of dentures and fillings. As he took his seat in the jury box, he wondered how many people in the Court would see him there, recognize him and nudge one another, with the spoken words—"look—see that. There's Vincent Cornibeer, the dentist." His fingers caressed his mean moustache. The Judge was looking straight at him . . . wondering, probably, why the jury hadn't made *him* foreman and not Vanbrugh! Clever man, Mr. Justice Lamacraft. He had always understood that. Good at assessing the values of different men. His legal training helped him there, doubtless. Would do. Had made him as exact and precise as one of those calculating machines that were used nowadays in all the offices. His brother-in-law (Cornibeer's) had just ordered one. This man that was talking now could speak all right! Who was it? Cornibeer shifted awkwardly in his seat. His thin, sallow face, eaten into many furrows by the years of his life, changed into something like grotesque piteousness and his features for a time became less ugly. He also moved restlessly . . . long, thin arms—crooked shoulders. His pale face grew paler until it became almost as the face of a dead man. The cold sweat gathered on his brow and he fancied that he could almost hear the rapid beating of his heart as he sat there. His arms shook and trembled and then he suddenly recovered himself again and his first unconcerned look came back together with a semi-scornful smile that flickered about the corners of his feeble mouth. His fingers went to the straggling moustache again as a sign of his returned confidence. He was Vincent Cornibeer, the dentist again. He'd have a story to tell Aubrey Lewisham next time that they met. Curse Lewisham . . . for a snob!

Mrs. Adamson, the proprietress of the Elite Café-Restaurant—"joint and two veg. tenpence"—sat with her fat podgy hands laid on her knees. She bent forward a little towards Mr. Justice Lamacraft as she listened, as if she were striving to look through and through something that was always a long distance away from her. She had heavy, rolling waves of dark brown hair, slumbrous eyes with full lips beneath them. She looked almost lifeless, something like a statue, so quietly and without motion did she sit. Claude Merivale, watching anxiously from the dock, saw her, looked hard at her, and partly understood her immediately. He thought that her face was cruel in its impassivity. As he looked and wondered, the bells of a near-by church rang. Their music struck into his heart, and a strange ghastly suspicion took a hold of him. If his suspicion were correct there was but one way that the verdict could go. The certainty of that, the cold certainty took hold of him and gripped him. He saw Mrs. Adamson's breast heave and her face drawn into the network of wrinkles that were not the wrinkles that age had begotten. For she, too, had heard the bells of the church as Merivale had heard them, and a sharp pang of memory had shot through her. She, too, was back for a moment in the place where she had been born, those broad marshlands around the River Lea. The country, that people who spoke carelessly and without thought, called ugly, but she herself was of that sad lowland country and, therefore, loved it. Claude Merivale saw her smile and the cruelty of her face slowly faded from it and lo, there was kindliness there in its stead.

Mrs. Bryce, the widow of the retired Civil Servant, had, it must be admitted, a red-tipped nose. Digestive derangement, of course. There could be no other reason. She was a strict Congregationalist and although adherence to that faith had brought her her duck-footed, dab-toed husband, she yet remained true to it. Her eyes were small and, it is to be regretted, bloodshot. She sat with her arms stretching straight down and the hands clenched. She had entered the Court that morning with the fixed intention of not looking at the prisoner. Her late husband had looked at little beyond his money and now he lay under the earth. She still thought that to die when he did, had been most inconsiderate of him, and she had made up her mind that this would be the first thing that she would tell him when they met on the golden floor. Mrs. Letitia Bryce sniffed at her thoughts. The sniff reached the ears of Mr. Justice Lamacraft. Mr. Justice Lamacraft frowned and looked across in the direction whence the sniff had travelled. The frown rested on the guilty Mrs. Bryce, who had great difficulty in preventing herself from screaming aloud and dashing precipitately from the precincts of the Court. Instead of doing so, however, she sat rigidly still, staring straight in front of her.

Veronica Burns was the remaining member of the twelve jurors. Her predominant feeling was to take an active and intelligent interest in the whole of the proceedings. To miss nothing. This trial was of Claude Merivale for murder, an event of importance in her life, and she was determined to make both the best and the most of it. From which general observations it will be seen and understood, that the trial of Claude Merivale before Mr. Justice Lamacraft had commenced.

"Call Dr. Moxom."

There was a stirring in the Court. Mr. Justice Lamacraft leant forward. Dr. Moxom took the Testament in his right hand.

Mrs. Bryce sniffed again. On this occasion, the foreman of the jury turned and frowned at her.

CHAPTER XI
THE VERDICT

CAMPBELL Patrick's speech for the defence was, in part, as follows. He called no witnesses beyond Claude Merivale himself. Merivale, in the witness-box, told exactly the same story that he had told previously. Anthony Bathurst, seated with Chief Inspector MacMorran in a place of privilege, watched him closely all the time that he spent in the witness-box, and especially whilst he stood there under the battery of Sir Percival Keene. Mr. Bathurst formed certain deductions. Here is the main substance of Campbell Patrick's speech.

"The prosecution has conducted its case with commendable fairness. As was but to be anticipated, seeing that it was in the hands of my distinguished colleague, Sir Percival Keene, whose chivalry and absolute integrity have never been questioned or surpassed." Campbell Patrick bowed. "But I would point out to the Jury, to the twelve members of the Jury, that the conscious and exclusive pursuit of material success nearly always finishes with disappointment, and its twin condition disillusionment. At the end of it, the ambitious man who has achieved his ambition, finds it but a Dead Sea apple in his mouth—or what I shall better term 'the substance of a dream.' You have heard the evidence of Dr. Moxom for the prosecution, and that of Dr. Quinton Gaskell for the defence. Each gentleman an expert. You have heard of the scratch on the throat of the dead woman and of the jagged finger-nail of the prisoner that was noticeable on the morning that he surrendered to the police. Is a man to go to the gallows because of a scratch? Such a happening is unthinkable. No intelligent jury would consider such a possibility. Think rather of a man asleep and dreaming. As any of us may. As many of us undoubtedly do. All dreams are not *bad* dreams or born of evil thinking. I would assert that, without the slightest fear of contradiction. The good dream, which is not always a day-dream, is a divine gift to the man who has learned, not only the final unreality of what seems most real to him, but also the super-importance of that which never can be seen or heard. I will quote to you the words of Lord Lytton."

Here Mr. Bathurst looked up in surprise and nudged Chief Inspector MacMorran in the ribs. Campbell Patrick's voice rang across the Court.

"*'The Now is an atom of sand, And the Near is a perishing clod: But Afar is a Faery land, And Beyond is the bosom of God.'* When a young man sees visions they spur him to action. When the old man dreams dreams, he is impelled to sacrifice. Hearken therefore to the words which I have just employed in order to illustrate my point. 'Spur' and 'impel'. Let us look at them from the point of view of special meaning. Each contains the nuance of meaning that is allied with a sense of force. Claude Merivale, whom you are trying for the wilful murder of his wife— and 'wilful' means 'deliberate' remember—dreamt that he was in danger. Personal danger! He met force with force. That is to say he acted naturally. Even though both these 'forces' were born in and of a dream. Consider tyrannies. God is tyranny. Evil is a tyranny. The obsession of 'force' can be a tyranny equally as potent as either of the other two. In the case of the prisoner at the bar, I contend that it *was*! Sometimes when one of these tyrannies comes to one in full consciousness, there is a natural resentment against it and the desire to fly from it. But, remember, Claude Merivale was *unable* to escape from it. He was caught in the inescapable entanglement of a force that attacked him in that thin border country that lies between the unconsciousness of sleep and the apprehension of wakefulness. He was entirely *incapable* of avoiding what he considered his inevitable obligation. His mind was fettered and his faculties bound."

Campbell Patrick dropped his voice almost to a whisper.

"The Angel of the Lord appeareth to Joseph in a dream. Then there came 'revelation' to Joseph. The dreamer was transformed and in the transformation became an effective man of action. Revelation came also to Claude Merivale and he, like

Joseph before him, also became an effective man of action. What other course of action was possible to him? The fact that the person at his side was his wife *meant nothing to him* as he turned in his sleep to contend with the enemies that attacked him but were only the figments of his dream. *He did not know that the person he had seized was his wife.* He could not know! How could he? He was asleep! More than that even—he was dead! Yes, I repeat it—*dead*. I make that statement with deliberate intent. Each one of us who sleep? at night—dies. Yes—every night that we fall asleep. To wake next morning is the daily recurring miracle of the blessed resurrection! Keep that eternal fact in your hearts and minds when the time comes for you to arrive at your verdict, ladies and gentlemen of the jury. That is all that I would ask. For while we are asleep and therefore, as I have shown you, *dead*, there is no satisfactory answer to the question as to where our minds actually are, or what our bodies actually do. There can be none! The dreamer is an effective man of action when he refuses to mistake the 'is' for the 'might be.' Properly understood, it is a matter for extreme satisfaction that a man's life is uncertain and at the best, so far as the world is concerned, of short duration, because it is not conceivable that so much has been prepared and so much has been promised for what after all is but a scanty fulfilment. If man be 'dream of a dream' and 'shadow of a shade' then the dream is a magnificent prophecy and the shade is the shadow of the Eternal. Now this brings us to a further point. It is inevitable that he who cannot dream should as a rule be impatient with the dreams of others and resentful of them, just as the blind are irritated by the clear vision of their fellows. To the people to whom the world is nothing but streets and front doors those others who find it heaven on earth are active annoyances. Poets, in their time, have given us dreams. But when a poet writes a poem and gives it the word 'dream' in its title, has he really *dreamt* as we understand the word at this trial, to-day? There is written evidence that 'Kubla Khan' was the result of a dream, brought on by the influence of opinion, but when Tennyson wrote a 'Dream of Fair Women' did he actually see them in a vision that came to him during the night? Dreamland *must* be associated with Chaos. Again, certain visions are not to be regarded as dreams. And there is, I contend, an essential difference between a dream and a day-dream. It is safest, perhaps, I suppose, to regard the poet when he is a dreamer as a being 'sui generis,' for who would be audacious enough to compare a poet's recorded dream, gorgeous in colour as a Tintoretto, suave and harmonious as a painting by Lorraine, with his own feeble dreams? Dreams that are almost always absurd, illogical, incomprehensible, and not infrequently accompanied by nightmare!

Boccaccio's Lorenzo appeared to Isabella in a dream, but did Porphyry melt into Madeleine's dream as Keats describes it, and can we believe that Endymion, lulled to slumber upon Mount Latmos, actually saw the moon stoop to kiss him? All entanglements of Beauty, ladies and gentlemen of the Jury, like the veiled maiden in Alastor, and the Damozel who always will be Blessed. Picturesque, tropical, allegorical imagination and even pathetic! Vastly different from the entanglement of the case with which we are dealing today. But, mark you, with the common factor of the dream itself. Turned sordid into an avenue, at the end of which lurked death itself. Claude Merivale, the prisoner at the bar, has told us that he slept that night and dreamed. The eminent counsel for the Crown, by repeated and clever questioning, has failed to shake him even infinitesimally on that story. Why? *Because it is impossible to shake the Truth!* Its foundations are too strong! Only Claude Merivale himself knows what he dreamt on the dreadful night when Mrs. Merivale died. To us are open two courses, one of which, you, ladies and gentlemen of the Jury, will shortly be called upon to take. You can believe the prisoner or you can disbelieve him. If you believe him, you will return a verdict of 'Not guilty.' I cannot visualize that you will disbelieve him. Supposing he had *dreamt* that he had killed his wife—supposing that the two parts of the dream had been reversed in point of time—what would have been the result? I demand the answer! Here it is! Mrs. Merivale would still be alive! Think of that—ladies and gentlemen of the Jury! The prisoner is, and has always been, a man of character. The

Prosecution has attempted to present you with a motive for the murder. The time-honoured one of jealousy. That Mrs. Merivale was wanton . . . a fair woman, like to Lamia . . . with the face of an angel, eyes like stars, breasts like the golden front in the Hesperides, but, from the middle downwards, shaped like serpent. I say to you that the Prosecution has lamentably failed to prove that motive. Does a man, jealous of his wife and fearful that he has lost her affections, make his mind up to murder her, and wake up in the middle of the night to carry out his purpose? The prisoner's character has never been assailed. Mrs. Merivale's character stands in like place. It cannot be said of her: 'She made it Plain that Human Passion was Ordered by Pre-destination; that if weak women went astray, their stars were more in fault than they.' One of the attributes of personal character is the care placed on the bestowal of values. Things belonging to others are valued because of that, even though to the valuer they may possess little or no significance. We must keep our judgment to ourselves and respect the dreams . . . all the dreams . . . of the dreamer. They may be his treasures. We do not know. Here, we are of the earth—earthy, and cannot understand. Here we see but dimly and darkly. There—wherever 'there' may be—we shall see face to face. *We* may see *then* that which the dreamer sees *now*. We may share the joy and the rapture that come to him out of his fantasies. We may cross the threshold with him, we may enter into his blessed intimacies . . . and when we do, we must 'take off the shoes from our feet, for the place whereon we shall stand will be holy ground.' Ladies and gentlemen of the Jury, I ask you for that verdict which I sincerely believe to be the only one possible to men and women of intelligence . . . a verdict of 'not guilty.'" Campbell Patrick hitched his robe over his left shoulder and sat down.

Mr. Justice Lamacraft's face was a study as he began his summing up. There was fire in his eyes and emotion on his lips.

"Ladies and Gentlemen of the Jury," he opened, "you have patiently listened to . . ." the nine men and the three women to whom he addressed his words waited upon them. Every syllable came to their ears clearly and distinctly. Mr. Justice Lamacraft spoke for nearly three-quarters of an hour. Then his voice changed:

"I will ask you now to retire and perform the duty which has come your way through the exigencies of the law. To find a true verdict, a true and proper verdict, according to the weight of the evidence that has been presented to you, and regardless of what the consequences of such a verdict may prove to be. Ladies and gentlemen, you will now retire and consider your verdict."

The members of the Jury filed slowly from their places, and as they did so, a warder stepped forward quickly and touched Claude Merivale on the shoulder. Claude Merivale turned and understood what was expected of him. Daniel Vanbrugh gathered his eleven members around him in the room to which they had been taken and began to talk to them.

"Now, ladies and gentlemen, I think that our best method of arriving at a verdict will be as follows. We must attempt to arrive, as quickly as we can, at unanimity. You all follow me?"

"That's O.K. with me," replied Arnold immediately. "I think it's the goods, and just what we ought to do. Give us your own ideas, will you, Vanbrugh?"

"I was just about to do so," replied Vanbrugh, "when you interrupted me. Kindly don't do so again."

"All right. Needn't get stuffy. And no reason to come the schoolmaster touch, either. Even if you are foreman. Suppose I've got a right to speak, haven't I?" Arnold turned away with an ugly look on his face. "Proper pig-o," he muttered as he turned.

Vanbrugh ignored the unpleasant tone in Arnold's voice and addressed the others of the party,

"Now, ladies and gentlemen," he said again, "I'll lead off by telling you my own impressions. When I've finished, I'll make clear to you what *my* verdict is. All those of you who agree with me, and I'm confident that there will be several, can say so at once. That means that the others, that is to say, those who disagree with me, can begin to argue their case. In that way, we can soon hope for a condition of general agreement to come fairly quickly. Does that idea find favour with you, ladies and gentlemen?" On his last words, Vanbrugh looked round enquiringly. There were subdued murmurs from which Vanbrugh understood that he was expected to carry on as he had suggested. Arnold's contribution was a sarcastic laugh, but Mrs. Adamson went and stood at his side. Vanbrugh noticed the movement and resented it. He recovered himself quickly, however, and began to place his various points before the eight men and three women who faced him. He spoke with but little interruption. Occasionally there came a question. One from Mrs. Bryce, concerning the scratch on Mrs. Merivale's throat. One from Richmond, the florist, with regard to Campbell Patrick's statement that sleep was comparable with a state of death, and another from Veronica Burns as to whether Mr. Vanbrugh, the respected foreman whom they had elected, ever dreamt himself. Daniel Vanburgh answered all these questions. He flattered himself that his replies were concise and to the point. He gradually came to the finish of these statements. He told the eleven jurors clearly what would be his verdict. They heard it. The different faces at which he looked registered varying emotions.

"Now, ladies and gentlemen, how many of you are with me? I'll put the question to you, one by one. Those who agree with me will signify their agreement by saying 'Yes.' Now—Mr. Claringbold?" "Yes." "Mr. Forrest?" "Yes." "Mr. Stokes?" "Yes." "Mr. Richmond?" "Yes." "Mr. Arnold?" "No."

Vanbrugh frowned.

"Mr. Vinall?" Arthur Vinall, fishmonger and poulterer, who had first looked on death in an Essex village, hesitated on his answer. "Er—yes."

Vanbrugh continued his inquisition. "Mr. Pollard?"

"No."

A cough from Arnold followed Pollard's reply. "Mr. Cornibeer?"

"Yes. Yes—I think yes."

"Now I'll put the question to the ladies."

"Mrs. Adamson?"

"No."

"Mrs. Bryce."

"No."

"Miss Burns?"

"Yes, Mr. Vanbrugh, undoubtedly 'yes.'" Miss Burns knew her mind.

"Thank you," said Vanbrugh. "Now let's see where we are. We have eight against four. I suppose now that it's up to me to convince the other four. Is that the wish of the others?"

"Certainly not," said Arnold. "You're not quite the Big Shot of the outfit, as you seem to imagine you are. Hold on a minute. You've had your say and put your case. Now let one of us have a say and put our side of the question. Fair's fair all the world over. Now, Mrs. Adamson—you have your go."

Mrs. Adamson, without waiting for any movement of consent or disapproval from the foreman, was in her stride at once. The eight heard her out. Discussion started. Argument became fast and furious. Mrs. Bryce gave way under an onslaught from Vanbrugh, and Pollard, the house agent, quickly followed her. Arnold and Mrs. Adamson, of the minority, alone remained. When the Jury had been in retirement for an hour and a quarter, Mrs. Adamson, under argument from Richmond and Stokes, showed signs of weakening. Her capitulation came ten minutes later and with his last ally gone, Arnold threw up the sponge.

Vanbrugh sent up the necessary message. The Court came to life again. The news was flashed quickly that the members of the Jury had at last reached an agreement and were coming back. Anthony Bathurst watched the nine men and the three women as they filed into their respective places. Mr. Justice Lamacraft entered quickly. His Chaplain and the Clerk of the Assize accompanied him. Anthony saw the ominous square of black silk ready to be used, if wanted. The Clerk of Assize rose and addressed the members of the Jury. The buzz and stir of the Court ceased with a suddenness that came almost as a shock.

"Ladies and Gentlemen of the Jury! Are you agreed upon your verdict?" This particular clerk had a good voice and it rang through the Court. Vanbrugh was determined that he would not play second fiddle. He cleared his throat magnificently.

"We are."

"Do you find the prisoner at the bar, Claude Rhys Ingram Merivale, guilty or not guilty?"

There was a pause. Vanbrugh intended that there should be. He had an eye and a mind for effect. He looked round the entire court before he answered the all-important question.

"Not guilty."

The stir that followed the foreman's announcement was silenced again—this time by the commanding voice of the usher. Mr. Justice Lamacraft leant forward towards Claude Merivale.

"Claude Rhys Ingram Merivale, as you heard, the Jury have arrived at their verdict. That verdict has been arrived at after a most thorough and searching inquiry into the whole of the evidence that has been placed before them. You, Claude Rhys Ingram Merivale, are acquitted of the murder of your wife, Vera Merivale, and are discharged." The Judge turned towards the Jury. He thanked them for their services, promised them the usual exemption from further service and discharged them.

Anthony looked askance at Chief Inspector MacMorran.

"Well, Andrew, and that's that."

MacMorran grunted. Anthony watched the people as they dispersed from the Court. He saw a knot of men together in a press, passing through one of the doors. Suddenly a face turned towards the dock and Anthony, looking carelessly across the Court, caught a fleeting glimpse of a line of determined-looking jaw. It struck a familiar chord in his memory. It was like somebody whom he knew . . . just in profile. Who was it? His mind worked lazily. Until the shattering truth hit him! The side of the face which he had seen for that quickly passing moment had been like the prisoner's. Catching Inspector MacMorran by the arm, Anthony Bathurst walked quickly towards the door through which the man had just passed.

"What's the darned hurry?" expostulated the inspector. "What's she like, or is it that you must congratulate Claude Merivale so quickly?"

"Don't be all sorts of an old ass," returned Anthony. "I saw so much of somebody just now, that I shan't rest quiet until I've seen some more. A man who was very like the man that's just been acquitted. Do you hear what I'm saying, Andrew?"

By this time, they had crossed the Court and had passed through the entrance doors. MacMorran frowned. Neither the haste of his movements nor Mr. Bathurst's explanation was pleasing to him. He shook his head wearily as Anthony brought him through the doors.

"These enthusiasms are, of course, not without interest, but—"

Anthony's restraining arm forced him to a standstill. The people were dispersing in all directions. There was no sign of the man whom Anthony had seen and tried to follow. Already he could hear the shouts of the newsboys outside.

"We've missed him, Andrew," he said.

"I'm not surprised. We've been missing things all through the case."

"Speak for yourself, you miserable old devil."

"I was. I was speaking for both of us." Anthony grinned.

"I'll clear it up before I've finished, Andrew. And I'll give you one of the biggest surprises of your life. You mark my words if I don't."

MacMorran shook his head thoughtfully.

"I'm better off than I was, Andrew," continued Mr. Bathurst. "A shadowy suspicion has become something much more like a certainty. While there's life, you know, there's hope."

"There's not much life about Mrs. Merivale."

"That isn't fair. She was dead before I came into it. You can't reproach me with that."

MacMorran turned and looked at him searchingly. "Come and have one," he said.

"You've taken the words from my mouth, Andrew," replied Mr. Bathurst.

PART TWO
THE PUNISHMENT

CHAPTER I
Mr. Bathurst Meditative

Anthony Lotherington Bathurst for a second time drank beer with Inspector MacMorran and P.C. Pike Holloway. MacMorran was talking. Holloway was content to let him. Why not? It wasn't his fault or his responsibility that the Inspector wasted time. The wastage could be well employed.

"As far as I am concerned," said the Inspector, "the case is finished. The Merivale murder can be put on the files and gradually forgotten. And I'll tell you why, if either of you is sufficiently interested to listen to me. It'll be a change for Mr. Bathurst to listen. Claude Merivale murdered his wife. He has been tried on that charge and acquitted. He can't be tried again. The law of the land won't allow it. So there we are. Merivale 1 MacMorran 0. No extra time need be played. All the results and full reports including Scottish League matches! Thank you, Mr. Bathurst—I don't mind if I do."

Anthony smiled and refilled the Inspector's glass. Pike Holloway, observing the activity, hastily emptied his own tankard. Consideration for others!

"Well, Andrew," returned Mr. Bathurst, "I won't deny the truth of what you say. I can't. All the same, I'm strongly tempted to keep going. In my own humble way. Do you mind if I ask you a question?"

"It wouldn't be the first time, now I come to think of it. Shoot!"

"Which, to your mind, Andrew, is the most significant point of the whole affair? No—I'll alter that—the *two* most important points? Take your time, have a good look round, and pick where you like."

Pike Holloway put his tankard on the corner of the mantelpiece, brushed his moustache and prepared to listen. Despite the prophecies of his grandmother, not often did he take part in the counsels of the great. MacMorran thought carefully over Anthony Bathurst's question. He had been told to take his time—and he would.

"Firstly," he replied with slow emphasis, "the scratch on Mrs. Merivale's throat, taking into consideration the fact, mind you, that we *know* Merivale had a jagged nail showing when he came down to give himself up and, secondly, the discrepancy in his 'times.' That is to say the difference in his own story compared with what we know Constable Holloway here has told us. They're the two points that I select." MacMorran finished his oration and drank more beer. "Well—what do you think of 'em yourself?" he added hopefully.

"I'll take one and reject the other."

"H'm! Not so bad for me. A bit above my usual form. I'm showin' improvement in my old age."

Anthony proceeded. "I'll take the scratch on the throat, and for *my* other, I'll take the disappearance of Merivale's light suit from the wardrobe at the Catena Club. First of all, we'll talk about the scratch on Mrs. Merivale's throat. And I think, my far from merry Andrew, that I shall probably surprise you with the opinion that I shall give you of it. Because in my opinion it would have been much more significant if Claude Merivale *hadn't* had that jagged finger-nail which all of you simply couldn't help seeing. You must have gaped at it!"

Anthony's tone was significant. MacMorran looked up at him curiously.

"What are you gettin' at?"

There was a smile showing in Anthony's grey eyes as he answered. "Why, *just* this, Andrew. That for truth's sake I should have preferred that the torn nail of Merivale's finger had *not* been there." Constable Holloway leant forward in his chair and put his elbows on the table. What was coming next besides more beer? Anthony Bathurst continued his explanation to the Inspector.

"Let me put it in a nutshell for you. It will assist you materially. What I think is this. That the nail was torn *because* of the scratch on the dead woman's throat." Anthony rubbed his chin.

MacMorran shook his head. "Of course it was. What are you talking about? I'm afraid I don't get you. Explain—will you?"

"Think carefully over what I said and you'll see what I mean. I said that the nail fitted the scratch. You assumed that the scratch fitted the nail. No nail—no scratch. Common sense, that. But I'm confident that no *scratch* would have meant no jagged *nail*! Merivale had noticed the scratch on his dead wife's throat and lo, he produced the nail to fit it so beautifully. Cart and horse, rather than horse and cart."

MacMorran shook his head in hopeless resignation. "I'm afraid, then, that the case is beyond me altogether. If what you say is correct—what about Merivale's dream? Where does that come in now?"

Anthony shrugged his shoulders. "Does it matter, Andrew? Especially to you?"

"I don't set much store by dreams," contributed Pike Holloway. "Give me plain facts and no fancy stuff. I've seen many a horse win a race in a dream but it was an also-ran on the course. Cost me no end of money! Once you start admitting dreams and such-like, where are you going to finish up? Pardon the liberty, sir, but that's plain talkin' from a plain man."

"You're too late with that," said Anthony, "you didn't hear Campbell Patrick for the defence. You missed a treat. He had the jury in the hollow of his hand. Personally, I was surprised that they were away as long as they were."

"Three of 'em stood out for a time—or so I've heard," interposed the Inspector. "That was the rumour that floated up to us. Strange how we usually get the 'low-down' on those things."

"It doesn't matter now," said Anthony. "Let me proceed with my second point. The disappearance of the suit of white duck from the wardrobe at the Catena Club. Perhaps, and I speak in all seriousness, the most significant feature of all that we know."

"All attempts to trace that telephone call which was supposed to have been made—failed. There's no doubt that it was put through from a call-box. I'm presumin', of course, that your man, Hill, the steward, was speakin' the truth. Similarly, I haven't yet run across a guy who's known to his intimates as 'Tollie.' Bad going—all of it."

"Perhaps he isn't, Andrew. Have you thought of that possibility? The name may have been specially reserved for Mrs. Merivale. There's a chance of it, you know. Such things have been known to happen before." Anthony broke off. For a few moments he seemed lost in thought. "I'd give a hell of a lot to know who wanted that suit of Merivale's—and *why* he wanted it. It looks as though he wanted the suit itself and not anything that was in it. As far as one can tell that is. A suit of white duck. H'm! Unusual! You say that you saw Claude Merivale in it regularly, didn't you, Constable?" Anthony Bathurst turned to Constable Holloway for confirmation of his statement.

Holloway nodded confidently. "For some time now, sir. Oh—yes! Some weeks I should say it is now, sir. Mr. Merivale used to come home regularly in it. It suited him too. Looked very smart in it he did."

"H'm! It beats me, Andrew, just as much as it does you." Anthony rose and walked to the window of the flat. "You had no success whatever, Inspector, you say, over the Maidenhead dance-club clue? The short plump man who used to escort Mrs. Merivale to Reveres? Answering to the name of 'Tollie'?"

"Picked up nothing, Mr. Bathurst, although I've put several feelers round. As I said just now, he couldn't have been *generally* known by the name, otherwise I should have picked something up. What made you come back to the point so quickly? Thought of something else—have you?"

"I was thinking of the man whom I saw in Court. Who, from the angle at which I saw him, reminded me so much of Claude Merivale. I had a vague, nebulous idea that he might—"

MacMorran interrupted him. "Might be the mysterious 'Tollie.'"

"No. He couldn't be. It doesn't fit. If 'Tollie' is plump and short, as Major Revere told us he was. No! The man whom I saw leaving the Court was tall, slim and well-built. 'Tollie' and he can't be the same man on those terms—can they? No. Not that. I thought that perhaps he and 'Tollie' might be acquainted. That was all. Nothing in the idea, probably."

"Any grounds for thinking like that?" inquired MacMorran gravely.

"No. No real grounds. Can't support it in any way."

"Then why worry? That's not like you, Mr. Bathurst. What's the idea?"

Anthony came back from the window and sat in his chair again. Constable Pike Holloway turned and watched him curiously. This was an Anthony Bathurst whom he had not previously seen or heard.

"Well, Inspector—it's like this. When the science of deduction fails you, and you can find nothing emerging out of it, you are turned in the direction of pastures new. You have a guess at things sometimes, Inspector. Why shouldn't I? Who am I to be excluded from the guessing gallery?"

MacMorran shook his head at the explanation. "It's not like you. That's what I mean. That's all."

"Thanks for the compliment, Andrew. Praise from Sir Hubert!"

There was a silence broken at last by Pike Holloway's almost ecstatic enjoyment of more beer. Suddenly Inspector MacMorran saw a light come into Anthony Bathurst's eyes. MacMorran waited with patience for revelation. He knew that it would come when the time was ripe. Anthony began to speak. "Andrew, I've missed something. And, which is more, I ought to be kicked for missing it! I only hope I've retrieved it before it's too late."

"What is it, Mr. Bathurst?"

"Something that I heard when I called at the Catena Club. That day I had the chat with Mr. Montague Jenkins. Goodness alone knows why I didn't fasten on to it before this. Have I been slow! Especially as the point touches the matter of the suit that Merivale wore. The now-notorious suit of white duck. I've just remembered what Jenkins told me about it. That Merivale was wearing it in connection with a picture on which he had been working. A new picture. Well—I'm beginning to find the fact interesting, Andrew. What do you think about it yourself?"

Constable Pike Holloway was all eyes and ears. He felt that the white duck suit was more or less his responsibility. And much more so now than before.

"Can't see that it makes much difference," replied MacMorran.

"It might do."

"How?"

"We can't tell. But the fact gives the suit a special significance. Takes it away from the ordinary. It might very well have more interest to some people, say, than an ordinary every-day lounge suit would have. Can't quite explain what I mean, but you can see the drift of it, can't you?"

Inspector MacMorran nodded slowly. "Yes, I get it. Brings the affair into the circle of the new picture, you mean. There was a newspaper reference to it only yesterday. It's nearly finished. One of A.J. Carstairs's productions. Plenty of ballyhoo about it. Like all the Carstairs stuff. He certainly does know how to get publicity."

Anthony looked at MacMorran with something that approached admiration.

"He sure does, Andrew."

MacMorran grinned feebly at the sally. "Well, you know what I mean, don't you?"

"I'm beginning to be interested in that picture. I know that. When it comes on, I think I must make a point of seeing it. What's it called—can you remember?"

MacMorran thought over the question. "Don't know. Can't remember that I've ever run across the title. I've a sort of idea at the back of my mind that the title hadn't been decided on until fairly recently. Think I read that somewhere."

"There's no time like the 'now-time,' as François Villon said," remarked Mr. Bathurst. "I can soon find out. If I'm going to see it, I may as well know the title now, in case it slips my notice when the first night comes on. Just a minute and we'll find out." MacMorran and Pike Holloway listened as Anthony telephoned.

"Lexham 2288. Thank you." Pause. "Is that you, Horace? Thought you might be at home turning some stuff out. Seems I was right. Marvellous how I think of things. You know who it is this end. What? Same to you—swine-face! Won't keep you half a sec., so don't get hot and bothered. But I've no doubt you can tell me something I want to know. That's why I rang you. What's the title of the new Carstairs picture? Yes . . . that's right . . . Claude Merivale was in the cast originally. What? Gone back to it? I'm not surprised. Carstairs wouldn't miss that chance. Good 'box-office,' of course. Exceptionally so. What? What's that? Is it, by Jove? Thanks a lot, Horatio. I don't know what I should do without you. Well, here's mud in your eye. Remember me to Hilda." There was a silence as Anthony replaced the telephone receiver.

MacMorran and Constable Pike Holloway wondered what it was that had caused the sudden change in the tone of his voice, as he had spoken to the invisible and seemingly omniscient Horace. The silence continued for an appreciable time. Anthony Bathurst, finger to his lip, gazed at the telephone, lost in thought. MacMorran was curious.

"Well," he inquired, "what's the hot news?"

Anthony was smiling as he turned to answer the Inspector's question. "The title of the Carstairs-Merivale picture, Andrew, is *The Painter of Ferrara*. Proving, my dear chap, that there are more painters in the world than you and I and Constable Pike Holloway here ever dreamed of. We might well have ransacked our brains for the 'Painter' connection, mightn't we?" His smile became a laugh.

The Constable began to see the meaning of Mr. Bathurst's remarks. He nodded his head.

"The word I heard Mr. Merivale use as he entered his house that night. Yes—I see now. Well, well—who would have thought that he was referring to the picture that he was working on? Funny how things turn out."

"It looks like that from what we know now, doesn't it? The information, too, serves a useful purpose. It lets light into a matter that we hadn't previously properly understood. Which is all to the good. At the same time though—" Anthony Bathurst hesitated. He seemed uncertain.

"At the same time—*what?*"

"We don't appear to be making *too* much headway, do we? On the most optimistic valuation. Everything that comes along and suggests that it might be promising, fizzles out. Turns out to be all above board and entirely ordinary. Consider this for example. Disappointing."

As he finished speaking, there came a tap on the door. Anthony looked up. "Yes, Emily? What is it?"

Emily entered with her usual quietness. "A gentleman to see you, sir. He asked if I would bring you up this card." Emily came across the room and handed over a visiting-card.

Anthony looked at it with some curiosity. Emily waited there, for his decision, at the side of him. Anthony's face twisted into a smile.

"It has been said that the occasion brings forth the man. Pausanias to wit. The present appears to be no exception to the rule." He carelessly flicked the card on the table in front of them.

Chief Inspector MacMorran picked up the card to read it. The sight of the name that it bore did not in any way please him. He showed his displeasure in a frown.

"Claude Merivale? The man himself. What the hell does he want here?"

"That," returned Anthony, "he will no doubt tell us when we admit him."

"In that case," replied MacMorran, "I think that I'd better be going." He rose and gestured towards Constable Pike Holloway. The latter rose also, without remark.

"On the other hand," countered Anthony, nodding to Emily, "I can't think of a better reason why you should remain."

MacMorran and the constable without fuss resumed their seats.

Mr. Bathurst evidently knew best!

CHAPTER II
Claude Merivale Belligerent

Emily departed to obey the instructions of Anthony Bathurst. Footsteps sounded on the staircase. Anthony went to the door to admit his self-invited guest. Merivale entered. He showed traces of his recent ordeal. But his debonair manner was still with him. He looked round the room.

"Good evening, gentlemen," he said challengingly. "I trust that I am not too much of a disturbance."

It was then that he noticed the presence of Pike Holloway and came to an abrupt stop. Anthony entered the breach.

"Chief Inspector MacMorran, whom you know, Police Constable Pike Holloway whom you have met—er—several times, and myself—with whom, you are, I believe, moderately acquainted. Sit down, do."

"In sooth," replied Merivale with mock grandeur, "I seem—almost straight from my cell—to have strolled into a nest of hornets. Two pros and a 'bloomin' amateur'! Ah, well, I can't expect the break every time. T'would be too much." He took the chair which Anthony had offered to him. As he did so, he faced Pike Holloway and looked him over with a curious scrutiny. "Your face certainly is familiar, officer, although for the minute I am not able to place it. Forgive me, won't you?"

MacMorran—uncompromising—glared at him.

Pike Holloway, however, quickly responded to Merivale's words and mood. "Used to meet you, sir, of an evening. Don't you remember? My beat covers Enthoven Terrace, where your house is. That's what you're thinking of, sir." The Constable's face beamed with satisfaction. It was plain at once that Merivale understood. His face cleared of its doubt directly Pike Holloway gave his explanation.

"Of course. I remember now. Used to pass you on my way home. Knew I'd seen you somewhere before. Couldn't place it. No wonder your face seemed familiar to me. Stupid of me."

Pike Holloway was not content to let the matter rest there. He pursued the subject still further. "Come to that, Mr. Merivale, don't you remember that I passed your front gate just as you were going in on the night—er—that you—er—" He suddenly realized that he had entered deeper waters.

Merivale, after hesitating for a moment or so, looked at him. Evidently the constable's last words had made but little impression on him.

"Which night do you mean?"

Pike Holloway's discomfiture at his *faux pas* increased. He moved one of his arms awkwardly. Merivale's direct question had been unexpected by him. He took what he considered was the best course.

"The night of your trouble, sir."

Merivale stared at him with a curious look in his eyes. "Are you trying to tell me that you saw me on that evening?"

"Yes, sir. Saw you going into the house on that very evening. Heard you mention the word 'painter' as you went in. Perhaps you didn't spot me, Mr. Merivale, as I went by, but I saw you."

Claude Merivale's eyes narrowed at the Constable's statement. "What time was this, officer?"

Anthony now was listening with both ears. This was critical. Pike Holloway pushed his hand through his hair. "In the early part of the evening, sir. About six-thirty, sir. As near to that as makes no odds."

Anthony watched Claude Merivale's face as he listened. He would have sworn that the man was making a calculation of a sort. What was it, Anthony wondered? A strange case this, all the way through. Then Anthony saw Merivale nod slowly in acquiescence.

"Yes," he said quietly and deliberately, "I do remember the incident now. Although you saw me as you say, I only just caught a mere glimpse of you. Out of the corner of my eye. That was it. I do remember now quite clearly. And the time would have been about half-past six, as you say. Yes, just about."

Pike Holloway nodded eagerly. He was glad that things had gone as they had. Felt rehabilitated. Shouldn't have liked Mr.

Bathurst to think that his story of his meeting with Merivale was unreliable. Or even Inspector MacMorran, come to that.

Merivale addressed the Inspector. It would seem that the Pike Holloway incident was almost forgotten by him. That it had been disposed of.

"You're wondering, I know, what has brought me here. Why I have come to see you. Why the mouse has crept into the lion's den."

"Some mouse," interjected a cynical MacMorran.

"I'll tell you," continued Claude Merivale, ignoring the interruption. "I'll clear away your suspense."

"Thank you," murmured Anthony encouragingly.

Merivale gave him a half-glance that might have meant anything. Anthony appeared to be unconscious of it. Merivale proceeded with his statement.

"I have been in prison for some time. You know that. I make no complaint with regard to that. It was inevitable in the light of all the circumstances. Nothing else could have happened. I have been tried for my life and in accordance with the traditions of English justice, I have been acquitted. And although I am not a lawyer, I have sufficient acquaintance with the law of this country to know that I cannot be tried again for the murder of my wife."

Merivale's voice was even and entirely without emotion.

Anthony looked at MacMorran, who smoked on steadily. Pike Holloway shifted uneasily in his seat.

Merivale went on again with his story. "All these things, as I said, have happened to me. Very few men, comparatively speaking, will be called upon, or have ever been called upon, to endure what I have endured. It is as well. Also, I would say this. That I have no complaint with regard to the manner in which the case against me was conducted. Everything was scrupulously fair and if Inspector MacMorran here were concerned in it in any way, I should like to thank him here and now for all that he did and to say how thoroughly I appreciated it." A courteous gesture towards MacMorran gave point to his remarks. The only sound that came from the Inspector's direction was the crackle of the tobacco burning in his pipe. Nothing disconcerted by the cool reception of his complimentary tribute, Merivale continued. "You will see that, up to the present, the sole burden of my song has been complete satisfaction. But I have dealt so far, only with that which is past. With that portion of my life, that I am thankful to say lies behind me." He paused again, to proceed slowly and more gravely. "These things, these foolish things, are gone as I said. But other things, less foolish, I hope and believe, lie in front of me. Life must be lived. There is no honourable escape from it. It will need all the courage and strength that I can summon to my assistance for me to live my life. I am an artist. In a way, I can claim that. I belong to the public. My position, therefore, is not quite an ordinary or conventional one. Which brings me to my first complaint. A complaint for which I seek redress. Redress! I cannot use a better or happier word. Something has been stolen from me. While I lay in prison." There was an edge now on Merivale's voice. Anthony's senses came to the alert. What was coming from Merivale now? Of course! Why had he wondered? He knew the answer before Merivale gave it. The word 'redress' had been the clue to it.

"On the evening of what Inspector MacMorran and others have been considerate enough to refer to as 'my trouble,' I changed my clothes at my Club—the Catena Club in Piccadilly. I have been a member of the Club for years. I left the suit that I then took off in one of the private wardrobes there. While I have been absent, gentlemen, that suit has been taken away from that wardrobe. I have inquired at the Club premises and I can get no satisfaction there. I was referred by the Club to the Police Authorities. Does that mean that my suit has been taken by the police in connection with the case for the recent prosecution? If so—I want it back." As he looked at them, Anthony Bathurst felt certain that Merivale was definitely anxious about something. The fact surprised Mr. Bathurst. Surely anxiety should not now rest upon Merivale's pillow? He had passed through the days of his danger, and fear should lie behind. What fear could haunt him now? The suit! The white duck suit again! Merivale was speaking once more. Nobody had replied to the question that he had asked. Merivale therefore repeated himself. "Have the police thought fit to take my suit from the wardrobe at the Catena Club? I should like to know, please."

Anthony glanced across at MacMorran. The latter nodded almost imperceptibly. Anthony knew what the nod signified. He took on himself, therefore, the responsibility of the answer for which Claude Merivale was waiting.

"The police have not acquired your suit, Mr. Merivale. I can tell you that with certainty. It formed no part of the Crown's case against you. Why should it?"

The trap was baited. Merivale eyed him suspiciously.

"Inquiries had been made at the Catena Club prior to mine today. I am basing my idea on that. I learned as much when I went there. I understood that those first inquiries were not unconnected with the activities of Scotland Yard. I apologize if I'm wrong."

Anthony answered him without hesitation. "In a way, that is quite true, Mr. Merivale. I made the original inquiries myself. In fact, I may as well tell you that my efforts met with no more success than your own have. The suit had been taken from the wardrobe prior to my arrival at the Catena Club, since when we have been unable to trace it. Unhappily, that is the extent of my information."

Merivale went a shade paler. "Am I to understand that you cannot help me, then?"

"About your suit?"

"Of course."

"I'm afraid that with regard to your suit, you and we are in the same boat. Somebody, utterly unknown as I understand, was sufficiently interested in the suit that you hung up in the Catena Club wardrobe, to telephone concerning it, first of all, and then to take steps to remove it. Whoever it was, was successful."

Merivale moistened his lips with his tongue. "How? How is it possible that anybody could—"

Anthony interrupted him. "Walk off with it? Let me suggest—by sheer audacity. *L'audace, l'audace*—you know the rest. For that is certainly how our unknown friend achieved his objective."

Merivale sat staring straight in front of him. He had no words for the moment. MacMorran, having heard all, bent down and knocked the burnt tobacco from his pipe. Anthony came in again—more directly this time.

"Was the suit tremendously valuable to you, Mr. Merivale? If so, perhaps we might be able to—"

Merivale recovered himself. "Oh, no, it had no value beyond the ordinary. At the same time, I'm by no means overjoyed to lose a perfectly good suit of clothes. It formed part of my wardrobe. I had recently, as you know, been at work on a new 'flick' and the suit was useful to me. That's about all that there is to it. Well, I'm sorry I troubled you." He rose, with the evident intention of departure. Anthony waved him back to the seat that he had vacated.

"Is there anybody of whom you can think, to whom the suit would have been valuable?"

Merivale's answer was ready. Readier even, than usual. "Not a soul. The idea's fantastic. I don't mix with people who wear each other's suits." The smile on his face, as he spoke, diminished the force of the gibe.

Anthony ignored it. He kept to his point. "Leaving the suit itself out of the question for a moment, then, was there anything *in* the suit, in any of the pockets, for instance, that might be valuable to anybody. Which is a somewhat different proposition, you will admit." Anthony's tone of nonchalance failed to mask the deliberation behind his statement.

Merivale's lip curled. "Mr. Bathurst, surely you are failing to live up to your reputation? I changed my suit at the Catena Club and left the one that I had taken off in the wardrobe on the Club premises. I have already told you that once. Should I have left anything of value in the pockets? Is it possible? Should I be so entirely lacking in intelligence? The pockets were absolutely empty, let me tell you. I transferred *everything* to the pockets of my other suit. I took care to do so. Really, Mr. Bathurst, the question does you less than credit." Merivale thrust his hands into his pocket with an impatient movement of his head.

Anthony listened to his statement gravely. Again he paid no heed to the implied criticism. "Value, Mr. Merivale, using the word that you have used, if you will allow me to say so, is a relative term. There are intrinsic values and there are values that are absolutely extrinsic. Those values may well be attached to the same article. There might have been something in one of the pockets of your suit that was utterly worthless as far as you were concerned, but which, on the other hand, might have been extremely valuable to another. Surely you will concede me that much?" Anthony looked at him interrogatively.

"Such as?" sneered Merivale.

Mr. Bathurst shrugged his shoulders. "Who can tell? I might make suggestions. Purely suggestions, you understand. Let me see now. What can I suggest? A photograph? A visiting-card? A letter? A telegram? Even a railway ticket in some circumstances? Any of those personal, intimate things that mean little or nothing in themselves but which have a definite exclusive meaning for one, two and perhaps even three people." Anthony deliberately stressed the word "three." "Are you following me, Mr. Merivale?"

Merivale had remained cool and collected. MacMorran realized more than ever as he listened that the man was an excessively hard nut to crack. Merivale nodded when Anthony finished.

"Oh, yes. Perfectly. But all the same, aren't you overlooking something? Something that I have already told you? I said that the pockets of the suit that I left behind were empty. No photographs, no telegrams, no letters. Nothing personal. Nothing intimate. Nothing private. Nothing important, sensational or incriminating. I'm afraid, Mr. Bathurst, that your theory, interesting though it may be, comes crashing down like a house of cards."

Anthony shrugged his shoulders. "Very well. We'll accept that position. For the sake of argument. So far, I've constructed, or attempted to construct. You've demolished. Suppose we reverse the activities? *You* make suggestions and let *me* have a smack at *them*. Why do you think your suit was stolen? I could bear to hear all your opinions."

Having turned the tables, Anthony lounged back in his chair. But Claude Merivale refused to pick up the gauntlet which Bathurst had thrown down. "I haven't the slightest idea why the suit has been stolen. And, because I haven't any idea, I can't see any reason *why* I should put up a string of fantastic theories. Even to please you. I refuse point blank to do such a thing. Because you have played at that game, why should I? It seems to me perfectly ridiculous."

"In that case then, Mr. Merivale," returned Anthony, "I am afraid that we cannot help you."

There was a silence, broken only again by the crackle of Inspector MacMorran's pipe. Anthony waited for Merivale. Mr. Bathurst considered that he had said all that need be said. It was for Mr. Merivale to play. Merivale, however, had lost the mastery of his own moods. Anthony felt certain that his dominant feelings were of annoyance. Why? That was the question. Anthony found himself toying with a new theory. On the whole, it attracted him. He broke the silence.

"I understand, Mr. Merivale," he said, "that you have returned to the cast of your picture. The picture upon which you were engaged when your crash came."

Merivale looked at him suspiciously. "Yes. That is so. But why—what's the point behind your mentioning that?"

"I read a notice about it, the other day. In the *Morning Message*, I fancy it was. But so much of the stuff in the papers is unreliable that it's refreshing to have come across something that's authentic. When's the *première*?"

Merivale was frowning. "Next week. The picture was almost finished when I made my temporary but enforced exit from the cast." His face clouded over—sadly.

The sudden change of it surprised Anthony. This man Merivale had many sides and many moods. One followed another with remarkable rapidity and often a mood came which was entirely new and for which one, even with experience of the man, was utterly unprepared.

"Let me see," said Anthony, "what is the title of the picture? It's eluded me for the moment."

"The title has been but recently decided. It is called *The Painter of Ferrara*."

Anthony raised questioning eyebrows.

"Matteo Dossi?"

Merivale nodded. "Yes. The picture deals with him. You are familiar with his work?"

"I have seen those fine examples of his work which have been exhibited in English galleries. I admired them immensely. But I must confess that I know little of Signor Dossi beyond that."

"I see. The film is good—exceptionally good—and I hope it will be a success. I'll go farther than that. I'll predict that it will be. A.J. Carstairs doesn't make many mistakes. You see if I'm not right. And now, gentlemen, I'll wish you good night. In a way, I'm sorry that I troubled you. Thank you for everything—and nothing."

MacMorran nodded his good night. Pike Holloway was inarticulate. Mr. Bathurst saw his visitor to the front door.

Chief-Inspector MacMorran and Constable Pike Holloway somewhat impatiently awaited his return.

"Well, Andrew," said Anthony a few moments later, "and what do you make of all that? What is it that's worrying our Mr. Merivale now?"

"Guilty conscience," returned MacMorran, curtly. "Nothing more and nothing less. And it bites too."

"You think so," replied Anthony. "I wonder."

"You can if you like. I don't. It's as plain as a pikestaff to me. Has been all the time. The man's a scoundrel and would have decorated the end of a rope. But he won't now, more's the pity."

Anthony smiled at the Inspector. "You never know, Andrew. As I'm beginning to see things, he may even do that yet."

MacMorran turned and looked at him with amazement. "How is that possible?"

Anthony smiled more broadly. "Well . . . he might form one of a tug-of-war team . . . mightn't he?"

MacMorran cursed softly as Mr. Bathurst opened another bottle.

Constable Pike Holloway reached for his tankard.

CHAPTER III
First Night

ANTHONY Lotherington Bathurst met Inspector MacMorran and Constable Pike Holloway somewhat unostentatiously in the box-office of the Illyrian Super-Cinema, Leicester Square. They were waiting for him when he arrived, which is not to say that Mr. Bathurst was late. Inspector MacMorran was relieved when he saw Anthony come in. The stream of cars, big and small, that rolled and purred to the entrance of the cinema testified eloquently to the extra degree of publicity that the picture had received as a result of the sensational trial of Claude Merivale. People who should have had many better things to do, stood on the scaffolding of a building opposite the cinema. Women had their coats torn from their backs. Handbags were lost and trampled underfoot. The trial of Merivale had weighed more with the picture-going public than even the magic name of A.J. Carstairs himself. It could be seen early that the gathering was to be eminently distinguished and completely representative. Almost all the stars of the theatrical and screen firmaments were there in the flesh. As Anthony said to Inspector MacMorran, you noticed them more this way than in the other. The Haymarket was crowded. The traffic was jammed. Thousands of eyes eagerly awaited the coming of the stars. Every motor-car that drew up was loudly cheered, in the remote chance that there was somebody inside who might merit the cheering. When Marilyn Garbrich appeared there came a full-throated roar from the crowd. An eminent and happily-married theatrical couple who by reason of their unimpeachable and long-endured domesticity had cast a halo over a somewhat discredited profession entered the theatre to the accompaniment of a burst of clapping.

"Time," said Anthony, "is a great healer."

MacMorran, alas, failed to comprehend. There were occasions when Mr. Bathurst's subtlety was too much for him.

Anthony paid for three seats in the upper circle, and as they took their places, a salvo of enthusiastic clapping heralded the arrival of Hansa Varenna. At length the curtain-set parted. *The Painter of Ferrara.*

The real performance had started. After a considerable period of time the picture itself commenced.

Anthony flooded his brain with a stream of cold reasoning and settled down in his seat to watch, to think . . . and perhaps, by the Grace of God . . . to understand! He knew that if ever his brain were to be one hundred per cent alert and resilient, that time must be to-night. He must pass nothing. He must miss nothing. Nothing at all. Pike Holloway was there with him, that was one thing. The man could help in one direction—that was certain. And all to the good. The names of the cast were studding the screen. They flashed and scintillated. Leo Meux. Hugh Assheton. Claude Merivale. Peter Hesketh. Richard Winston. Leslie Vining. Bradley Cole. Flack Lewis. Michael Kingshott. Holt Banbury. Horace Dickie. Victoria Garland. Beatrice Belmont. Constance Norman. Jessica Mortimer. Helen Meredith. Joan Bryan. Edyth Woodforde. Anthony took in everything. Every name. Every activity. Every announcement. Dresses. Photography. Adaptations. Technical processes. The picture itself started on a quiet note that was both artistic and effective. Anthony's eyes never left the screen. The author, he quickly perceived, was a brilliant realist. Atmosphere not only quickly came, but was maintained. Followed by tension and excitement. Strong stuff. Pathos, pity, and then again romance and quickly-fluttered sensation. The Italian scenes were well done. Victoria Garland, in the wedding ceremony scene, radiated beauty, charm, and an unerring sense of comedy. The pace of the picture grew fast and furious. Claude Merivale, from his first appearance, until the quarrel scene in the wine-shop, was adequate and convincing. Peter Hesketh, Leo Meux and Hugh Assheton supported him admirably. The quartette played with force allied to sincerity and above all with an admirable sense of restraint. Joan Bryan, as the young peasant girl doomed to die so soon, was adorably delightful and acted with a spirituality that was unforgettable. Unlike so many pictures which are almost entirely episodic, the story had coherent continuity and

Anthony remembered Claude Merivale's confident prediction, made in his flat, that *The Painter of Ferrara* would be a box-office success. Leslie Vining as the type of publicity agent that any social or professional aspirant would find invaluable, was magnificent. Music, pretty frocks, witty and daring lines were all there, to delight a sophisticated audience. Anthony's eyes took in every movement of every changing scene. Claude Merivale showed depth of emotion and considerable dramatic power. He was much in front of Anthony's expectations. MacMorran moved restlessly in his seat.

"Give me 'Variety,'" he muttered to himself, "every time. Now Marie Lloyd—"

Anthony was attracted, too, by the performance of Leo Meux. Here, surely, was the highest art that conceals art! Only the finest intelligence could simulate stupidity as Meux did, only real depth of character portray the shallowness. Beatrice Belmont, Jessica Mortimer and Hugh Assheton fitted beautifully . . . more than that . . . fitted *perfectly* into a superb setting, within which anything at all short of sheer brilliance would have "stuck out a mile." The scene changed suddenly from the marble quarries to the orange groves of Niume. Anthony still watched and waited. Vicky Garland, now impersonating her brother, and Meux were holding the picture. There entered to them, Claude Merivale, Hugh Assheton and Leslie Vining. All the men in this scene were wearing suits of white duck. Anthony leant forward eagerly. Surely . . . from now onward. . . . His hands gripped the edges of his seat. He must watch from this moment onwards with even more vigilance than he had shown before. The second quarrel between Merivale and Meux was superbly played. Anthony was irresistibly reminded of the famous "three men" scene in Sir Squire Bancroft's adaptation of Sardou's *Diplomacy*. The author of the present picture had employed almost the same technique. The entire scene held the rare gift of quality. These were real people, these people of shades and echoes, behaving exactly in the circumstances as real people would behave. They never became tedious or wearisome. The shooting of Vining by Jessica Mortimer was shown with terrific dignity. Vining's death scene couldn't have been bettered.

Anthony craned forward more and more so that he should miss nothing. The story gained in virility every moment. Claude Merivale's insidious attack on Meux as he lay sleeping was superbly conceived. The master-hand of A.J.C. and his trick-technique of taking short sharp shots and joining them were apparent therein at every turn. So the picture ran until the intervention of Assheton, in the struggle that had developed between Claude Merivale and Leo Meux. As Assheton plunged into the affray the impact of his body knocked Merivale to one side and he was swung right round. Assheton then came to grips with Leo Meux. Their faces came close together. Meux faced the audience, his head down, as a bull about to charge an hereditary foe. Assheton's was in profile, his hand raised high above his head, his chin uplifted. It was at that instant that Anthony Bathurst saw something that he had seen once . . . if not twice before. Assheton's face, at this angle, was very like Claude Merivale's. The full side of it bounded by the strong ridge of jaw. When you saw the full face the likeness did not occur to you, but when the face was presented as it was now, there was no mistaking the similarity. Anthony felt his heart beating faster. If what he thought were true, Assheton was the man whom he had seen leaving the court at the conclusion of the Merivale trial, and . . . extending the idea logically, Assheton *may* have been the man of the photograph seated in the deck-chair at the side of the late Vera Merivale. Here were possibilities, indeed! Anthony leant over the side of his seat and whispered again to Inspector MacMorran. "Anything strike you, Andrew?"

"Aye!" replied that worthy. "Yon's the famous suit of white duck. Is that your meaning?"

Anthony, secretly amused, shook his head and relapsed into his seat again. In time, the white duck costumes gave way to fancy dress and plumed hats. Hugh Assheton wore a big hat, broad-brimmed and with a sweeping feather. As he looked at the picture, Anthony exercised his mind again. Another fugitive likeness had begun to haunt him. Whom was this Assheton fellow like now? A man? Then it must be Claude Merivale surely! Anthony shook his head and rejected the suggestion. Assheton didn't resemble Merivale now. A woman? Yes . . . a woman! Which woman? A woman . . . whom Anthony had seen . . . to whom Anthony had talked not so very long ago. Who the dickens was it? Anthony whipped and cudgelled his brains. Somebody who had made recent contact with him in this case of Claude Merivale. Not Eva Lamb who had had "the evening off" on the night that Vera Merivale had died. Who else was there? Of course . . . of course . . . revelation came to him now incredibly swiftly. There was no doubting it. Jill Merivale, sister of Claude Merivale, the man who was taking part in the film play that was taking place in front of his eyes at that moment. Into what entanglement of relationship had he unwittingly stumbled? He assessed ages. As he judged the two men from what he had seen of Merivale and from what he could see of Assheton playing on the screen, there were about ten years between them, Merivale being the senior.

The picture came to a crescendo. Then it finished in a blaze of triumph. Truly, a great picture. As Marilyn Garbrich left her box to leave the cinema, there came yet another terrific burst of applause. People stood and unashamedly stared at her as she came through a door and descended a flight of stairs. Anthony, as he made his way out, heard foreign accents and broken English all round him. The people surged towards "La Garbrich" when she reached the foyer. Outside, the streets were even more crowded than when the performance started. Undisciplined cries came from them, "Marilyn!" "Marilyn!" Anthony felt sickened at this revelation of mass hysteria. He piloted MacMorran and Pike Holloway to his waiting car.

"Well," remarked the Inspector, as he took his seat at Anthony's side, "as I said when I was in there, give me Harry Lauder and dear old Marie Lloyd before all that flummery. Why, if Dan Leno . . ."

Anthony smiled and shook his head at the Inspector's judgment. "Different, Andrew! Different altogether. No fair comparison. Different technique, laddie! Each has a value and each has a place. To me, you see, the music-hall makes but little appeal."

MacMorran continued with his grumble. "Waste of time! Sheer waste. I might ha' been playin' darts." He turned and spat scientifically through the car window.

"So you didn't notice what we went to notice, Andrew? I'm disappointed in you."

MacMorran looked at him suspiciously. "Eh? What's that? You're not going to tell me that I missed the boat, are you?"

"I won't go so far as to say that. But the man whom we've been looking for . . . the man who was in Court the day Claude Merivale was tried . . . the man who is sometimes *like* C.M., Esq., but not always . . . glad to find that you're interested, Andrew . . . well, that man was playing in *The Painter of Ferrara* and you've been watching him for best part of this evening."

MacMorran swore. "Do you mean that, Mr. Bathurst? Honour bright?"

Anthony nodded. "As bright as it ever can be. Like a good deed in a naughty world. So you missed it, then?"

The car had cleared the jam and made greater speed. Anthony continued what he had to say. "I'm not altogether surprised at you. I missed the point myself for a long time. My eye didn't catch the likeness until the fight in the orange-grove. Remember the scene I mean?"

MacMorran was silent. He was lost in thought, attempting to recapture the details of the picture.

"Who's the man, then? What's his name?" he asked at length.

"Hugh Assheton," returned Anthony Bathurst. "The cousin and rival painter of Merivale in the film."

"You mean the tall fellow . . . who wore the big hat in the final scenes?"

"That's the bloke, Andrew. Question now is—where does he fit in the scheme of 'things Merivale?' That is where I think our friend the Constable sitting behind us might perhaps be of assistance. We'll get him to keep a sharp eye on Master Assheton. It's up to us to solve this case if only for your sake, my dear chap. There's no knowing what Pike Holloway may pick up for us. If he gets down to business. We'll make it clear to him before he leaves us to-night. What do you think yourself?"

MacMorran nodded assent to Anthony's suggestion. "Sound idea. Now that we've started, we may as well see the job through to the finish. You can drop me here, Mr. Bathurst. And the Constable. Suit me nicely. I'll pop down the Underground and be home with the old woman in a jiffy. Holloway can manage easily too. And thanks for the evening out."

He got out of the car and Pike Holloway followed him. MacMorran's tone was dry. Anthony grinned at the implication which it held. "Glad you enjoyed yourself, Andrew. Next time I'll take you to see *The Lion Comique* and hear the 'Jingo' song. Stone-Age revivals."

MacMorran came back to the kerb and leant on the ledge of the car window. "Yes . . . and I remember my old man's stories of him, Mr. Bathurst. Great, he said he was. Used to come on and wave a silk handkerchief to the gallery boys. Give 'em a sort of salute—'Ah-ha, my royal birds.' And they'd give it to 'im back, 'Good old George.' Many a time my old dad's talked about him. Music-halls *were* music-halls in those days. The old boy was chairman more than once. Good night, Mr. Bathurst."

Anthony waved "good nights" to them and the car sped homeward. Back in the flat, Anthony turned to his *London Telephone Directory*. "'Hugh Assheton.' Thank God," murmured Anthony to himself, "he spells his name in the unusual form. Gives me more chance of finding him." He turned the pages of the directory. "Assheton, Arthur, Assheton, Francis. Here we are, Assheton, Hugh, 8 Linklater Mansions, W.1. Good. Close at hand if wanted. Distance will be no object because it won't exist." Anthony replaced the directory on the telephone-table and mixed himself a drink. Where would the case eventually lead him? Why bother about it? Claude Merivale had been tried for the murder and been acquitted. Why not leave matters at that? Anthony thought hard and then shook his head. No! There was work for him to do. The case with its complexities attracted him. It held a problem after his own heart. A problem, the kernel of which, he was determined to extract.

Anthony filled his pipe and settled down in his chair to an exercise in intense thought. Eventually he came to a certain decision, thought of MacMorran and smiled.

CHAPTER IV
Major Revere Sees a Picture

For the second time in the space of a few weeks, Anthony Lotherington Bathurst came in his car to the riverside town of Maidenhead in the county of Berkshire. For the second time also, he drove that car to Major Revere's. On this second occasion, Revere's reception of him was distinctly warmer and more friendly.

"I'm honoured," said the Major at Anthony's appearance, "you're the second 'distinguished personage' who's called on me here today. I shall begin to think that 'Revere's,' of Maidenhead, is becoming the Mecca of all good Society people. I shall—really. If the practice continues." He smiled at Anthony affably.

"Good," said Mr. Bathurst. "Pleased to hear that prosperity is winging towards you. Hope it not only arrives but stays. If I may ask, who's the other caller to whom you refer?"

"No less than the great A.J. Carstairs himself. The famous film producer."

Anthony heard the name with considerable interest. Coincidence or something more? Dare he investigate further? Or would Revere shy and run out? Anthony determined to take the chance.

"I suppose he's a fairly frequent visitor down here? Unlike a good many of us."

Revere's cordiality remained. The day had been a good one for him.

"No," he replied. "As a matter of fact he told me just now that he'd never been down here before."

"Strange," answered Anthony with forced nonchalance. "You surprise me. I wonder what brought him here today?"

"Something to do with a house-boat, so he told me. He intends to rent one next summer, I believe. Miss Garland had one last season. Said he'd heard about my little place from a friend of his and couldn't pass it when he was so near to it, without giving me a look-up. Damned decent of him. Told him so. Now what can I do for you this time, Mr. Bathurst?"

Anthony hesitated a moment before he replied and checked a question that had almost been upon his lips.

"Well, it's like this, Major Revere," he said, "instead of being your guest, as I should be in ordinary circumstances, I want you to be mine. Instead of coming down here at your invitation, which would be the usual course of things socially, I want you to come up to town at mine."

Major Revere stared at him without understanding. "What on earth for?" he demanded eventually and with little courtesy.

"You would like me to be more explicit? Is that the idea?"

"Naturally. It's reasonable, isn't it?"

"I suppose it is. Well, I'll put the invitation into definite terms. Then you may judge for yourself. I want you to be my guest in town at the Illyrian Cinema. Picture—*The Painter of Ferrara*. Producer, by a strange coincidence, your acquaintance of this morning—A.J. Carstairs. There—surely that's an attraction in itself?"

Revere looked at him curiously. "What's the game? Put your cards on the table."

"Remember the time I came down here before?"

"Certainly. I rarely forget a face."

"Good! Remember, too, what brought me down here?"

"Yes. The Merivale murder case. You came down here before the trial of Claude Merivale."

"Excellent. Better and better. That means you remember the main idea behind my visit."

"Of course. It concerned the visits that the murdered woman had paid here. You asked me about the man who came with her—her dancing partner. Is that right?"

Anthony nodded. "Yes. You told me about the man known as 'Tollie'. Well—you were absolutely right in all that you have said."

Revere looked a little annoyed. "I see. And now that we've got that far, where are we?"

"I'll tell you, Major Revere. I want you to come with me to *The Painter of Ferrara*. I want you to see the picture. I've a 'hunch.' I am wondering whether you will be able to help me over a point that is troubling me. I must make this clear, though. You will be my guest for the entire evening, of course."

He looked at Revere almost whimsically. Revere made no answer.

"Well," said Anthony. "What do you say? Are you on?"

"I hate pictures," uttered Major Revere.

"Too bad," murmured Mr. Bathurst.

"I loathe them. All that Yank stuff gets on my nerves. Offends my ear. Makes my blood boil."

"'The Painter of Ferrara,'" prompted Anthony softly, "is an entirely British production."

"That's no recommendation. British pictures are slow. Too slow to catch cold. Lack guts. Want more pep. Producers—no vision. Leave me cold."

"You are critical."

"Am I?"

"Almost, shall we say, hypercritical."

"Perhaps I am. I certainly don't worship the microbe of mediocrity if that's what you mean. I know a good thing when I see it. And also a damned bad one. I don't go into raptures over what is ordinary in the extreme, and laud it to the skies. If all that's being hypercritical, I'll plead guilty to the charge."

"*The Painter of Ferrara*, as shown at the Illyrian, is in the front rank of pictures. You can take that from me. Whatever opinions we may hold of A.J. Carstairs privately, you've got to hand it to him as a producer. This picture, to which I'm inviting you, has pace, pep, guts *and* vision. All four of 'em. Even a judge of picture art, such as you yourself seem to be, would be bound to agree with me. I'm certain of it."

Anthony waited patiently. This man Revere was no easy proposition to handle. Far from it. Revere swung round on him.

"How can I help you . . . by looking at a film performance? I can't see the idea. Sounds ridiculous."

"I don't want to prejudice your judgment by giving you information in advance. If you'll do me the honour to accompany me I'll tell you more when we're there. If, of course, you refuse to help me . . . it doesn't matter . . . I must try in other directions. Sorry to have taken up so much of your time."

Anthony turned away. Major Revere half-checked him. Anthony stopped. "Yes?"

"All right. You can count on me. When do you want me to come?"

"Any time that suits you. But if you want to please me, the sooner the better."

Revere took a small book from his pocket and examined it. Anthony saw that it was a diary. Revere made certain calculations.

"If it's O.K. with you, I could manage this evening. I've a comparatively light programme down here today and I think I can make it." Anthony extended his hand. "I'll meet you at Paddington then, unless you prefer to come up by road?"

Revere took Mr. Bathurst's hand and shook his head. "No, I'll come by train. Better for getting back. Meet me at Paddington at ten minutes past six. That's a good train. I nearly always catch it when I go up West. I caught it when I . . ." Revere broke off suddenly and looked at his watch. "By George! I had no idea it was so late. You must excuse me, Mr. Bathurst, if you don't mind. I've one or two important jobs that I must attend to. Especially remembering what's on this evening. See you later then, as arranged."

They shook hands again and Anthony returned to his car. A smile played round the corners of his mouth. "Good work that! And Carstairs here, himself—eh? It's a small world, that's sure."

He made good time back to town. He had much to occupy his thoughts. Also he considered, as he weighed the various "pros and cons" of the case, that at last he had a certain amount of cause for self-congratulation. This club at Maidenhead, which he had just visited, under the supervision and management of Major Revere, did not seem to be entirely unconnected with the death of Mrs. Merivale. She had visited there. Fairly frequently.

He knew that. With a cavalier. Whom she had called "Tollie." Now—he had found A.J. Carstairs there and fixed up an evening with the proprietor. Of these people Carstairs touched on Claude Merivale, almost intimately. On the outskirts of a town, Anthony came to an A.A. name sign. He had set the trip-counter of his speedometer at the start of his journey, so that he might reckon the car mileage. At this distance, he looked at the sign and was satisfied. Mr. Bathurst always remembered that nearly all speedometers are mechanical optimists where matters of both distance and speed are concerned. A hundred real miles will read often enough as no; it has always been his opinion that few owner-drivers know the margin of error of their particular instrument and take care to allow for it. Anthony has always argued that properly-taken times over known distances are the only reliable factors when one is reckoning "averages." If you count stops, for meals or for other reasons, you must note their duration accurately, otherwise your average calculations will be inaccurate. The car that Anthony drove made for a high average. It had flexibility, ease of handling and was always quickly into its stride from traffic-stops and at the conclusion of speed limits. These qualities count more, perhaps, than the power for high "top" speed.

He brought the "Lanchester" into town eventually in excellent time. As he garaged the car, two thoughts played together in his mind. There was no relationship, strangely, between them. Firstly, he thought of the time when he had investigated the affair of the three Somersets and the tragedy of Brutton Copse, when Diane Fortolis had met him just in this place where he was now standing, and secondly, he thought in the terms of a question. Who at this precise moment was wearing Claude Merivale's missing suit?

When early evening came, he gave Emily, his faithful maid-attendant, certain explicit instructions in case MacMorran should particularly want him. Anthony came to Paddington at six o'clock, with ten minutes to spare for the arrival of Major Revere's train. When the train did arrive, Anthony was at the barrier, and had little difficulty in identifying the Major's burly figure as Revere made his way down the platform. When Revere joined him, Anthony glanced at his face and felt moderately certain that he was by no means in the best of tempers. "A hard nut, the Major," thought Mr. Bathurst, "with the bump of obstinacy most beautifully developed."

"Evening, Bathurst," remarked Revere, "now what's our first port of call?"

"Murillo's."

"Suits me."

They came to the waiting "Lanchester."

"Murillo's?" repeated Major Revere. "Some years since I was there. Is it as good as it was?"

Anthony turned the car into Praed Street. "Nothing is. How can it be? If it were, none of us would know what to say about it. The conservation of civilization rests mainly on approximately four foundations, one of which is 'they were giants in those days.' Surely you will agree with me with regard to that?"

Part of the frown disappeared from Revere's face. "Not for a moment would I disagree. Good Lord—no!" He settled down more comfortably in his seat and uttered a question that Anthony found surprising. "So Merivale was acquitted of his wife's murder after all? Damned lucky chap, I should say, if ever there were one."

"You expected the verdict to go the other way, then?"

"Most certainly I did. Didn't you?"

Anthony considered for a moment before answering. "No, I think that I can honestly say that I anticipated a verdict of 'not guilty.'"

"Based on what grounds?"

Anthony, as he half-turned in his seat, detected an unusual gleam in the eyes of Major Revere. He gave question for question. "Do you mean justifiably—or as the case was contested?"

"Say rather as the case *went*."

"Oh—entirely on the grounds of the likely line of defence. I mean by that, that the defence, Campbell Patrick's defence, and the medical evidence that was put in by Quinton Gaskell, were exactly as I expected they would be."

Revere sat silent for a time, digesting the terms of Anthony Bathurst's reply. The car came to a stop. Revere looked out.

"Here we are," said Anthony, "this, if I mistake not, is Murillo's."

The dinner passed pleasantly enough. Anthony's arrangements, telephoned in advance of their arrival, were impeccable. He would have been a curmudgeon indeed who would have faulted them.

Revere thawed a little under the influence of Murillo's master-hand, and became distinctly more companionable. For an appreciable time he kept off the Merivale case. Anthony let him have his head and Revere touched on several widely dissimilar subjects. He ranged, within the space of but a short time, from Jack Churchill, Duke of Marlborough, and his campaigns, to the Great Plague of London.

"I am a Winchester man," he said, when the sorbet came, "and I can tell you this, Bathurst, with certainty. Outside the ancient West Gate of Winchester, a few paces distant from that frowning portal, there stands an old obelisk. And believe me, Bathurst, on the very stone which forms its base the country folk in that terrible Plague year of 1666 laid their produce. Honest to goodness they did. The stricken citizens placed their payments on this stone and the coins they used, to settle their dues, were duly immersed in bowls of vinegar. As a youngster, this stone used to exercise a considerable fascination for me. Don't know really why, but many a time I've weaved romantic histories round it."

Anthony heard him out, and the finish of the meal found Major Revere almost good-tempered. Anthony paid the bill and drove him to the Illyrian with studied care. As they entered the palatial building, Revere's despondency and depression seemed to return, for he unaccountably relapsed into a forbidding silence. Anthony looked at his watch.

"If they're running to time," he said serenely, "we're just about right. I did my best to judge things closely."

He and Major Revere were conducted to two seats in the circle. To his satisfaction, Anthony saw immediately that his judgment of the time had been correct. *The Painter of Ferrara* would be showing again within a few moments. Revere took his seat awkwardly and with an ill grace. Anthony watched him with some uneasiness. *The Painter of Ferrara* started. There was no flamboyant atmosphere within the cinema such as had characterized the opening night. The picture rolled forward to its development. The quiet note at the beginning. The scenes in the Italian villages. The wedding, with Vicky Garland at her own inimitable best. Joan Bryan's big scene came and then Anthony noticed that Revere moved suddenly in his seat and half-turned towards him. Anthony did not desire interruption at this stage. He motioned to Revere to hold what he had to say until later. Revere understood at once and remained silent. So the picture ran on to its appointed end. The quarries. The orange groves. The second quarrel between Leo Meux and Claude Merivale. The "three men" scene that Anthony had found so attractive on the previous occasion. The death of Vining. All that Anthony had seen before. *The Painter of Ferrara* finished. The audience rose for *The King*.

Anthony piloted Major Revere to the bar at the back of the circle. He ordered whiskies with Perrier Jouët. As Major Revere raised his glass to his lips, Anthony judged that the moment had come to put the long-delayed question to him. It was monosyllabic.

"Well?"

Revere nodded.

"Yes. You're right. He's there in the picture."

Anthony nodded. "Tollie?"

"A-ha. He's there right enough. The innkeeper chap. Congratters on your idea. It's certainly turned up trumps. Peter Hesketh, the name is. I watched for the names at the beginning."

Anthony gave him a sharp half-glance and nodded again.

"Yes. That's true. Peter Hesketh. The plump 'Tollie.' So he has been cavalier to Claude Merivale's murdered lady, has he?"

"You've said it. Many a time as I can vouch for. Now you have one with me. It's about time I stood you something."

Major Revere called the girl and gave the order. Again came whiskies and mineral water. Revere proceeded to amplify his previous statement; the whiskies were warming him. "Many a time and oft, my dear Bathurst, has the plump and well-filled Hesketh, if that's his real name, talked soft nothings to the late Mrs. Merivale under my hospitable roof. I'm dead sure of that."

Anthony thought. "The last occasion was some time ago?"

"Yes," returned Revere, "I must admit that. Still you haven't over-far to look for Claude Merivale's murder-motive, have you?"

"No. That's very true, I suppose. Well, Revere, you've clarified the situation for me as I hoped that you would be able to, when I came down this morning. To have identified Mrs. Merivale's companion on her Maidenhead excursions, is to have accomplished something. My best thanks. We'll have a 'binder' before I drive you back to Paddington. How do you go for trains?"

Anthony watched him closely.

Revere glanced at his wrist-watch. "I'm all right. I can spare another ten minutes or so. Thanks."

Anthony ordered and they drank again. Strangely enough, Revere, at Paddington, for his return journey, was in the best of spirits.

"A most enjoyable evening, Bathurst. Glad I came up after all," he said to Anthony as they parted at the barrier. "And more glad still that I was able to be of real assistance to you. I was *afraid* it would be a wild-goose chase—but you knew best after all. Good-bye, Bathurst, and the best of luck. Good huntin'."

Anthony waved a hand to him as he walked down the platform to the door of his compartment. The last that he saw of Revere was his tall form bending to enter the train that was to take him back to Berkshire. Anthony walked slowly back to his car. If he faced the truth, the evening had brought him complications indeed! Nevertheless, he had made definite progress.

He had something for Inspector MacMorran at last.

CHAPTER V
THE WATERS GROW DEEPER

"ANDREW," said Anthony Bathurst to Chief Inspector MacMorran, "waggle your ears. I have news for you. I've made an appreciable advance in the Merivale case. That's the main reason why I asked you to come round here. The other reason is, of course, that I like you. Though God knows why."

MacMorran rubbed his nose and grinned delightedly. Anthony, in this mood, invariably pleased him.

"I'm listening," he said, "tell me the good news."

"I will. I've discovered the identity of Mrs. Merivale's boy friend. The lad who used to trot her down to Revere's place at Maidenhead."

"Go on." MacMorran's tone was steady, but his eyes held the flicker of interest.

"And I'll tell you this. You know the man, Andrew."

"I do?"

"Yes, you do. Fact."

"This is getting interesting," said MacMorran with slow emphasis.

"More interesting, you mean! Yes, I was with you when we saw him the other evening. Likewise you were with me."

MacMorran assumed the defensive. "You're alludin' now, I take it, Mr. Bathurst, to the individual who is supposed to have answered to the nickname of 'Tollie'? That's so, isn't it?"

Anthony nodded. "Quite right."

"Short and plump fellow supposed to be, wasn't he?"

Anthony nodded. "That's the chap."

MacMorran shook his head.

"Well, I don't get it. Can't think of anybody. Who fits the bill all round. Tell me, Mr. Bathurst. Who's the man?"

"By name, Hesketh. Peter Hesketh. You saw him in the cast of that picture we saw. Merivale's picture. With the word 'Painter' as part of its title. Now can you remember him?"

"Help me," asked MacMorran with characteristic curtness.

"Peter Hesketh is the man that plays the part of the innkeeper, Bruno Grassi. Most of his work is in the early stages of the picture. When Merivale came into the inn with the girl that afterwards dies in the quarry, Hesketh is leaning across the counter of the wine-shop with a leather apron on and his sleeves rolled up. Can't you remember him now?"

MacMorran nodded that he understood. "Aye! I can well remember that scene. Those big casks of wine. Yes. I've fixed the fellow." He whistled softly under his breath. "Where does this take us to, Mr. Bathurst? We mustn't chase too many hares, you know. If we do, we shall lose 'em all. Bound to." The Inspector looked so serious as he spoke that Anthony felt a strong temptation to laugh immoderately.

"Your reception of my news surprises me, Andrew. Do you know what I thought you'd do? I thought you'd wag a sententious finger in my face and say with all the solemnity of the MacMorrans, 'there you are. What did I tell you? Motive—jealousy. Merivale discovered that his wife had a lover so he took matters into his own hands and strangled her, first taking care to scratch her throat artistically with his jagged finger-nail.'"

The Inspector made no reply. The bombardment had been too heavy for him. Anthony rallied him.

"Well—what about it, Andrew? Why so coy to collect the empties? Not like you, you know."

MacMorran took a match and prodded the tobacco in the bowl of his pipe. "Why need we thrash our brains and bother ourselves? Why chase those hares I mentioned just now? Is any of it necessary? Merivale has been tried and acquitted. But that Merivale murdered his wife *deliberately and with malice aforethought* I'm as certain as I am that there was a king whom we knew as Edward the Eighth. So all this jabber of boy friends and lovers and jealousy and scratched throats is so much 'blether' to me and I'm not carin' two hoots about it."

Anthony affected admiration of the Inspector's effort. "Good man. But that's only *your* lookout. I'm more of a free lance than you are. With—ahem—something of a reputation. And before I've shuffled off this mortal coil and reached the bourne from which no traveller returns, I mean to solve the Merivale case all the way through, covering every corner of it, and then some. It's a case after my own heart, Andrew, and it hasn't ended for me just because Claude Merivale has been acquitted. No matter how *you* feel about it. No, sir!"

MacMorran shrugged his shoulders. "Be-yutiful. Hear his brave words. What devotion to a cause! What a difference there is between working for your living and playin' at soldiers."

Anthony smiled broadly, at which MacMorran went on.

"What have you picked up when all is said and done? Since you started? Sweet Fanny Adams."

Anthony challenged swiftly. "That's not true, Andrew—and you know it! Listen! This man Hesketh. The dance-tickets for Revere's. The stolen suit. The man like Merivale. There are at least four significances. Add them to what we knew comparatively early. The deck-chair photograph. The scratch on the woman's throat. The discrepancy in times, counting Pike Holloway's story. Good Lord, Andrew, when you sit there and talk as you did just now . . . well it's not like you. Have a heart! And in addition to all the points I've just enumerated, with your permission I'll name one more. Something upon which I've been dwelling for the last day or so."

MacMorran secretly delighted to have roused Anthony to the pitch of so defensive a declaration, put the question.

"And what may that be, Mr. Bathurst?"

"Why, just this. That neither you nor I has paid anything like enough attention to Merivale's movements on the last day of Mrs. Merivale's life." Anthony leant forward towards MacMorran's chair. "I'll tell *you* something! Claude Merivale, that evening, *had an appointment* at Brighton with Max Zinstein. This appointment was important to him in every sense of the word. But he didn't keep it, Andrew!"

"I know he didn't keep it."

"Why didn't he keep it? Have you thought of that, Andrew?"

"Because he went home to Enthoven Terrace, instead."

"Yes, I know he did. But *why*? *Why* did he go there? What made him change his mind?"

"You can search me," replied MacMorran.

"What happened to Claude Merivale . . . during the day . . . that made him change his mind? That made him cancel an appointment? An appointment which was of extreme importance to him. To his entire career. Max Zinstein, as I've no doubt you know, Inspector, isn't a man to play fast and loose with. He's at least in the A.J. Carstairs class. Yet Claude Merivale, in the comparatively early days of his career as a screen actor, his reputation still in the making, deliberately breaks the appointment that he has made with the great Zinstein himself. As far as we know, merely to spend part of the evening at the Catena Club and the latter part at his house in Enthoven Terrace. Once again, Andrew, why did he do those things?"

MacMorran took his pipe from the corner of his mouth, blew down the mouthpiece, and uttered deliberate indictment. "What makes a man change his plans suddenly and dash off home? Especially a married man. Married to an attractive woman. Suspicion!" He thrust his face quite close to Anthony's as he emphasized the word. "If we trust too much we may be deceived. But if we trust too little, we give ourselves a hell of a time." Anthony nodded acceptance.

"Agreed on that. Suspicion of what?"

"Of his wife's infidelity, of course. What else do you think? A hundred to one on it."

Anthony rejected the terms of certainty. "Doesn't follow. A likelihood, I grant. But your odds are wildly extravagant. There might be other reasons. It's quite possible. Credible reasons."

MacMorran immediately challenged. "Such as?"

"That he'd left something of value in the house and remembered it at the last minute. Even a matter of keys. Or then again—that something had suddenly *acquired* a value. A third possibility—that he had tremendously important news for Mrs. Merivale. News that might concern dozens of other possibilities. There are three main lines for you, Andrew."

MacMorran puffed steadily at his pipe. "Bet mine's the right one—all the same. In spite of all you say."

"You *may* be right, of course. If you *are*—then there's something about the whole affair that beats me all together. Take Merivale's movements right through, as we think we know them. After he came off the set he went home to Enthoven Terrace. As per invoice Pike Holloway. Wearing the white duck suit. This would be somewhere about half-past six. Then he arrives at the Catena Club in Piccadilly about seven-thirty. Why? What took him there? See evidence of Montague Jenkins. *Still* wearing the suit of white duck. If he wanted dinner at the Club, why did he go home first? Then—mark this point carefully, Andrew— the *next* that we hear of Claude Merivale, is his *second* arrival at Enthoven Terrace, in the region of eleven twenty-two. Left Catena Club, he states, about eleven o'clock. But, on this last occasion, *not* wearing the white suit. That suit, he leaves in a wardrobe at the Catena Club. Because he wanted to *change* his clothes. Why didn't he change them at home when he went there for the first time? Now, my dear Andrew, do you still think that Mrs. Merivale's infidelity is a hundred per cent watertight proposition that's going to cover all those points? Because I'm hanged if I do."

MacMorran scratched his head. Anthony had certainly shaken his confidence. "Well—the way you put it—"

"I've merely given you facts, Andrew. No theories of any kind. You know my invariable rule. No theorizing unless it's based on data."

MacMorran shrugged his shoulders with impatience. "Yes. I've heard all that before. But at the same time, Mr. Bathurst—" MacMorran stopped abruptly. Something unusual about Anthony had arrested his attention. Anthony had risen from his chair and was standing motionless in the middle of the room. His hands were thrust deeply into his trousers pockets and he was staring straight at the window in front of him. MacMorran watched him silently. He recalled that he had seen Anthony Bathurst like this before. Something was afoot. He would hear what this was shortly, if he were patient. Seconds ticked by. Anthony relaxed slowly and then turned towards him.

"Andrew, you doddering old idiot, I believe I've got it. And don't mind what I called you, because there are two of us."

"What's the big idea, Mr. Bathurst?"

"I've seen through something, about which I had been completely blind before. That's all there is to it at the moment. Don't rush me. Even now, I'm only on to the outside of things. But I must see this man 'Tollie.' Peter Hesketh. Our leather-aproned innkeeper. And the sooner the better. Get his address for me, Inspector, as soon as you can, will you? He's not on the 'phone. I've already looked."

MacMorran took out his note-book and made a note of the name. "You shall have that early to-morrow morning, Mr. Bathurst. I'll get into touch with the studio at once."

"'Phone it through to me here, Andrew. Then I'll get busy on it without delay. Have a spot before you go, will you? Hang on, while I get the glasses."

When MacMorran had departed, Anthony turned out the light and sought the seclusion of his most spacious arm-chair. He stretched his long legs lazily towards the hearth. If the idea that had just come to him were correct, much of his doubt and difficulty would be explained away satisfactorily. He checked up again on Merivale's movements as he had just detailed them to MacMorran. Of course! This would explain, too, why the suit had been of such vital importance *after* the murder. Or rather *might* have been. If he could only have seen Merivale's hands on the morning that he walked into the room at Scotland Yard and made his confession! The gloves, of course, had been destroyed. Burnt for a certainty. The girl Lamb was away. Merivale had been aware of that. *And* Mrs. Merivale knew it. A man doesn't carry gloves to his bedroom *unless* he has a definite purpose in his mind. The first thing he takes off when he gets indoors and removes his outdoor clothes—his gloves. Without exception. Ninety-nine men out of every hundred. So far so good. If he were on the right track, it explained the deck-chair photograph, the scratch, Claude Merivale's false defence, his lies about Worthing, and all the principal points in the monstrous collusion. Anthony slowly refilled his pipe and smoked on into the night. That which had been amorphous was now slowly taking shape.

CHAPTER VI
Peter Hesketh Betrays Confidences

In the matter of Peter Hesketh's address, MacMorran was as good as his word. The information was in Anthony Bathurst's possession by the following midday. Hesketh, Anthony noted with some satisfaction, lived at Harrow. "Wheatley, Castlemar Gardens, Harrow." Anthony had a quick lunch, therefore, got out the "Lanchester," and made for Harrow and Hesketh, at a reasonable speed. When he came to the house of his quest, he had determined what questions to ask Hesketh, should he be lucky enough to find him at home. He drew the car to the kerb and walked up a trim, well-kept garden path and pressed the bell. The girl who answered his ring at once yielded the information that Peter Hesketh was within, and invited Mr. Bathurst to enter. As he had judged, Mr. Hesketh, following the completion of the shooting of *The Painter of Ferrara*, was "resting."

Anthony thought that Hesketh looked a trifle scared when he came face to face with 1pm. The man was short and plump and fair. To Anthony, he immediately suggested the perfumed hairdresser and that the best bay rum ran riotously in his veins. His soft, curling, flaxen hair, and smiling round pink face, accompanied a noticeable pair of big and absurdly-bright blue eyes. Also, he was what Anthony always described to himself as "rosy-gilled." Peter Hesketh's face, however, was "different," in the impression which it produced. In his own style, the man was handsome. There was no denying this. His face was plump, it is true, but every feature of it was definitely removed from the ordinary. He advanced towards Anthony with an odd kind of buoyant, deliberately measured step. Almost as though he were attempting to keep time and touch to a dance-number which only he himself was hearing. He extended to Anthony excessively casually, and in the manner of a man preoccupied, a fat, comfortable hand.

"Delighted to meet you, I'm sure. *The* Mr. Bathurst, of course! Oh—boy! I've heard of you from poor dear old Claude, poor laddie—what a ghastly time he's had. Very, very trying—makes me shudder."

"You have a flair for words, Mr. Hesketh."

"Eh! What did I say? Oh . . . of course . . . yes. Unintentional on my part, believe me. Wouldn't dream of joking at dear old Claude's expense." He looked, as he spoke, straight into Anthony's face.

Anthony bore the optical raid with his usual composure. He made no reply.

Hesketh protested. "Oh—you're not going to be apathetic . . . please. My dear fellow—it's not done. Come and park yourself somewhere and let's talk."

Anthony sighed. "I feel cold and callous this afternoon, but heaven forbid that I should be apathetic in your company, Mr. Hesketh."

"Good," replied Peter Hesketh. "That alters everything—you have lifted a burden from my very soul."

Anthony assumed that particular expression of his that suggested a continuation of indolent melancholy and unresentful disenchantment. As though all the scales of illusion had long since fallen from his eyes, and that he had accepted the implied conditions with a regret that, in felicity, was tempered by amusement. Hesketh took him into a deep-toned, book-laden room and indicated to him where he might be comfortably seated. Anthony settled himself.

"I take it, Mr. Bathurst," said Peter Hesketh, "that you are curious . . . yes? Concerning this Merivale murder . . . yes? Of which Claude, dear old Claude, one of the whitest and very best . . . has been acquitted." The last few words were spoken with studied emphasis.

"Curiosity," returned Mr. Bathurst, "is a vice. It is said to be destructive. I was recommended during the days of my youth to suppress it. But, of course, that recommendation was in relation to that type of curiosity which was merely idle and, therefore, unpardonable."

"Oh, good! An answer after my own heart. Tell me some more. I was ever one to seek learning."

"I agree."

Hesketh regarded him suspiciously. "Er . . . go on, will you?"

"I will," said Anthony. "The impulse has seized me."

"Intelligent impulse," murmured Hesketh.

Anthony ignored the interruption. "Will you agree with me, Mr. Hesketh, when I say that to reach the truth behind the Merivale murder . . . as you yourself described it, is immensely desirable? For everybody concerned?"

Hesketh swayed his head and shoulders, becoming instantly, in expression, the innkeeper of his recent picture.

"It depends, rather, doesn't it?"

"Upon what?"

"Upon whom the truth harms or hurts."

"It can hurt or harm only the guilty."

"Oh, no. Don't be too confident about that. The truth, conceivably, might injure the innocent. I can imagine a set of circumstances where that might well happen."

"Let us understand one another. You mean—you won't talk?"

Hesketh spread out his hands. "Was ever a man so directly inhuman? I know nothing! I have nothing to say. I am, you see, entirely negative. There are occasions, my dear Bathurst, when silence is the most perfect herald of both joy *and* discretion."

"Exactly. You will continue, then, to affirm that you know nothing?"

"It is the truth."

Anthony decided to join issue with him at once. "What can you tell me, then, Mr. Hesketh . . . not about the Merivale murder, but concerning Major Revere's establishment at Maidenhead?"

Peter Hesketh's face fell. Then he flung his plump hands towards the ceiling. "Oh . . . hear the man! He has an ignoble soul." Into his voice he crammed the suspicion of a sob.

"Major Revere is interested in you," said Anthony. "He has seen your performance in *The Painter of Ferrara* and he sometimes refers to you as 'Tollie.'"

"Really! Tell Major Revere from me, since you know him so well, that it is considered rather low to spread tittle-tattle behind a person's back. Also, that he's most ungallant. 'Major' . . . what a misnomer!"

"Ungallant! Judging by the word that you choose there's a lady in the case, then?"

Hesketh suddenly shed part of his mood of artificiality. "If you could bear to *hear* the whole improbable truth in one ear-full . . . the lady was the late Vera Merivale. But, of course, I am wasting my time—you already know that." Hesketh frowned heavy disapproval.

"Proceed," said Anthony.

"I will," said Hesketh and Anthony saw something and liked him better at that moment than ever before. "Mrs. Merivale was a lady of the highest possible character. You can get that, and hold on to it, right from the pistol. Character, mark you, not reputation. She was young, dark, beautiful, and the epitome of personal charm. She thought me the nicest man she'd ever met—*next to her husband,—dear old Claude*. Remember that! But, of course, I'm willing to admit that she'd never met you, Mr. Bathurst."

Anthony smiled inwardly at the touch. Not at all bad, he thought. Hesketh went on.

"She adored my acting and eternally delighted in the many brilliant things which I so constantly say. I am sorry, but you force me to mention these things." He paused and glanced sideways at Anthony.

Mr. Bathurst looked admirably blank. Hesketh was quick to take up his parable again. He dropped his voice half a tone and became more serious.

"Vera Merivale was no fool, either. Get that, too. I've heard her say things herself, that weren't half bad. And besides calling me 'Tollie,' she was a thunderin' good accompanist. Didn't just bang the notes down as they do in the Parish Hall, but fitted in, with insight and real sympathy. And now she's gone. A case of remembered kisses after death."

"A showman," thought Anthony as he listened to him. "A showman—and once a showman, always a showman." He spoke.

"Then, for which of these qualities of hers, Mr. Hesketh, did she die?"

Hesketh bridled at the implication. "You have deliberately placed a false construction on all that I have said. Can't you recall that significant remark which I made to you a moment ago?"

"Which one? So many of the remarks you made were almost desperately significant."

"'*Next to her husband,*'" Hesketh asserted with emphasis. "And when I say that, I say everything. For the simple reason, that in that particular direction there is nothing else *to* say. Look here, Bathurst, old chap, if you don't mind my telling you, you've got a hell of a lot to learn. '*Cherchez la femme,*' doesn't always work out as you would like it to. Yes, sir. If you've got into your fat head that I was running round with Vera Merivale, as her very best boy friend that ever was, all *sub rosa* and not *coram publico*, you can drop that line of thought as quickly as ever you like. For your own sake, my dear Hawkshaw! Because you're barking up the wrong tree. When I carted V.M. anywhere, it was to please dear old Claude, and the dear old boy always had both eyes open to it. You weren't aware of that, were you?"

"I was not. As you say, I have a lot to learn. It was to remedy some of these, my deficiencies, that you have so courteously pointed out, that brought me here to see you. What you have just told me clears up much of my doubt and difficulty."

"Good! So you can remove all the little pictures that you'd been painting for yourself, of dear old Claude rolling home one night after a day on the set, tired and done to the world, and seein' red against V. all on account of this little Peter fellow cuddlin' her on a luxurious divan. Never on your life, Bathurst. And that's that."

Anthony carefully thought over Hesketh's last statement. He put a simple question to him. "Then why did she die, Hesketh?

You must have a theory. Besides—think how Claude Merivale's suit was stolen."

Peter Hesketh took it calmly. He did not turn a hair. Instead, he partly lost his temper.

"*You know* how V. died. Good God—how many more times do you police wallahs want it rammed down your throats? The truth I mean. You've had nothing on dear old Claude and you'll get nothing on me. Claude told you the truth and nothing but the appalling truth, but of course it was so strange to all of you, you didn't recognize it. What a farce it all is. Lord—you sleuthing fellows make me tired." He flung up his arms with a gesture of abandoned helplessness.

But Anthony was not to be denied. He persisted in the attack. "You made no comment on my remark about Merivale's stolen suit, Mr. Hesketh. It was a suit of white duck. It disappeared most mysteriously from a wardrobe at the Catena Club in Piccadilly. And nobody can reason why."

"Well, what the hell's that got to do with the death of poor V.?"

There was a point of almost frank interrogation in his eyes.

"I don't know. I wish I did. That's what I'm trying to find out. Look at it for yourself. Claude Merivale, you say, told the truth. He strangled his wife in a dream. While he's in prison awaiting trial, one of his suits is stolen. He couldn't have stolen it. Ergo . . . somebody else stole it. Why? Because it probably might have had eloquent testimony to give with regard to the murder. Or something in one of its pockets might have had." Hesketh listened and smacked his lips as though at an unutterable recollection.

"Couldn't somebody have recovered the suit, acting on behalf of dear old Claude? Has that struck you? Even I might have."

Anthony cut in almost peremptorily. "I'm afraid that your suggestion is almost without value, Mr. Hesketh. I've actually seen Merivale on the matter, or rather, he's seen me. He came to my flat, as a matter of fact, and definitely broached the—" Mr. Bathurst stopped abruptly. Hesketh was staring at him. As he stared, he brushed nonchalantly with the back of his hand at his fair curling hair. "Effulgent egotist," thought Anthony and deliberately returned the pointed stare.

"Well," prompted Peter Hesketh, "go on. About dear old Claude, I mean."

Anthony's voice was severe. "There's not a great deal more to say. By the way, I've seen your picture, *The Painter of Ferrara*. Twice. I must offer you my most sincere congratulations. A grand piece of work. Very much above the ordinary."

Hesketh stood away. He raised his eyebrows. They hinted challenge. Two, however, could play the eyebrow game so Anthony raised his. Hesketh wavered in the contest.

"Thanks. Good of you. I'm glad you liked it."

"Oh, I did. Immensely."

"Carstairs is a genius. I had no doubts of its success right from the first 'shots.' To me, it is an incomparably beautiful picture. It inspires one. Consider the research alone that contributed toward its making. Carstairs and Merivale and Vicky Garland spent a month in Italy simply and solely soaking up 'mentality.'"

Anthony nodded. "They deserved success, then. Such thoroughness."

"Absolutely. Everything is so 'right' about 'The Painter.' Costumes. *Décor*. The very happenings that it depicts all bear the hammer-hard ring of authenticity. And in addition, its artistry is superb. The whole thing to me is life-like—but lovable." Hesketh paused but for a mere second, lo continue quickly in his eulogy. "Take it comprehensively. Settings. Perfect! Direction, inspired! Photography. Beautiful! The script! An overwhelming triumph of both word-loveliness and serene simplicity. As regards individual acting there are many magnificent performances. I can think of at least seven or eight. Vicky Garland, Meux. Joan Bryan, Helen Meredith, Jessica Mortimer, Hugh Assheton and dear old Claude himself—all out of the top drawer, my dear Bathurst, every one of 'em, you must agree."

"Yes. I accept all that you say. As I told you, I liked it so much that I saw it twice."

Hesketh flashed resentment at him. "I don't count *you* or your judgment. It wasn't the excellence of the show that attracted you. You were nosing round, looking for a murderer."

Anthony smiled at him. "Which according to your private gospel, was a pretty thankless task."

"Naturally."

There came a silence.

"Assheton," said Anthony quietly, "Hugh Assheton, isn't it? One of the cast that you picked out as having played a good show."

"What about him? If you ask me, old Hughie played a blinder. An absolute blinder. Good boy, Hughie Assheton."

"I'm not doubting that part of it, by any means. I wouldn't fault anybody in the cast whom I saw. In fact, on the other hand, Assheton caught my eye several times. It must have been, as you say, because he put over such an excellent show."

Hesketh nodded exuberantly at Anthony's agreement with him. "Oh—Hughie's the goods. Marvellous bloke—really. The ideal conversationalist. Never dull. Always racy. Knows something about everything and everything about something."

"Good. What's his particular speciality, then?"

"Astronomy. The stars in their courses. That suits Hughie Assheton all the way and then—some. Gives him the whole blinkin' Universe to study. See the idea? He can talk to you in detail about a hundred and twenty-two things, and after he's been talking like that, he'll leave you wondering whether it's the real man to whom you've been talking or the actor. Which is dashed clever. Get me?"

"I think so."

"But don't misunderstand me. No. I don't want that to happen. Old Hughie isn't always acting. Oh, dear no. I didn't mean that. Much too clever in every way. He's an intellectual. But his moods are nearly always so vital and they so continually change, that he becomes enigmatic. The old Sphinx himself, you know, his sand and his smile. Says that the artist must dig deep and then deeper into every part that he's called upon to play. He's lucky, I must say. Audiences like him—which always makes him a sound box-office proposition. I'll make a confident prophecy about Hughie Assheton. He'll top the bill in a couple of year's time—you mark my words." Hesketh paused. "Have a cigarette—I want one." He handed Anthony his case.

"Also—there's this. Hughie's got a wonderful sense of humour, a marvellous memory and also an incredible capacity for hard work. The combination of his qualities is irresistible. He can be humble. He can be arrogant. And right down in his heart he's deeply grateful to the cinema for giving him 'his chance' as he calls it. Also, in addition to all that I've told you, he's actuated invariably by a most active, refreshing sincerity. That fact alone sets him apart."

Anthony coming to the point of interrogation. "Here's a little feature about him that occurred to me as I watched the picture. I wonder if the same idea has ever struck you? That, sometimes, when you catch him side-face, he's not unlike Claude Merivale. Years younger, of course. And naturally slimmer, and in better condition. But the likeness bit me. Ever noticed it yourself?"

Hesketh pursed his lips and wrinkled his brows. "Erm—erm—perhaps yes a shade! I can see what you mean, certainly. The nose and just round the jaw here." Hesketh made a movement with his hands along the line of his jaw.

"That's it," said Anthony. "You've got it. That's just where I do mean."

Hesketh smiled. "Funny how these things strike some people and not others. I've played in shows with him and dear old Claude and scarcely spotted it. But now that you draw my attention to it—I can see it."

"I'd like to meet him," said Anthony quietly. "This Assheton—there are one or two things that I'd like to ask him."

Suspicion flitted rapidly across Hesketh's face. "How do you mean?"

Mr. Bathurst affected nonchalance. "There are just one or two matters that I'd like to discuss with him. Nothing terribly important. Should I find him communicative, do you think?"

Hesketh was silent. "I can't think what there is that Assheton could tell you that I can't," he said at length. "Don't see your idea at all."

Anthony made no reply. Chiefly because he had no intention of replying. Hesketh was forced to the issue. "I said that I couldn't see what Assheton could say to you that I can't."

All the artificialities of Hesketh were now things of the past. The actor and poseur had gone. Behind the masks, the actual man remained. Anthony smiled at him almost indulgently. For the first moment of the encounter, perhaps, he was definitely on top. Hesketh again reiterated his difficulty.

"I don't mind that at all, Mr. Hesketh," said Anthony, "and don't you bother your head about it, either. You have quite enough to worry you without my adding any of my worries to your burden. Good-bye—and thank you."

But Peter Hesketh's face when Anthony left him was far from pleasant. Also he rubbed his head very thoughtfully.

If Assheton talked too much. . . .

CHAPTER VII
Death at the Catena Club

Hill, the steward of the Catena Club in Piccadilly, had passed through what he himself always described as a "chequered existence." An old soldier, whom a grateful country had rewarded but scantily for his efforts on the fields of Flanders, he had seen much, heard much, and done much during his career, that he would have liked to forget. There had been a period of some weeks when Vile Destruction and Violent Death had been Hill's daily companions. It will be seen, therefore, from this statement, that Hill was by no means afraid to come home in the dark and would enter a third-class smoking compartment on a winter evening with the utmost equanimity. But on the evening of the sensation at the Catena Club, Hill had as nasty a shock as he had ever experienced during the whole of his career. It was on the evening of the "A.J. Carstairs Banquet" to the cast of the recent successful picture *The Painter of Ferrara*. Everybody who was anybody in the cinema world was present. Each table, at A.J. Carstairs's specially expressed request, seated ten persons. At the second table, marked "B" on the plan, were seated Claude and Jill Merivale, Peter Hesketh and Vicky Garland, Hugh Assheton and Joan Bryan, Leo Meux and Trixie Belmont, the exotic Max Zinstein and Jessica Mortimer. The dinner, all the way through, had been a tremendous success. It had run to its finish without a single untoward incident. The speeches were made and the various parties at the different tables had broken up into smaller sections. Dancing was due to start within a quarter of an hour.

Hill had received a message that there was a soap and clean towel shortage in one of the gentlemen's lavatories in the basement. Inasmuch as the message came from somebody who *was* somebody, Hill had no option but to obey the instruction more readily than it was his habit to obey most messages. He descended the short flight of stone steps that led to the particular lavatory, the supplies of which required replenishing, almost light-heartedly, and with a soft snappy whistle on his lips. For him, the evening had been a good and profitable one. Tips had been many, and, on the average, much more lucrative than was the case usually. Hill, soap in hand, and towels over his arm, pushed open the rather heavy door of the lavatory with his stock all ready to be placed in the proper places—and his snatch of song froze and died on his lips. The reason was as follows. The body of a man lay prostrate on the floor of the lavatory. Familiarity with death meant that Hill had no doubts with regard to the matter. Whoever the man might be—or better—might have been, he wouldn't be anybody again. Nothing at all—beyond a name and a memory. Hill knew at once, without being told, that the man at whom he looked was as dead as mutton. Hill kept his head. He quietly put his soap and towels on the ledge in front of the mirrors, went out, pulled the door behind him and locked it with the master key—his own personal property—that he almost always carried with him. Hill went straight upstairs and reported what he had found to H.B. Austin, the secretary of the Catena Club who had remained on duty late that night owing to the exigencies of the Carstairs dinner-party.

Austin listened to Hill's story with almost open-mouthed amazement.

"Dead, you say? Good God, man, are you sure? But this is pretty awful. The man may be no more than faint or ill. You ought to have—"

Hill shook his head in such a way that Austin was immediately silenced. Hill spoke.

"No. Mr. Austin, sir, this bloke downstairs is a 'goner' all right. You can take it from me. I've seen too many of 'is kind over the other side not to know 'em when I see 'em. I haven't made any mistake—don't you worry about that."

Austin rose. "Well, then, if that's the case, Hill, I had better come downstairs with you and investigate matters for myself. You haven't mentioned this to anybody, I hope?"

Austin was anxious.

"Haven't breathed a word, sir. Came straight up 'ere to you, sir, directly I clapped eyes on 'im. Come down with me now, sir, will you, and see for yourself?"

Austin locked a drawer that was open in his desk and followed Hill out of the room. The buzz from the main room as they passed the door told them that dancing was now in full swing. Austin and Hill were unnoticed as they made their way to the regions below. Two men were trying the door of the locked lavatory as Austin and Hill went down the stairs. Words were passing between them.

"Blasted door's locked. Try that other one, Puffin. Damned silly idea, I call it. Over there, look."

They turned away and passed through the other door. Immediately they were out of sight, Austin indicated to Hill to unlock. Hill produced his master-key and did so. Austin and he passed through the door and again Hill locked the door behind him.

Austin, the secretary, looked at the prostrate body on the floor and nodded.

"You're right, Hill. This man's dead enough. Heart case, I should say, from the look on his face. I've seen all I want to see. Unlock the door again and I'll send for a doctor. Quietly now, Hill. Don't let anybody interfere, will you."

Without fuss or argument, Hill obeyed. The door was unlocked and locked again.

Doctor Batchelor was on the spot in incredibly quick time. Unostentatiously, he was conducted below and once more the door was unlocked and locked again. Dr. Batchelor went on his knees beside the body.

"Quite dead," he said after a moment or two. "Cardiac failure. Sudden seizure of some kind. Who is it? Any idea?" Austin knelt down on one knee by the side of the doctor and looked at the dead man's face.

"Yes, of course I know him. I scarcely looked at him the first time. It's Hugh Assheton, the screen actor. One of Carstairs's guests here this evening. Good God, how terrible! Just as he was making his name too. Rotten break—absolutely." He turned suddenly to Doctor Batchelor. "How long's he been dead, Doctor? Can you tell me that?"

"Oh no time at all. Your man must have found him almost at once. Body's still warm. Half-an-hour at the outside."

Austin nodded. "It works out like this, then. He must have come down here directly after the dinner finished—and toppled over." He noticed that the doctor was busy with Assheton's mouth. Austin watched him closely. It was obvious by this time that Dr. Batchelor was puzzled by something. Hill, standing behind the two men, also observed the fact.

"What is it, Doctor?" asked the Club secretary eventually, his impatience overcoming him. "What's troubling you?"

"Why this," returned Doctor Batchelor, "didn't you say a moment ago that this man is Hugh Assheton the screen actor?"

"Yes. This is Assheton, right enough. I know him. He's a member of the Catena Club. Why, what's the point?"

"Has he been playing in anything recently?"

"Yes. Of course he has. Very much so. He's in the recent screen success at the Illyrian—*The Painter of Ferrara*. The A.J. Carstairs picture. But why? What's the point?"

"Well," returned Doctor Batchelor. "Just this. Come and look here for yourself. This upper denture—see what I mean? It's ill-fitting. A ghastly affair. Look—it moves." The doctor touched Assheton's teeth with the point of his fore-finger. "Hardly what you would expect in a screen actor. What kind of parts did he play? Character stuff?"

"No. He just did *not*! Juvenile lead—or similar. And I'm beginning to see what you mean, Doctor. Funny—as you say."

"There may be explanations, of course. Still—" Dr. Batchelor paused. He turned to Hill. "You found him lying here, you say, just as he is now?"

"Yes, Doctor. Exactly as you see him. I came down here with soap and a consignment of clean towels, and saw him lying there. Dropped my soap and towels over on the ledge there, where you can still see them, and went straight up to tell Mr. Austin here. May as well take 'em back for this evening. No good leaving 'em here. You won't want this place used again tonight, I suppose, sir?"

Austin nodded assent. Hill turned and walked over to the ledge where he had laid the clean towels. He picked them up one by one to lay across his forearm again. Then, and suddenly at that, he stood there, as though transfixed. Austin, the secretary, noticed that there was something unusual about the man. His ordinary self-confidence seemed to have suddenly deserted him. Austin at once questioned him.

"What's the matter, Hill? You look as though you have seen a ghost. What's the trouble?"

Hill's face was set in a curious expression. "Not quite as bad as a ghost, sir. But something very peculiar, sir. About these clean towels, sir. That I brought down here, just now. I brought down half a dozen, sir, and put 'em on this ledge. Directly I saw Mr. Assheton lying dead here." Hill stopped abruptly.

"Well, what about it?" demanded Austin.

"Well, sir, there's only five here now, sir." Hill blurted the last sentence in one almost incoherent breath.

"What are you talking about? You must have made a mistake."

"What's this," said Dr. Batchelor curiously. "Say that again."

Hill repeated his statement and again counted the towels one by one, this time in front of the two other men.

"There you are, sir, and you, Doctor sir, one—two—three—four—five. And that's the bundle. You can't get away from it, sir."

The doctor dropped again by the side of Assheton's body. Austin and Hill saw him place his face close to that of the dead man and sniff round Assheton's lips and nose. Then shake his head as though doubtful and full of misgiving.

"Mr. Austin," he said quietly, "I'm not satisfied, by any means. Send for the police, will you? I don't care who comes along. But as I'm seeing things now I don't feel that I should take any risks."

Austin raised his hand. "Just a minute, Doctor, before we cross the Rubicon. This may prove extremely serious for the Club. Let me have another word or so with Hill here. I must get this straight."

The Club secretary turned to the steward. "These towels, Hill. Are you absolutely positive, Hill, that you did bring six towels down here?"

"Absolutely positive, Mr. Austin."

"Did you count them?"

"Yes, I always do."

"You might have made a mistake."

Hill shook his head. "I might have done—but I didn't."

"We must make sure of our ground, you know, Hill. Before we set the police ball rolling. Can't afford to make a mistake. You know what I mean, Hill."

Hill was obdurate. He stuck to both his guns and his towels, "I am certain, Mr. Austin, sir. I would swear to what I said, anywhere, and at any time."

The Doctor nodded quickly. "The police, Austin. Yes—yes. I insist on it. Lock the door again behind you after you go out. Hill and I will stay here by the body until you return."

Hill handed over the key.

Austin nodded and walked slowly to the door. He unlocked the door. He opened it and passed through. They heard him lock it again. They heard his steps outside. Hill looked at the dead body of Hugh Assheton lying on the floor. He pursed his lips in a feeble attempt to whistle. The endeavour was not an overwhelming success. Doctor Batchelor frowned severely on him. Surely this was no place for such an exercise! Clowns are out of place in cathedrals. Hill relapsed into silence. Then, after what seemed to each of them an interminable time they heard the footsteps of Austin . . . returning to them.

"The police," he announced quietly, "are on their way."

CHAPTER VIII
White Heat

Anthony Lotherington Bathurst was at Chief Inspector MacMorran's side shortly after breakfast on the following morning.

"Facts, Andrew. Facts, please! Any of 'em and all of 'em. When I got the news, I made up my mind to come along to you at once. Now what have you got for me?"

MacMorran plunged into his story. Anthony listened attentively.

"You went, you say. Yourself?"

"I did that. I was on duty when the call came through from the Catena Club. In a way, I jumped to it and *at* it. Thought of you and your interest, you see."

Anthony rubbed his hands and his grey eyes gleamed.

"The Catena Club, Andrew. Notice that? Oh what a gem of a problem! I wonder if I shall ever look on its like again?" Mr. Bathurst settled down comfortably to hear the further details of the Inspector's full story. Occasionally he came in with a sharp interruption.

"Who was the first doctor?"

"Batchelor. Austin, the secretary of the Club, sent for him. Lives close handy. Only a few doors away. Pretty good man, I should say, too. I was impressed, rather."

"And your doctor?"

"Moxom again. I took him along with me. He wanted to come."

"Good. Go ahead, then."

MacMorran went ahead as directed. "Just a minute, Andrew. Top denture?"

"Yes. Wasn't a perfect fit. I shouldn't call it altogether 'ill-fitting.' Wouldn't go as far as Doctor Batchelor did. He pointed it out in the first place to Doctor Moxom."

Anthony nodded again. "O.K. I get it. Go on. Give me more."

MacMorran got to work again. He came to the matter, of the missing hand-towel. Anthony listened with suppressed excitement.

"Just a minute, Andrew, please! Let me get this right. Hill, you say, went down with the towels and the soap. Found lavatory empty, save for Assheton's body. Yes?"

"That's so, Mr. Bathurst."

"Right. I see it. Let me continue, then. Hill came out, locked door, found Austin. Austin and he went down there again. Unlocked door to enter. Locked it again behind them when they went inside. Yes, yes. Then they went for the doctor. Door unlocked for them to get out. Locked again. Behind them. Batchelor arrives with Hill and Austin. Door unlocked. Door locked. Yes . . . I get it. It's pretty obvious what happened. Assheton was murdered in some way that we don't yet understand. But which, in time, we *shall* understand. When Hill went down for the first time, with the towels on his arm and the soap in his hand, murderer was still there. Of course he was. Inside one of the inner apartments. You see what it all means, Andrew, don't you? Murderer had a key or keys."

"Agreed on that, Mr. Bathurst. I saw that directly I had the facts put before me."

"Of course. Heard Hill coming and hid inside one of the private lavatories. When Hill went out for Austin, he came out . . . and that's when he used the towel. Oh, MacMorran, this is all damned good."

"You think so, Mr. Bathurst? I'm not so sure. As I've told you before, it's my living—this job—and not a pastime."

MacMorran's voice had a rueful note.

"Who was there, Andrew? At the dinner-party? That's something I *must* know. It's what I have come for, most of all. Did you bring away a plan of the tables?"

"There you are, all ready for you." MacMorran pushed a square piece of paper over to him. "I brought that away with me last night. Also, I interviewed personally every person shown on that plan there, whose name is marked with a cross."

Anthony mentally noted the names. "Did you pick anything up, Andrew, from anybody?"

"Not the tip of a cat's whisker. Not the square root of ruddy nothing." MacMorran shrugged his shoulders.

Anthony went through the list of names. "Table B," Claude Merivale and his sister. Ah, that would be Jill Merivale. Charming girl! Anthony remembered her. He had meant to see her again. Peter Hesketh and Vicky Garland. Familiar names again. From the cast of the picture. Assheton, the dead man, and Miss Bryan. Leo Meux and Trixie Belmont. Yes . . . most of them here. Max Zinstein—hallo—unexpected this, and Jessica Mortimer. The plan of the seating was as shown here.

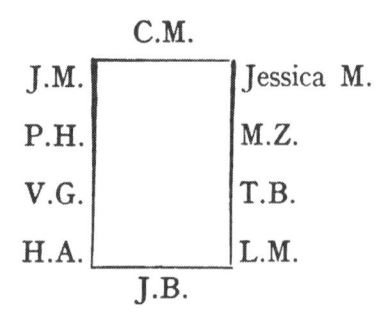

```
             C.M.
      J.M. ┌──────┐ Jessica M.
      P.H. │      │ M.Z.
      V.G. │      │ T.B.
      H.A. └──────┘ L.M.
             J.B.
```

Anthony studied the plan of the seating carefully. Claude Merivale at the head—naturally. Yes—nothing surprising about that. Facing him from the other end—Joan Bryan—Hugh Assheton on her immediate left. Leo Meux on her right. Assheton's other immediate neighbour—Vicky Garland. A girl—that was—either side of him.

"Plan for 'Table A,' Andrew, please," Anthony extended his hand.

MacMorran passed it over.

"H'm. Carstairs, the great A.J. here. Yes—that fits all right. On his right, Marilyn Garbrich. Naturally. On his left Hansa Varenna. Equally so. Next to her Alexander Sursum. Yes. All in order. All the stars in their courses and out of them too. O Glamorous night! I suppose that such honour had never before come to the Catena Club to seat so many celebrities on one single evening." Anthony handed back the two plans.

MacMorran took them without a word. Anthony realized the problem. He would learn nothing now from Hugh Assheton himself, that was a certainty. Dead men are notoriously inarticulate. Where and what was the genesis of this dark and sinister case that had first come to the notice of the public, from Vera Merivale's bedroom?

"Tell me of your interviews, Andrew. Besides the guests here whom you've marked. What about the staff? Did you see Hill?"

"Yes. Tested him thoroughly."

"How was he?"

"Sound as a bell all the way through."

"What about Austin, the secretary? Also satisfactory?"

"Yes. Discovered nothing to make me think otherwise."

"Any others?"

"Several. I asked about movements of the guests, for instance, within and towards the lower regions."

Anthony raised his eyes. "Surely, Andrew! As bad as that was it? How did you fare with Charon?"

MacMorran answered. "You know what I mean and where I mean. So don't be funny. Near the lavatories."

"I beg your pardon! Any luck?"

"No. Nobody had noticed anything at all unusual. Nobody had been seen wandering about. Or prowling about. Or—"

"Behaving in a suspicious manner?"

MacMorran nodded. "Nobody."

"Of course, there's this to be considered, men going downstairs to the lavatories at various times would not be noticed.

There must be always a certain amount of passing to and fro after the various dining-parties have broken up, for washing, and so on. Who would be noticed by anybody? It's the unusual, the abnormal, the extraordinary that engages attention. The ordinary does not. It should not! Our criminal is clever."

MacMorran nodded quick agreement. "That's so."

"When's Moxom doing the P.M.?"

"This morning. I shall know all there is to know about that, some time today. It's on the cards that it may come through on the 'phone here. I told him I might be with you."

"I'll tell you something, Andrew. I called on Master Peter Hesketh a day or so ago. Tuesday to be exact. He told me all sorts of things. Amongst them these." Anthony recounted incidents from his interview with Hesketh. "And now you see, Andrew, just as I'm warmish, I've lost Hugh Assheton."

MacMorran slowly filled his pipe. "Yes. Afraid you're right there. Still, can't be helped now. The milk's spilt. No use moaning about it."

Anthony studied the dinner-table plans again. Tables A and B. "I must see the body, Andrew. It simply screams for my attention. If only I could have seen it last night."

The telephone bell buzzed on MacMorran's desk. Anthony gestured towards it. "Here you are, Andrew. Moxom's result very likely. Take it, man, as quickly as you can and put me out of my misery."

The Inspector answered the call. "Yes. Chief Inspector MacMorran speaking. Yes. Tell him I'm here and that I'll take it now." Pause. Anthony listening. MacMorran's face showed that he was about to speak again. "Yes. Yes. Right-o, Doctor. What's that? Poisoned? How?" Anthony came round and stood at the Inspector's side. "May I?" he whispered. MacMorran nodded. Anthony took the receiver from the Inspector's hand. He introduced himself to Doctor Moxom.

"What?" he said at length. "Is that a fact?" Mr. Bathurst whistled. Eventually he replaced the receiver.

"Well, Andrew," he said, "you heard something of what the doctor said. Before I took over from you. Here's the rest. Assheton was poisoned but Doctor Moxom isn't sure *how* the poison was administered. Do we progress—or don't we?"

The Inspector looked at him. He made no comment.

"I'd like to see the body, Andrew, if I may, before Moxom's finished with it. I mustn't waste any more time. Take me along with you now, will you?"

MacMorran nodded. "I'll come along in the car with you at once."

They reached the mortuary within two minutes. Luckily for Anthony, as he entered the building, Doctor Moxom was still there. He nodded to Anthony as Mr. Bathurst joined him by the body of Hugh Assheton. The two men talked, and while they talked Andrew MacMorran listened to them. He heard terms and descriptions that he didn't quite understand. Terms of medicine, of vegetable poisons, of toxins, known and comparatively unknown. He saw Doctor Moxom nod two or three times. Then Anthony looked carefully at the upper denture which Moxom handed to him. It was as clean as possible. There was no sign anywhere of it having been tampered with.

"It fits badly, Bathurst. Which is strange, to say the least of it. There's no arguing about that. Dr. Batchelor pointed it out to me in the first place. Have a look at it for yourself."

Anthony did so. He told Moxom that he saw nothing whatever in its condition to excite any suspicion.

"The poison, whatever it was, must have acted very quickly," remarked Moxom. "Something similar to the vegetable poisons that are mostly found in South America. The 'curare' group, I mean."

"Any puncture or scratch of any kind on the body, doctor?"

"Can't see one, Bathurst. I had the same idea. Looked everywhere."

"It's damned extraordinary. All of it. Why kill him if he—" Mr. Bathurst paused suddenly. "And how administered—that's the point? Yes. Yes. That might explain the lavatory. And the towel." He went across to the slab again and stared fixedly at the dead body of Hugh Assheton. Then he turned away and beckoned to Chief Inspector MacMorran. "Take me to the Catena

Club, Andrew. For the second time in my history! I would talk with Hill the steward, Austin the secretary, and even could I endure for a time the conversation of the redoubtable Montague Jenkins. That is, of course, if the worst came to the worst, which God forbid!"

Anthony and the Inspector came to the Catena Club on this second occasion with more data than it had been their fortune to have before. Austin, the secretary, who received them was the epitome of courtesy. Anthony Bathurst remembered that Inspector MacMorran had commented previously on the entirely satisfactory way in which Austin had dealt with his every request. After a quick introduction to Anthony, the latter proceeded to question Austin.

"In the matter of keys, Mr. Austin. It seems to me that considerable importance attaches to the question of keys. I refer, of course, to the various incidents of the lavatory."

Austin looked up curiously. What exactly did this man Bathurst mean?

"Have you a set of keys on the club premises? Keys, I mean, for every door in the place?"

Austin nodded. "Oh, yes! All the keys of the premises hang on various nails in a glass case. That case is kept in the porter's box on the right of the vestibule just as you come in."

"Accessible? Easily accessible?"

"H'm. You would call it accessible, I suppose. But I wouldn't admit the truth of your second question."

"The door of this porter's room wouldn't be locked, I presume?"

"No."

"And the porter himself wouldn't *always* be on duty in his room?"

"No-o. He might be called away temporarily for a variety of reasons. But he wouldn't be away for long. Ever."

"Thank you, Mr. Austin. That settles two questions with which I was seriously concerning myself." Anthony turned to MacMorran. "What was found on the dead man's person, Inspector?"

MacMorran enumerated the articles on the tips of his fingers. "Cigarette-case. Lighter. Silk handkerchief in breast pocket of coat. Ordinary white handkerchief in sleeve. Left hand. Yale door key, of his flat, we've settled that. Small leather wallet containing stamps to the value of sevenpence ha'penny and thirteen pounds in currency notes. Oh—and half a dozen visiting cards. His own—every one of 'em. In his trousers pocket, four and ninepence in loose cash."

"Nothing else?"

"Nothing whatever, Mr. Bathurst. No letters. Nothing in the way of correspondence at all—if that's what you're thinking of."

Anthony looked disappointed. Austin interposed. "The Inspector's list is exactly as I should have expected. Assheton had with him just those articles that a man coming out to dine here would bring with him."

"Overcoat, Inspector? What about that? He wore a light overcoat, no doubt. Anything, shall we say, in any of the overcoat pockets?"

"Gloves. Light chamois. Size eight and three-quarters. Two old bus tickets. One to Victoria Station on a 25. H.M. 2857. The other F.B. 3991—between somewhere and Champion Hill, Dulwich."

Anthony smiled at the precise details. "Good man, Andrew. That's the stuff I like. Attention to detail."

Austin looked quickly from one man to the other. He had not encountered this particular set of double harness before. Almost a second late on the beat, he realized that Anthony Bathurst was speaking to him.

"Would you be good enough to conduct me to the lavatory where Assheton died and tell Hill the steward to come down with us, Mr. Austin?"

"Certainly, Mr. Bathurst. Only too pleased. I'll send for Hill at once." Austin gave an order on the telephone and as a result thereof, the contingent of three picked up Hill at the top of the first staircase. They at once made the journey to the quarters below.

"Assheton's lavatory—as we call it now—has been locked ever since the affair," explained Inspector MacMorran, "and I've had a man on duty down here ever since I came away from the place on the first occasion."

"Good man, again, Andrew. I salute you! *Bayete!*"

MacMorran grinned but the grin was semi-rueful. He went forward and following a brief conversation the uniformed man of MacMorran's stood on one side and the door was opened. The four men entered.

"Now, Hill," said Mr. Bathurst, "show me the exact place where you put the clean towels, will you, please?"

Hill stepped towards the ledge under the line of windows and gestured with his open hand. "Here, sir. They were all in one pile here, sir."

Anthony's quick comprehensive glance took in the various points of the apartment that he desired to master and understand.

"Now tell me, Hill, please, where exactly the dead man was lying when you found him here. Show me, for instance, where his head was and where his legs were."

Hill went on one knee and made the necessary indications. Anthony glanced at the secretary, Austin. Austin nodded the corroboration that he saw Anthony desired.

"Yes. I agree. That's how the body was when I arrived with Hill after he had come and reported to me."

Anthony used chalk on the floor and his eyes to measure relative distances.

"I'll present you with a piece of information. When you came down with your towels, Hill, the person that killed Assheton was surprised by your entrance and just had time to hide in one of the private apartments there. If I had to name it, I should say that one." He pointed to the right-hand compartment.

Inspector MacMorran turned and sought enlightenment.

"Explain, Mr. Bathurst—please. Why was the murderer surprised and why did he hide *there*, rather than in here?" MacMorran pointed in the two other possible directions.

Anthony at once accepted the challenge. "I'll answer your first question first, Inspector. Which, you will agree, is but appropriate. When Hill here arrived with his arm-load of clean towels and fresh soap, the murderer, we say, was surprised and hid in one of these two compartments. The lavatory door, that is the main door through which we all just passed, was unlocked. Remember that. Hill met with no resistance as he entered. Would a murder be committed behind an *unlocked* door? Under circumstances and conditions where detection and discovery would be easy and simple? Ask yourself the question. Of course not. The murderer had only just *unlocked the door* in order to get away when he heard Hill's approaching footsteps and was forced to scurry back into hiding *without having time to lock the door again*. He could not risk those few seconds that the task would have entailed. Do you follow me, Andrew?" Anthony Bathurst smiled as he asked the question. "I'll vow that my explanation is the right one."

MacMorran received it by nodding slowly as each point had been made. Austin and Hill the steward were obviously impressed.

"All right, Mr. Bathurst," returned the Inspector, "I'll take it from you. Now let me have the rest. Why do you say that he hid in *there*?" He stabbed with his forefinger at the right-hand compartment. Anthony immediately pointed to the floor.

"Why, that point is even plainer to me than the other point. Reconstruct the picture. The murderer is at the door. About to clear out. He hears Hill's footsteps coming this way. He turns back quickly in something like a semi-panic. He has no time to lose. *The body is lying there. Like this.* Hill just showed us and there are the marks. Our murderer then obviously takes the path where he the better avoids it . . . and that path takes him *there*. He must be *slick*!" Anthony pointed to the right hand compartment.

MacMorran, Hill and Austin followed the direction of Mr. Bathurst's pointing finger. Then their eyes, as one man's, went back to the position on the floor where Anthony had drawn the chalk line after Hill had described how Assheton's body had lain. MacMorran nodded. It was the last contribution that he felt called upon to make. Anthony had succeeded in convincing him of the justice of each of the two statements. He yielded him the tribute of his admiration.

"Yes. You're right, Mr. Bathurst. I might have known."

In turn, Anthony put a question to him. "Combed out Assheton's flat?"

"Yes. Nothing at all."

"Been to his dentist's?"

MacMorran stared at the query. "Why? Oh . . . I see . . . well . . . I suppose I know why. . . . but what can a dentist . . . ?" He paused and Anthony, evidently, switched off the point for the time being.

"Well, Mr. Austin, I must thank you for your courtesy in showing me round. And you too, Hill—many thanks for explaining everything so clearly."

Anthony walked with Inspector MacMorran to his car. "Well, Andrew," he said quietly, "can you tell me this? *Why* was this man Assheton killed? And—mark you—just before I was about to have an interview with him. Most unfortunate! Don't you think so, Mac?"

MacMorran shrugged uncompromising shoulders. "I'm with you, Mr. Bathurst. All the way. Most significant, if you ask me. Find the people who knew of your intended talk with Hugh Assheton and get busy with *them*. That procedure, as you yourself would say, is most certainly indicated. You'll get results."

"Quite so, Andrew." Mr. Bathurst nodded approval. "But don't forget also that there are such things as Horses *and* Carts. They have an accepted order. And one mustn't come before the other."

At that precise moment Montague Jenkins was entering the Catena. "Has anybody been enquiring for me?" he asked the porter.

"No, sir," replied the porter gravely, "but several members have asked me to let them know directly you leave."

"What?" exclaimed Jenkins. "What was that?"

But the porter and his face gave nothing away.

In which respect he was not unlike the man who had accosted him.

CHAPTER IX
The Upper Denture of Aubrey Lewisham

At a touch on his arm from Inspector MacMorran, Anthony stopped the car.

"Here," said the Inspector. "This is the place that we want. I've had three men on the job for two days—and as things turned out they weren't wanted. I came across the bill in Assheton's flat."

Anthony nodded. "So that all we have to do is merely confirmatory, eh? The man shall look upon his handiwork—and acclaim it—or otherwise. You shine on these jobs, Andrew. They're your métier. Remember Simon Gildey, the cuddlesome coffin-maker of Mill End, in the county of Essex? When we looked into that little mystery of the three Somersets? By Jove, how you took him to your heart! I shall never forget it." Anthony grinned at MacMorran's straight face.

"There's a morbid strain in you, sir, that's not in me. We can't all be alike, I suppose. Just as well. I'm getting out. But you can't park the car here. I'll wait for you by the railings over there."

Anthony parked the car appropriately and then rejoined the Inspector. They walked up the stone steps of the establishment. At the top was a brass plate affixed to the wall and suitably inscribed. "Aubrey Lewisham, L.D.S."

"Love," murmured Anthony, "but not always for this Mr. Lewisham."

MacMorran produced a document from his breast-pocket. "Here's the account. Paid and receipted, you see. There's no mistaking it. Look for yourself."

Anthony glanced at the paper. "Hugh Assheton, Esq., 17 Clarges Terrace. To one upper Denture £21." Below the narration was the scrawling signature of "Aubrey Lewisham," over the customary receipt stamp.

Mr. Bathurst pointed to the date and the address. "Not so very long ago, Andrew and a false address. Note that—will you?"

They passed into a passage through an outer door.

"Are we a trifle early, Andrew? It's a fault of mine, I'm afraid. Rather than to be late."

MacMorran glanced at his watch. "No. On the tick. Nothing to worry about. I arranged with him to call at half-past two—it's on the stroke of that now."

Anthony nodded satisfaction. "Good. I don't feel like waiting long. Getting impatient in my old age. Kicking my heels in a dentist's waiting-room has but a small attraction for me. I have certain reminiscences, for the vivid resurrection of which, I have no desire. One of these days I'll tell you the story of Charlie Thompson, the biscuit-barrel and the Banshee."

As they crossed the threshold of a room that faced them, a young lady came forward to meet them. "Mr. MacMorran?" she enquired pertly.

"Quite right. An appointment to see Mr. Lewisham at half-past two."

"Will you step this way, please?"

They obeyed. Their period of waiting was not prolonged. A big beefy man, with large hands, who wore horn-rimmed glasses came in to them. Anybody less like a dentist in appearance, Anthony found it difficult to imagine.

"Good afternoon, gentlemen." He looked quickly from one to the other of them. "Inspector MacMorran?"

"That's right," replied the Inspector, "and this is Mr. Anthony Bathurst. You remember that I said he would come along with me when I spoke to you on the telephone this morning."

Lewisham nodded briskly. "Yes. Yes. I remember." He gave his broad shoulders a heave. "Good afternoon, Mr. Bathurst. Now take a seat, gentlemen. We may as well be as comfortable as we can. Sit there, will you?" He indicated two chairs. Anthony and MacMorran took them. "Now what can I do for you gentlemen? I hope that your business with me won't take *too* long." His heavy features broke into a smile.

"I trust not, Mr. Lewisham. There is no reason why we should be too long over the job. At any rate, we'll hope not. I'll give you the facts." MacMorran made himself more comfortable in his chair and opened the ball.

"I believe, Mr. Lewisham, that the late Mr. Hugh Assheton was a recent patient of yours? As you are probably aware, Mr. Assheton was recently found dead on the floor of a lavatory in the Catena Club."

Lewisham nodded. "Yes—to both of your statements. In relation to the first of them, Mr. Assheton was a very recent patient of mine. If you will allow me to turn up my accounts, I shall be able to tell you the exact date."

"Don't trouble to do that, Mr. Lewisham. As a matter of fact I have your account here with me now. I know the date. You supplied Mr. Assheton with an upper denture?"

"That is so. An excellent piece of work, too, if you will pardon my saying so."

MacMorran glanced across at Anthony. The latter signified his approval.

Anthony Bathurst turned to Lewisham, the dentist. "Was Assheton a regular patient of yours, Mr. Lewisham? Did you know him?"

"No. He had never come to me before. He told me that he had been recommended to me by a friend of his. Another . . . er . . . film actor I believe, speaking, that is, entirely from memory."

"You couldn't remember the name of his friend, I suppose?"

Lewisham considered. "No—I couldn't. It's no good pretending that I could. Actually, I have no clear recollection that he ever mentioned the name."

"Pity! That name might have been valuable information to us."

Lewisham immediately became more communicative. "Please get this right. I don't want you gentlemen to go away with any false impressions. I made no extractions for Mr. Assheton and I feel bound to tell you that there were certain other unusual features of our . . . er . . . association. I think that perhaps you gentlemen ought to know that."

Anthony's senses tingled at the admission. "Please tell us, Mr. Lewisham, all that you can."

"Well . . . Assheton, as an actor . . . was extremely careful with regard to his teeth—they, of course, affected his elocution and er—diction, generally. His present set was satisfactory but he had a great fear, he said, of suddenly breaking the plate or even one of the teeth and being left high and dry as it were, in consequence. You see the idea?"

Anthony and MacMorran expressed their understanding. Lewisham went on.

"But very strangely, he brought me a plaster-cast impression of his upper denture. Already made for me. It appears from what he told me that he can't stand the impression being taken by the hot wax. It makes him retch terribly. Many of my patients, I may say, are affected similarly. So the result was that I made him the second set from his own impression. He actually paid for it before it was made, for which payment I gave him a receipt."

MacMorran produced the denture from his pocket. "Is this the denture that you made for Assheton?" He handed the artificial teeth over to the dentist.

Lewisham examined the denture closely. "Yes. This is mine. No doubt about that. I call tell by several features of it. Why? Is there a doubt about it?"

"No. I just wanted your confirmation—that's all."

Anthony came in again. "How did the denture fit when it was ready for him?"

"Oh—all right. At least he made no complaints about it. As a matter of fact, I never saw him again."

"What!" exclaimed Mr. Bathurst.

"No. He arranged to call one afternoon for the denture, but 'phoned to tell me that owing to a special rehearsal or something, that had been called for suddenly, he couldn't possibly keep the appointment. So I sent the order at his own special request down to the studio, where he accepted it. He said that he would let me know if any alterations would be required. I heard nothing—so I presume that the denture was entirely satisfactory. Of course I knew it would be."

Mr. Bathurst rubbed his hands. "Who took the teeth to the studio?"

"One of my mechanics here. I sent him down with it as Assheton had requested me to. Assheton was waiting for him when he arrived. He fixed a time and my chap kept it. Tipped him well too. My chap quite enjoyed the experience—so he told me. Something novel for him. All the cast were made up for their various parts when he got there—I tell you my chap was full of it when he got back."

Anthony leant forward towards Mr. Aubrey Lewisham. "Let me get this straight, Mr. Lewisham, please. Let me detail the entire procedure that Assheton adopted with regard to this denture, right from the inception with you? It's tremendously important, so that I shall be extremely obliged if you will listen carefully to what I have to say."

Lewisham, impressed by the gravity of Mr. Bathurst's tone, nodded his acceptance of the situation. Anthony commenced his statement.

"Point No. 1—Assheton comes to you for a new upper denture—although the one that he had was entirely satisfactory and despite the fact that you had never given him dental treatment before. Correct?"

"Absolutely."

"Good. Point No. 2—he told you that he feared that an ordinary, everyday accident might deprive him of his teeth and, as an actor dependent on the quality of his elocution, desired to be prepared against such an unpleasant contingency should it ever arise. Right?"

"Yes. Right."

"Good again. Point No. 3—instead of your taking the impression for the new denture, Assheton brought you one which was already prepared in the form of a plaster cast. Yes?"

"Yes. Again—quite right."

"Good. We're doing well. Now we come to Point No. 4—Assheton paid his bill before he actually had delivery of his order. I understood you to say that, Mr. Lewisham?"

Lewisham again nodded his agreement with Mr. Bathurst's statement. "Yes. Yes. That is entirely correct."

"Excellent. Now for Point No. 5—you didn't see Assheton again. But when the order was complete and the new denture ready for him, one of your mechanics took the teeth down to the studio where Assheton's picture was being 'shot' and delivered them straight into his hands. Yes?"

"Right again. You have the whole thing now exactly as the various incidents occurred."

Anthony rubbed his hands. "Thank you, Mr. Lewisham. And I mean that. Your information has been invaluable. Now I wonder whether you'd mind answering me another question. Do you often go to the pictures, Mr. Lewisham?"

Lewisham showed surprise.

"Never, Mr. Bathurst. I'm afraid that I'm not interested in such things. My one interest outside my work is yachting. I have a little craft of my own down at Burnham-on-Crouch that takes up almost all of my spare time. My son and I are down there almost every week-end."

"Thank you. Now this. Could you tell me the name of the picture that was being 'shot' when your mechanic took Assheton's teeth down?"

Lewisham shook his head. "No. I certainly couldn't. But I haven't the slightest doubt that my chap that went down could—if you asked him."

"Would it be troubling you too much?" inquired Mr. Bathurst, almost casually.

"Not at all. I'll get him now if you'd like a word with him. I know that he's here."

"Thank you. I would."

Aubrey Lewisham rose and walked through a connecting door. Anthony and MacMorran heard his voice coming from the farther room. Anthony winked at the Inspector. Then Lewisham came back to them again.

"I've sent for him. He's coming along in a moment or so. He's a very decent chap, you'll find. Name of Dawson."

Anthony and Inspector MacMorran awaited the coming of Aubrey Lewisham's mechanic. Lewisham himself said no more to them until Dawson arrived. The man was short and dark and quick-moving. Lewisham outlined the position. He concluded with the request that Dawson should answer the questions that Mr. Bathurst would put to him.

Anthony at once took Dawson back to the day of the delivery of Assheton's upper denture. "Where was the studio to which you took it?"

"I went down to Driffield, sir. To the new A.J. Carstairs picture that was being put on. At the moment, it's called *Death at my Elbow*, I believe. I happened to hear that when I was down there. Almost the same cast in it as in *The Painter of Ferrara*."

"Good. You delivered your order there into Mr. Assheton's hands, I understand?"

"That is so, sir. When I got there, Mr. Assheton was just going on the set. I gave him the order then and there. He was in his costume. As a matador. At least, I think it was a matador. One of those guys. It's a story of the Spanish bull ring. Rivalry and jealousy between the various matadors, picadors, and—er—toreadors." Dawson smiled with bright intelligence.

Anthony nodded. "I see. Thank you, Dawson. Your information has helped me considerably." At a gesture from Lewisham, Dawson withdrew.

Lewisham spoke to Anthony. "You're satisfied then, I take it?"

"Oh—yes—entirely. Your Dawson's a good boy. The Inspector and I are in your debt, Mr. Lewisham. All I hope is that I haven't detained you too long. I know how busy you gentlemen are."

In the car journeying homeward, Anthony's first words caused MacMorran a shock of surprise.

"Well, Andrew—do you see now where we are and what our immediate problem is?"

The Inspector shook his head almost despairingly. "I'm afraid that I don't, Mr. Bathurst. That is to say ... *exactly*. I can see that Lewisham's confidence in the quality of his own work was a bit misplaced. But even admitting that—I don't see quite where it gets us to. And that's a fact."

Anthony swung the car skilfully round a corner. "Then I'll endeavour to help you, my excellent Andrew. Our little problem that was, has developed. It has developed so much, and so unexpectedly, that we now have to find an unusually clever murderer. That's my task. For we are dealing, Andrew—and I'm *certain* of my ground now—with two murders. And as I said—we have to find one murderer."

MacMorran was roused into abnormal alertness. Anthony Bathurst went on unconcernedly. "Surely you were able to solve the mystery of the upper denture and why our friend Assheton needed it?" MacMorran shook his head.

"No. Not altogether. I've never been an actor. Why did he need it?"

Anthony chuckled at the Inspector's question. "It was his passport?"

"Passport? How do you mean? Where to?"

"Into another class of society. To the uncouth cell where Brooding Darkness spreads its jealous wings . . . and, friend Andrew, where the Night Raven sings. The Night Raven . . . unpleasant bird . . . think of that."

MacMorran looked uneasily at his companion. "Why must you always . . . ?"

Anthony checked him, a far-away look in his grey eyes. "Something I could bear to know, Andrew. As quickly as you can get it for me. And that is, the names of all the cast of this new picture of A.J. Carstairs. This picture of blood and sand . . . of matadors . . . and picadors and even toreadors . . . upon which Dawson, the mechanic of Lewisham, was privileged to cast his intelligent eye. Will you do that for me?"

MacMorran noted the request. "I'll get a man down to Driffield first thing to-morrow. I'll make a special point of it. Do you want the names of all the cast . . . or only those of the men?"

"Oh—only the men, Andrew. When you take into consideration *all* the circumstances of Assheton's death at the Catena Club, you must realize that there is no possible question of a . . ." Anthony stopped with an abrupt suddenness. His mind, with one of his strange lightning-like flashes, had reverted to the two evenings when he had looked upon *The Painter of Ferrara*.

"No, Andrew," he remarked with an almost ominous quietness. "I've altered my mind. Something you said made me alter it. Let me have the names of all the cast, women included."

The car came to the door of Anthony's garage. "Come and see what Emily has for us. Sometimes, you know, she approximates greatness," invited Mr. Bathurst.

Chief Inspector Andrew MacMorran needed no second bidding. Emily wielded a mighty rolling-pin . . . but only in the right direction! Her puff-pastry was superb.

CHAPTER X
"Death at my Elbow"

Anthony Lotherington Bathurst scanned the names on the list that had been sent to him by MacMorran from the "Yard." He compared them with the names on a second list that lay conveniently to his hand. The first list he saw had been compiled by the careful and steady hand of MacMorran. He had tabulated the names in two columns. First—men. Second—women. The first list contained the following names. MacMorran, true to type, had placed them in scrupulously alphabetical order. Hugh Assheton (deceased), Holt Banbury, Bradley Cole, Michael Kingshott, Flack Lewis, Claude Merivale, Leo Meux, Leslie Vining and Richard Winston. When he had finished reading this list, Mr. Bathurst frowned at what he saw. Something had caused him momentary displeasure. He turned to the list of the ladies. Beatrice Belmont, Joan Bryan, Victoria Garland, Bim Martindale, Helen Meredith, Jessica Mortimer and Constance Norman. Anthony then examined his other list and carefully placed a tick against certain names. The names that received this tick were Claude Merivale himself, Victoria Garland, Joan Bryan, Hugh Assheton, Leo Meux, Beatrice Belmont and Jessica Mortimer. "Seven names," reflected Anthony. "Seven. Three men and four women." Then he carefully placed his pen through the names of three of the women. At that his frown returned to take possession again of his features. A moment's thinking and Mr. Bathurst rose and walked to the telephone. He asked for a number. "Give me Driffield 2288." He was some little time before the connection was established. Mr. Bathurst, when the time came for him to speak, asked a question. This was what he heard after the asking. "Changes did you say? In the cast do you mean?" "Yes. *Any* changes that have taken place. Say, from the original cast." "H'm, I see. Half a minute now. I must think over that. Let me see now. Changes. Wait a moment. I must collect myself." Anthony Bathurst waited patiently. At length there came over the telephone the information that he desired. "Yes. You're quite right. Trust you.. There *were* two changes. Now what were they? Oh—I know—Hilda Bray and Peter Hesketh were in at the beginning but have since dropped out. Been superseded. Kingshott and Bim Martindale have come in and taken their places. Eh—what was that?" Anthony repeated the question that he had just asked. "When? Oh—I couldn't tell you that with any certainty. Not very long after the start, I should say, in the case of Hesketh—and it would have been about a week later when Bim Martindale came in on it. What? Oh—that's O.K.—only too pleased at any time. Call on me when you like. Don't mention it."

Anthony Bathurst replaced the receiver and returned to his lists. So Hilda Bray and Peter Hesketh had been members of the original cast but had seceded from it. Things were better perhaps, from his point of view, than they had at first seemed. Mr. Bathurst made an additional note on his two lists of names. Michael Kingshott and Bim Martindale in. More definite inquiries on the particular point that concerned him would yield him, doubtless, that additional degree of information that would be significant or otherwise.

Mr. Bathurst now determined to examine the notes that he had had from MacMorran concerning the Carstairs dinner-party at the Catena Club. The Inspector had sent them to him at his request some days before. Mr. Bathurst looked again at the plan of the table that MacMorran had drawn from him. On either side of Assheton there had been sitting a girl. Yes . . . he remembered that he had commented on that before. On his left, Miss Garland, on his right, Joan Bryan. Directly opposite to him had sat Leo Meux. Anthony visualized certain parts that he had seen twice of the story of *The Painter of Ferrara* before turning seriously to MacMorran's own notes on the case. The notes ran as follows: "Claude Merivale." "Appearance well-known—needs no description. *An old acquaintance.* Has no recollection of ever speaking to Assheton at any time during the dinner. Saw so much of him usually that each was pleased with a change of company. When the party broke up remembers that he saw Assheton talking to Max Zinstein. But he *thinks* that this conversation of theirs was of 'but short duration.'" "Jill Merivale."—"Dark hair. Lashes long and dark. Nose straight. Grey eyes. Very little information obtained. Says that she did not speak to Assheton after the dinner had started and corroborates her brother's statement that he didn't speak to Assheton either. When dinner was over, danced with A.J. Carstairs, Peter Hesketh and Leo Meux in that order of succession." "Peter Hesketh." "Could give little information that was in any way important or significant. States that he was occupied all the time of the dinner with his two dinner-table companions, Miss Merivale and Victoria Garland. Before dinner commenced was in the bar and had first a 'Clover Club' and then a 'White Lady' with Claude Merivale (this confirmed subsequently) Hugh Assheton and Leo Meux (unconfirmed, up to the present) before the majority of the ladies came in to the dining-room. When dinner finished, Hesketh says that he went to the bar for drinks unaccompanied (unlikely procedure for a man of Hesketh's type—but you never know) and then danced for some long time. This last remark partly vouched for, of course, by previous statement from Miss Jill Merivale. This information by Hesketh all given without the slightest hesitation and with every semblance of truth." "Vicky Garland." "Fair, blue-eyed and fluffy. Talkative and rather feather-brained young lady—*off* the screen. *But*—this to be noted carefully—says that Assheton was *not himself* all the evening. Says that Assheton hasn't been himself for *some considerable time*! When questioned more closely as to her exact meaning of this statement affirmed that he was 'pre-occupied.' Gave her (and other people) the impression that 'he *feared* something.' That he had something on his mind. To support this, claims that Assheton spoke *very little* all the time that the dinner was being served. Only spoke *when spoken to*. Replied to conversation that was addressed directly to him but seldom 'started anything going.' Can't assert, that as far as she *knew*, Assheton had any enemies." "Joan Bryan." "Of different type from Victoria Garland. More serious altogether. Probably steadier, better character and more reliable. Has had (according to report) a long uphill struggle to reach the point in her profession that she has reached. Recent protégée of A.J. Carstairs, whose influence has probably helped her considerably in her career. With regard to the evening of the dinner, agrees with Miss Garland that Assheton was 'distrait' and not himself. She also says that he 'said but little.' But won't go as far as Miss Garland about him having been like it for some time beforehand. Re movements on the dinner evening, says that she saw Assheton in close conversation, after the dinner was over, with Max Zinstein, thereby confirming Claude Merivale's statement to that effect. Then goes on to say that she danced several times with Carstairs and occasionally with Vining who came in to the gathering later." Here followed a special note made by MacMorran evidently as an afterthought and marked with an asterisk. "Am impressed with Joan Bryan's statement generally. Girl created excellent impression on me all the time that I was in conversation with her. *Much* superior, to my mind, to many of the girls of her profession who have enjoyed similar measure of success. Not so *fast*."

Anthony Bathurst smiled, read the Inspector's note carefully, and passed on. "Jessica Mortimer." "French-looking girl. Dark. Black hair, black eyes. Pallor of face. Restless fingers and hands. *Latin*—all the way through. Although at times, just a touch of the Japanese. Speaks fluently. Never at a loss for a word. Impresses one with great strength of personality. Rumoured love affair with Assheton that belonged more to the past than to the present—but this believed by everybody to have blown over *long* before. Could tell but little of what happened at the Carstairs' dinner. Stated (this struck me as strange) that Max Zinstein is one of the most fascinating men that she has ever met and that his conversation through the dinner was a perpetual delight to her. Can remember nothing about Assheton except that she *thinks* she saw him walk out of the room when the dinner finished. Can't remember if anybody there went with him or even followed him out."

Anthony Bathurst paused here to underline heavily two of MacMorran's statements. He then passed on to the next name on the list—"Max Zinstein." MacMorran had more information here than in any of the other instances. "German-born of Jewish origin. Seemingly able and well-informed man. Short. Stout but actually of poor physique. White face, broad in the brow and tapers to a thin chin. Age—in the fifties probably. Eyes the most remarkable features of him. Deep-set and shining and very dark blue. Perhaps blue-black. The eyes shine under the brows of the man. Lips usually curled into a smile under a long, fine, slightly hooked nose. Fat but sensitive hands. Specialist and expert, doubtless, in his own business. Everybody thinks so and almost everybody says so. Peculiar voice. Usually a little *resentful*. I think this is the best word that I can use. Speaks with a pronounced foreign accent. Smile strange and *steely*. Not loquacious. When interrogated, seldom used two words when one would do—and one usually did. To employ a hackneyed expression, has an extremely well-developed 'superiority complex.' I found that he had a knack of turning most of my emotions into curiosity. Corroborates Jessica Mortimer's statement as to what happened during the dinner. Also—and I think that *this* is important—agrees that directly the actual dinner part of the affair was over, Hugh Assheton came over to him and discussed the recent Carstairs picture, *The Painter of Ferrara*, with him. Is inclined to think that this conversation with Assheton lasted for at least 'a quarter of an hour.' Note—seeming discrepancy, or 'part' discrepancy, between *this* statement of Zinstein and that of Claude Merivale (interviewed first of all). Max Zinstein says that when Assheton left him at the *conclusion* of their conversation, Assheton went out of the room with (he thinks) Leo Meux, which fact (if it be a fact) nobody else seems to have observed." Anthony placed MacMorran's document on the table and sat there thinking for a time. He let the paper lie untouched and closed his eyes. Eventually he returned to his previous task.

"Trixie Belmont." "Pale brown hair. Short, square-cut and curling up underneath. Gives curious impression that hair is not her own but a cleverly manufactured wig. Pale. Alabaster pale. Staring, startled but candid sort of eyes. Colour of them uncertain. Either dark blue or brown. Sometimes they seem one, at other times the other. Lips—usually parted. Faint rose. Pretty and *interesting* girl. Speaks simply and without the slightest trace of affectation. Supposed to be close friend of Assheton's. This attachment fairly recent. Great favourite of A.J. Carstairs. Says she sat 'almost opposite' to Assheton at the dinner-party and agrees with the others, who have made the statement, that the man 'wasn't himself.' Didn't see what his movements were when the dinner had finished but knows for certain that he didn't dance at all. Is sure of this because she looked for him on the dance-floor and not seeing him, was disappointed. Had he been dancing at all he would most certainly have danced with her." Last but not least—"Leo Meux." "Fine-looking young fellow. Strong and exceptionally upright. Hazel eyes with dark eyebrows. Hair glossy and well-brushed. Straight, well-shapen nose. Voice crisp and full of the confidence and control and reserve that the man undoubtedly has. Splendid type of what A.L.B. would call *jeune premier*. I think that's how he spells it." (Anthony grinned happily at this touch of the real MacMorran.) "Decided and concise in all his statements. Unhesitating about every answer. Talked to Assheton at dinner but when the general party broke and split up into its various sections, lost sight of him, and of course, never saw or spoke to him again. For his own part, went into the dance-room and danced with, amongst others, Miss Belmont and Miss Garland. Note—important—Leo Meux did *not* confirm that he had cocktails in the bar with Hugh Assheton, Claude and Jill Merivale before the dinner started. When pressed more closely for this corroboration, Meux admitted that he might have had *one* 'Clover Club' with them but, if this were so, he was on the fringe of the crowd, as one might say, and didn't particularly notice who bought the drinks or who the actual people were that formed 'the crowd.' 'Said' that the drink might have been passed over to him. From his manner I formed the opinion that Meux's doubt was genuine and that the incident of the cocktails coming before dinner started, had not made as much impression on his mind as it might have been expected to do. Final summing up—'much cry' of examination with 'little wool' of result." Anthony pushed MacMorran's paper away from him with a quick movement of his hand and carefully filled his pipe. He thought that he saw at last how the murder had been committed and he thought also that he knew the motive that lay behind it. Risky! Undoubtedly! Yes—but at the same time, audacious. And audacity so often spells success. Perhaps, though, when the whole of the circumstances came to be reviewed, the risk was by no means so great as it appeared to be at first blush. There was present all the time, the point about the keys at the Catena Club and the evidence of the locked door. The door that had been tried and found to be locked. As he thought over these matters, Anthony Bathurst nodded several times to himself. Then he rose, walked to the window and drew the curtains. He threw off with practised ease the strain of the process of dissection through which he had so recently passed, the strain of all those multiple threads which he had been called upon to disentangle so that each one of them might find its proper place. To his clear intellect, trained by long experience to an almost instinctive rejection of all but the essential, there must come times of rest and mental tranquillity. Any other condition must eventually lead to disaster. Anthony Bathurst finished his pipe, placed it carefully on the mantelpiece, closed his eyes, stretched out his legs and found that rest.

When he awoke the fire had burned low on the hearth and his body had grown cold. His right elbow was numb and he felt thoroughly uncomfortable. The supreme mental effort that he had made was now beginning to take physical toll of him as well. He mixed himself a strong "peg" of Scotch before going to bed.

He was worried. There was no denying it. The way that he had to travel was by no means clear. Obstacles were there on it. For he could see no chance of bringing two murderers to Justice. It was—he felt—beyond his power.

CHAPTER XI
JUST FANCY!

ANTHONY Lotherington Bathurst possessed the qualities of both patience and perseverance. His worst enemies would have conceded him this much. But the more that he considered the difficulties of his present problem, the more he became convinced that the solution to the Merivale affair, no matter if it came soon or late, must eventually be an unsatisfactory one. That is to say, judged by his own standard. He discussed certain tactics with Inspector MacMorran. He even took Major Revere, partly, at least, into his confidence. Other people, whose names are familiar to the reader, were carefully looked at and their possibilities carefully considered and assessed, only to be regretfully discarded one by one. For it is dangerous to enlist an ally concerning whose reactions there remains even the slightest element of doubt. It will be enough to say that Andrew MacMorran was in Mr. Bathurst's company when he opened the letter bearing the Maidenhead post-mark and containing an invitation from Major Guy Revere to a certain Mr. Anthony Bathurst to attend a "Fancy Dress Revel" that was, as the ticket informed those who read it, to be held on the following Tuesday evening at Reveres, Copas Place, Palethorpe Road, Maidenhead, Berkshire. Anthony looked for a second time into the envelope.

"Ah," he said in a tone of satisfaction, "as I had hoped. A ticket for you, Andrew, as well. Couldn't have endured that you should have been left out. Revere is a man that knows his job. No half measures for him. Does the thing thoroughly."

MacMorran grunted. Neither he nor Anthony knew what the grunt was intended to convey.

"Not keen at all," grunted the Inspector. "Know several better ways than this of spending an evening. There's a darts—"

"Cheerful little soul, aren't you? What about me? Shan't I be all the better for your sparkling company? Or must I suffer alone?"

MacMorran sought the more practical side of the issue. "I'm nothing like as confident about the finish as you are, either. That's another thing."

"All right, Bright Eyes, take off your black tie, pull the crêpe favours from your hat and make Whoopee again. And that's three other things."

"All the same," conceded MacMorran, "I'm willing to admit that I'd give a good deal to put my hand on the murderer of Mrs. Merivale and know that I was sure of my ground. I know what *you* say and I know what *you* think. I've heard 'em both often enough. But I know also what I myself say and think!"

Anthony turned and faced him. "You have had your hand on Mrs. Merivale's murderer already. And he never protested his innocence. Your mistake was that you removed your fin too quickly. Always in such a damned hurry, you old sinner."

"Wasn't my fault that I took it off. Had no option. What a jury says—goes."

Anthony smiled at him enigmatically. "That's O.K. then, Andrew. We know where we are. I'll rail for you in the car. And see that you're dressed like a policeman and not as a gentleman. Otherwise, if you attempt a disguise you'll give the whole game away from the start. Your feet tell such a plaintive story." He dodged adroitly an empty tobacco tin which the Inspector threw at him. The tin hit the wall with a crash and rolled to the floor.

"That's right," said Anthony, "break up the happy home. I regard that as 'the most coarsest cut of all.'"

MacMorran looked shocked. "It's all right," remarked Mr. Bathurst. "The authority is William of Stratford himself."

The tables at Revere's were all fully occupied. The cabaret—B.C. Cobora's Young Ladies—had given their show, had mingled with careless camaraderie with the guests, and the floor had been cleared for dancing. The fancy dresses were daringly original. Anthony Bathurst had, so far, been unnoticed. For the reason that everybody, save Claude Merivale, regarded him as a waiter. Mr. Bathurst's costume demanded that this tribute should be paid to him. He had thought carefully over matters and had decided that this was the best course for him to adopt. Many of the Carstairs group were present at Major Revere's. Leo Meux, Vicky Garland, Peter Hesketh, Carstairs himself, even the exotic Max Zinstein, who had once been more than ordinarily interested in Claude Merivale. There was, as yet, no sign of Chief Inspector MacMorran. If he were actually there, on the premises, he had not so far disclosed himself. Mr. Bathurst was by no means displeased at this. If he had decided to alter certain plans that he had previously made, well, that was his funeral, and should subsequent events prove him to have been wrong he might still have time and opportunity to put himself right again. Let us glance at the costumes that decorated Revere's on this particular evening. Zinstein appeared as the "Le Petit Caporal." An admirable representation, thought Mr. Bathurst. Vicky Garland showed as the Orange Girl of Old Drury. Leo Meux and Peter Hesketh, having heard evidently of Zinstein's intention, were arrayed as "The Brothers of Ajaccio." Revere himself, a fine figure of a man, careered round as a Colonel of Dragoons. William Schwenk Gilbert, had he seen him, would have written an extra verse. Claude Merivale, ever original, had arrived as a species of Robot, similar to those in the pages of Kapek. His face, however, and his head were unmistakable. Jill, his sister, tall, slim and straight, looked radiantly happy as Queen Christina of Sweden. She was well suited by her choice. Garbo herself might well have envied her her beauty.

Dances started. Dances finished. No doubt the spirit of Vera Merivale, in ghostly rout, took part in most of them. Mr. Bathurst, as one of the many who stood, moved, served and waited, called one of the guests to his side for the purpose of conversation. When it came, the conversation that passed between them seemed strictly private. In time it was clear that agreement had been reached between Mr. Bathurst and his companion. A girl broke away from the dancing and also came to Anthony's side. Anthony spoke grave words to her. Her white, scared face showed that she understood.

"Must I?"—she asked of him—"do you *demand* that I do this?"

Anthony, in reply to her, shrugged his shoulders.

"Is it the only chance you will give me?" she asked again.

"It is. Don't you think that you should be eternally grateful for that chance?"

She turned away and as she did so, Anthony saw her brush away tears from her cheek.

Punctually at twenty-two minutes past eight, Anthony approached no less a person than the exotic Max Zinstein. Zinstein looked somewhat askance as Mr. Bathurst spoke to him. A few words from the latter were enough to clear the air.

"Where?" said Max Zinstein.

"In Major Revere's office . . . if you will be so kind. Thank you, Mr. Zinstein."

Zinstein accompanied Anthony to the room at the back of the dancing-hall. Anthony closed the door and waved him to a chair.

"But I understood," expostulated Zinstein, "that if Merivale has been tried for the murder of his wife and acquitted . . . then you police are not able to have a trial of him again." His English was heavy, thick and guttural.

"That is so, sir. But, you see, we might have other strings to our bow. In more ways than you are in a position to perceive. All that I want of you now, is a piece of information."

Anthony was very close to him now and Zinstein seemed uneasy. He tried to edge away, Anthony thought. With his black hair and sallow face he looked like a bird of prey that had made a social mistake and fluttered into the wrong cage. There was little of the Emperor about him now.

"If it is possible for me to give you the information that you are seeking I will give it to you, of course. But if not—well—what will you do then?"

He spread out his hands and his race was there for all to see and understand.

"You *can* give it to me," answered Mr. Bathurst. "That is why I asked you for it. Take your mind back to the evening that Vera Merivale was murdered in her bed. Remember?"

Zinstein licked dry lips. How undignified to be questioned in this matter! There was little of his superiority complex now.

"Yes," he permitted himself to answer.

"Am I right in understanding that Claude Merivale had an appointment with you on that evening?"

"You are."

"At what time was the appointment to be kept?"

"Just after nine o'clock."

"Where, Mr. Zinstein?"

"At Brighton. I live at Grand Avenue, Hove. I had arranged to meet Mr. Claude Merivale at Brighton station. By the train that arrives soon after nine o'clock."

"Mr. Merivale did not keep that appointment."

"He did not."

"You did?"

"I did. I did not murder my wife instead—if that's what you mean. But that was probably because I am a bachelor." Zinstein looked decidedly unpleasant.

"What was the reason that Merivale gave you for not keeping the appointment?"

"He has never given me one from that day to this. But surely—" again Zinstein spread out his fat hands—"that is all understandable. What might be a breach of courtesy at an ordinary time, in circumstances such as those that I have just outlined, becomes understandable. Surely that is so? How can I put it? The lesser event becomes, as it were, swallowed up, submerged in the greater. A naked man exposed to the fury of the elements, who suddenly finds clothing to his hand, does not worry if the suit that he finds lacks a gardenia in the buttonhole. I have, perhaps, expressed myself badly, *clumsily*—but I am sure that you will see what I mean."

Anthony Bathurst nodded sympathetically. "I understand you perfectly, Mr. Zinstein. But I venture to assert that you are overlooking one most important point in the matter of the death of Mrs. Merivale."

Zinstein's cheeks that had puffed out, subsided. "What is that?" The words came from him jerkily.

"The *time* when Mrs. Merivale died."

Zinstein sat and stared blankly. "The time?" he repeated.

"Yes," returned Anthony. "Don't you remember? Or didn't you invest the point with the importance that it merited?"

"I don't know that I ever gave it a thought. Merivale failed to meet me. Then I heard of the . . . trouble. I see." Zinstein paused. After a moment's thinking, he proceeded. "Yes. I see where I was wrong. I jumped at a conclusion. A conclusion that you are going to say was a false conclusion."

"More than *say*. *Prove!* Listen, Mr. Zinstein. Your appointment with Merivale was for nine o'clock . . . or as near to that as makes no odds. But according to his own statement, he didn't leave the Catena Club until something like two hours after that to arrive at his house in Enthoven Terrace at about twenty-two minutes past eleven! Something wrong somewhere, isn't there? Don't you agree with me?"

"There is just this." Zinstein formed his words carefully and spoke slowly. "Is that statement of Merivale's about the time that he left the Club corroborated . . . or is it merely his own and unsupported?"

"The evidence is conflicting. I will admit that readily. But the conflict is beside the point in regard to what you and I are discussing."

Zinstein's deep-set eyes bulged with suspicion. "Why? What grounds have you for saying that?"

Anthony brought down his hand firmly on to the table. "This! The medical evidence that I have in my possession satisfies me that Mrs. Merivale was not only alive at nine o'clock *when you were waiting for her husband at Brighton station*, but also at eleven o'clock, when Merivale claims to have left the Catena Club! And it's the nine o'clock time that *matters*! Now do you see where I'm getting, Mr. Zinstein?"

Zinstein shuffled in his seat. "I can see where I was wrong. But, as I said, I scarcely gave the matter a thought. Why are you labouring it so? I was wrong . . . there's an end to it."

"Yes. That's perfectly true. And there was an end to Mrs. Merivale."

Fear showed in Zinstein's eyes. Anthony leant over to him and spoke gravely.

"This is my point! *What happened to Claude Merivale that evening before his wife died*, to make him break his appointment with you . . . such an important appointment too?"

Zinstein fluttered. "How should I know? For I assure that I *don't*!"

Anthony rose and patted him on the shoulder. "I'll take your word for that. Because I think that outside Merivale himself, I am the only person in the world who *does*." Anthony bowed to the little man, thanked him and left him.

Within a moment, Inspector MacMorran was at his side.

"Well, Mr. Bathurst," he opened questioningly, "and what have you to tell me now? Is my journey to be rewarded?"

Anthony glanced at his watch. For a moment or so, there was a far-away look in his eyes. He replied to the Inspector whimsically.

"Virtue, Andrew, according to King Robert of Sicily, finds a sure reward. The sentiment is echoed at Pentecost."

MacMorran smiled hopelessly. "Which means?"

"Just this, Andrew. For the moment, come to the bar with me and name your own particular brand of poison."

CHAPTER XII
MacMorran Makes His Arrest

Half-an-hour later, Chief Inspector Andrew MacMorran noticed that Mr. Bathurst was very much more concerned about the time than was his usual habit. The Inspector put down his glass for the fourth occasion. Each time that he did so, he observed that Anthony was looking at his watch.

"You mentioned 'virtue' to me a little time ago, Mr. Bathurst. I am beginning to think that you must have meant 'patience.'"

Anthony pushed the Inspector's glass over for further replenishment. "You're a good scout, Andrew, and I shall never regret our associations. We've worked together too long not to understand each other properly. I only hope that I've helped you as much as you've helped me."

MacMorran cocked an inquisitive head over his glass. "What are you trying to tell me? That you've brought me down here on a wild-goose chase?"

"No, Andrew. Come over here to this table. Bring your drink with you."

MacMorran took the chair on Anthony's left. The bar was filling more and more every minute. The Inspector recognized many of the more familiar faces.

"Who's here this evening, Mr. Bathurst?" Anthony replied with the names. Suddenly MacMorran leant over to him with a sharp gesture and seized his wrist.

"You have solved the case, Mr. Bathurst! I can tell by your manner. I'd lay a hundred to one on it."

"Yes, Andrew. I have solved *our* case." It was at that moment that Nelly Gwyn entered with one of the Corsican brothers.

Anthony whispered to the Inspector, back in the comparative shadows. "Victoria Garland and Peter Hesketh. 'Tollie' to you and me—and the late Mrs. Merivale."

MacMorran nodded quickly. "Go on."

"Go on where?"

"Tell me more of your solution. Are you certain of your man?"

"Utterly and completely. I know who killed Hugh Assheton. I know, too, who killed Vera Merivale. By the way, how do you like Claude Merivale's costume this evening? The R.U.R. stuff. Does it appeal to you as appropriate? For an evening of this kind? Revere has certainly come up to scratch and done the thing well. I shall be eternally in his debt."

MacMorran eyed him curiously. "What's behind all this? What's the costume got to do with it? You're as bad on this as you were on that suit of white duck."

Anthony shook his head, emptied his glass and smiled. "No—that was different. There's only one Robot here this evening, Andrew. I want you to be sure of that."

"Am I to make an arrest?"

"Got a warrant?"

MacMorran tapped his pocket. "You can leave that safely to me."

"You are content to act upon my instructions?"

"You've never let me down yet."

"Do your job quietly, then. With no fuss. On no account must there be anything like a scene. I must study Major Revere a little, you know. *You* should, too, if you take my advice. I recommend the idea. Look at what he's done for me."

"That goes with me, Mr. Bathurst."

"Right."

Anthony took an envelope from his pocket and scribbled words on it. He pushed it over to MacMorran. The latter read it and looked up in amazement.

He tapped on the envelope. "So here . . . in this case . . . I am helpless?"

"I told you before that you were, so that you shouldn't be disappointed now. Don't you remember? Still, we can't always get the verdict to go our way. Mightn't be good for us."

"When?" queried the Inspector.

"Whenever you like. Only do it quietly, as I said. Suggest a chat in Revere's office. That may sound attractive. You never know. There are such things as strange tastes. I'll be in there waiting for you. Abyssinia!" Anthony strolled off nonchalantly in the wake of Peter Hesketh and Vicky Garland. But his heart was racing perilously with excitement. If his plans had miscarried, he was on the brink of disaster.

MacMorran rose as Anthony left him. He watched Mr. Bathurst's broad shoulders disappear through the doorway. He re-read the few words that Anthony had just scribbled to him. He frowned. He couldn't afford to make a mistake. Then he took the cigarette stub from his mouth and ground it under his heel. He squared his shoulders to his unpleasant task. His mind was made up. His confidence in Anthony Bathurst had never yet been misplaced. There was no valid reason why it should be on this occasion. He deliberately left the bar apartment and walked back into the dance-hall. There was no sign of Major Revere. He had half-hoped to have been able to have a word with him.

The band had just stopped. Knots of people were drifting towards seats in various parts of the room. He could see neither Hesketh nor the girl who had just partnered him. Strange, he thought, all the people whom he saw now around him were strangers to him. All the "familiars" seemed to have vanished for the time being. At last he saw the figure for which he had been looking. He walked slowly over to the Robot. Claude Merivale was joking and talking with Leo Meux and A.J. Carstairs. As he neared the group of people, MacMorran couldn't help thinking how high-pitched and bordering on the hysterical, Merivale's laugh was. Almost, as though he had some inkling of what was about to happen. MacMorran touched him lightly on the arm. Merivale turned quickly at the summons and moved away from Carstairs and Meux. The Inspector saw him raise his eyebrows.

"Yes?" he said sharply. His voice was thin and eager. "What can I do for you?"

MacMorran answered quietly, but a grim smile played round the corners of his mouth. "Pardon me troubling you, Mr. Merivale . . . you know me . . . we've met before . . . but would you be good enough to step over into Major Revere's private office? I want a word with you. Take my advice and come quietly."

"What do you want to say to me? What is it about?"

"A little matter of murder, Merivale. Don't tell me that you didn't understand that."

Merivale's face flushed. "All right. I'll come with you. But I warn you—you're making a very big mistake."

"We'll see about that! Thank you." The Inspector and the Robot figure walked across the dance-floor towards Major Revere's private office.

Laughter, fear and excitement are imperceptibly infectious! A mysterious hush settled over the room. Many pairs of eyes turned to watch the two retreating figures as they slowly made their way out.

CHAPTER XIII
Disaster

Anthony Bathurst waited in Major Revere's private office. Twice he looked at his wrist-watch. What he saw appeared to please him. He smiled. Everything that he had arranged should be in order now. He lit a cigarette, preparatory to MacMorran's coming. Well . . . Andrew was home at last . . . if not in the way that the Inspector had himself anticipated. He tossed the burnt match that he had used for his cigarette into the grate. Women were strange, subtle creatures, to be sure. Female men, perhaps . . . but something more than that when it came to the finest and most sympathetic analysis. He heard the sound of approaching footsteps. The critical moment of the whole inquiry was at hand. Anthony went and stood by the door. He then heard the subdued tones of the Inspector's voice; he could catch nothing in the nature of a reply. The door began to open. Anthony helped. He pulled it back by the handle. MacMorran entered behind his companion. He closed the door with an almost exaggerated care. Anthony turned and then swung round on to the Inspector with something suspiciously like apprehension.

"Inspector," he said sharply. "We must waste no time. We must get to the truth at once."

The Robot-like figure that stood by them did something to its hair. "I am sorry to hear what you said about wasting time, Mr. Bathurst. Because I'm very much afraid that's just what you are doing."

MacMorran stared in amazement. "Who are you?" he exclaimed.

"My name is Merivale," came the reply. "Jill Merivale."

"Where is your brother," demanded MacMorran.

"I've no idea. He left me some time ago. Did you really want him and not me? If so, why didn't you say as much when you first spoke to me?"

MacMorran cursed scientifically. He turned towards Anthony Bathurst, evidently for guidance.

"Sit down, Miss Merivale," said Anthony, indicating one of Revere's leather arm-chairs. "I'll apologize to you on behalf of the Inspector. But we wanted a little chat with your brother, Claude, and the Inspector here is disappointed that he'll have to go without it. You must make allowances for him."

Jill Merivale smiled. MacMorran stood there—stony faced.

"The Inspector didn't know that you and your brother had changed places." MacMorran glared. "Any more than I did." MacMorran came near to fury.

"That's all right, Mr. Bathurst," returned Jill Merivale, "but what was it actually that the Inspector wanted to talk to Claude about? I might be able to answer any questions . . . that the Inspector desired to ask."

There ensued a silence. It was eventually broken by Mac-Morran.

"I don't think that I need trouble Miss Merivale, thanking her all the same for the offer. I'll reserve my questions until I meet her brother again."

Anthony looked disappointed. "That's awkward, Inspector. I'm afraid it may be some considerable time before that is likely to happen."

"That reminds me," contributed Jill with the suggestion of an afterthought, "my brother left a note behind for somebody. I'd forgotten every word about it. What was the name, now? I must look."

She fished in a dim recess of her person and produced a letter. She glanced at the inscription on the envelope.

"Why it *is* for you, Inspector, all the time! What an idiot you must think me."

The Inspector accepted the letter suspiciously.

"Read it," said Anthony with peremptory directness, "let's hear what he has to say."

MacMorran opened the letter.

"My dear Inspector," [he read], *"our last bout goes to you—and yet in a way to me! What a game of topsy-turvy it has been. I gave myself up to you in the first place. You were on top. Then you lost your grip and I got on top. 'One all' as we might say in sporting terms. That was the first encounter. Then we joined swords again. I was on top to begin with. Then you turned the tables on me. You win. I lose. As a result of this second contest, I am left with nothing to say to you beyond—Good-bye! Not au 'voir you observe, but most definitely "good-bye.' I have the honour to remain, Yours sincerely, Claude Merivale. P.S.—My sister will have mementoes of me for both you yourself and Anthony Bathurst, for I knew that both of you would be inclined to beg a hair of me in memory and bequeath it as a rich legacy unto your heirs. C.M."*

MacMorran handed the letter to Anthony without comment. Mr. Bathurst in turn read it and stood there thinking hard. Jill intervened.

"Well . . . is everything all right now?"

"Oh, yes," remarked MacMorran. "Quite. I'm merely done on both sides. Public Pie-can No. 2. Thank you very much indeed. All the same, your clever brother hasn't finished with me yet. I'll see you outside, Mr. Bathurst, in ten minutes' time. Good night, Miss Merivale . . . and . . . er . . . congratulations."

"O.K., Inspector, I'll be there." This from Anthony.

The Inspector stalked out in high dudgeon. The moment he had gone, Jill Merivale came across to Anthony Bathurst. Her right hand was outstretched and her eyes were shining.

"Thank you, Mr. Bathurst," she said simply. "Thank you from the bottom of my heart. Claude will have left Croydon by now."

"Over half-an-hour ago, Miss Merivale. I gave him plenty of time before I let MacMorran move."

"I shall never be able to thank you enough. Never! No matter how old I live to. That idea of yours worked out splendidly." She held out her hand again. "Good-bye. I don't suppose that I shall ever see you again. But I shall never forget what you have done for us tonight."

Anthony smiled at her gravely. "It took me a long time to make up my mind, Miss Merivale. I always feel that I must stand on the side of justice. I consider that I am doing so now. That is why I have acted as I have. Believe me, I did not come to my decision, either lightly or wantonly. I am delighted to have helped you. Good-bye."

She took his hand in hers and held it there. "Even now, Mr. Bathurst, I am certain in my heart of hearts that my brother is not a murderer. For I *know* that that is the charge which would have been brought against him for the second time. He did not murder Vera and he did not kill Hugh Assheton—and I don't care what evidence you brought against him."

"He did," replied Anthony.

The girl stopped and stared. "Did what?"

"He did kill Hugh Assheton. Poisoned him."

"But why . . . why . . . why?" Her incredulity was almost hysterical.

"Oh . . . for an excellent reason. You see, Miss Merivale, Hugh Assheton strangled your brother's wife. I am sorry. Good-bye." Mr. Bathurst turned and left her.

MacMorran had given him ten minutes and that ten minutes was nearly up.

CHAPTER XIV
Disclosure

Anthony took the wheel and regarded MacMorran at his side with due solemnity. MacMorran stayed silent.

"Well?" MacMorran shook his head.

"Emily?" questioned Mr. Bathurst. . . . "or shall we eat out somewhere?"

"Either suits me."

"Good. That's nice and sociable of you. We'll make it Emily then. I'll talk during the meal, Andrew."

"You're tellin' me," returned the Inspector. "I'll do the dumb act better than ever in history. An oyster compared with me, will be one hundred per cent all singing and talking." He slumped into his seat and Anthony drove home on a mileage of monosyllables. The car was garaged and under the influence of Emily's technique over four courses, the Inspector threw off his mood and warmed to something more like his usual cordiality.

Anthony poured out more beer. MacMorran melted like snow under warm sun. In the end, a smile crossed his features.

"Spill it," he murmured. "Not the beer. I give in. I know that you're dying to. It's been your show really from start to finish."

Anthony shook his head. "No, Andrew. No bouquets please. I don't deserve any. I've cleared the case up, possibly, but for a long time I was wandering round looking for the right turning, and when I found it, it was luck rather than any skill on my part that showed it to me."

"In your own words, Mr. Bathurst, I can bear to hear it all."

"You shall, Andrew. Fill up your tankard again and if you'd like a 'Laranaga' take one out of that box over there."

Inspector MacMorran, still smiling, accepted both invitations.

Anthony knocked the ash from his cigarette-end and settled himself more comfortably in his arm-chair.

"Assheton was one of three things in relation to Claude Merivale's wife." Anthony paused, "I am not sure which."

MacMorran's curiosity was excited. "What do you mean?"

"I'll tell you. He was *(a)* Her lover, *(b)* her prospective lover or *(c)* her discarded lover. I incline to the last. I think that Mrs. Merivale had allowed him to ... er ... cherish ... certain anticipations for a considerable period of time, which she suddenly withdrew from him. The result was tragedy. It was he whom Constable Pike Holloway saw entering the house—not Claude Merivale—on the evening of the crime. Merivale's admission that it was he himself was a lie. You and I both know that there was a likeness between the two men. I suspected, after a time, that Holloway had seen Assheton. In some ways it was my first deduction."

"Peculiar coincidence that," contributed MacMorran. "About the likeness, I mean."

"No," returned Anthony quietly.

"No?"

"More than that. Assheton was Merivale's half-brother. His father died when Merivale was a boy. His mother married again. This second boy was born to her. When she died, she committed him to Merivale's care. Her passion had been for her second husband and she adored this child of her second marital adventure. On her death-bed, Merivale promised her that he would stick to the youngster to the end. The love, you see, was intercrossed. He worshipped her. She adored Assheton. Merivale told me all this at Revere's this evening." Anthony paused.

MacMorran took up the questioning again. "I suppose Merivale went home and found Assheton with his wife. Was that the bundle?"

Anthony shook his head. "No. Merivale's interest in the case started on that late afternoon, when the finish of the day's work came, by one of those strange mischances that do occur in life. Merivale and Assheton changed from their costumes, used in *The Painter of Ferrara*, washed and cleaned up close together . . . and Merivale went away . . . in Assheton's white duck suit. Assheton went in his. I don't know, of course, who made the original mistake. The suits were exactly alike and the two men of similar size. You know that. You've seen the picture. Assheton went to Vera Merivale, quarrelled with her and strangled her. Merivale went to the Catena Club, and changed there into another suit that he kept in the wardrobe there so that he could keep his appointment at Brighton with Max Zinstein." MacMorran nodded.

"That is where I made my second step in deduction," went on Anthony Bathurst. "I knew that something had happened to Merivale that evening, that had caused him to go home, and throw his important appointment with Zinstein to the four winds of heaven. It was obvious from all his movements, that when he left the studio, he *intended* to keep the Brighton appointment. The question was—*what had* happened to him? Now the last thing that he had done at the Catena Club was to change his suit. A suit which subsequently was stolen from the wardrobe. I became most interested in that suit, Andrew, as you know. As he changed, from the *wrong suit*, mind you, he found a *letter from his wife to Assheton*. It was the hope that he hadn't found it, that made Assheton get the suit back in the manner that he did. I *think* that Merivale left the letter there. I am not sure. I meant to ask him but it slipped my mind. You can imagine now what happened next."

MacMorran nodded and drained his tankard.

"After a time, Merivale mastered his shock and went home. He went home in a condition of semi-stupor. He was amazingly fond of his wife and his discovery had stunned him. You know what he found when he arrived. He felt certain from what the letter had told him that Assheton had strangled her. The house was empty. It was Eva Lamb's evening off, remember. Assheton had used gloves for the killing and had *left the gloves behind* when he made his way from the house. Merivale found them. What was he to do? If he denounced Assheton, on the strength of the letter that he had found—he sullied the reputation for all time of the woman that he loved, the mother of his children—and—at the same time—broke the oath that he had sworn to his own mother! Was there a way out? He felt little desire to live as he looked at his wife's dead body lying there on the bed. He would confess to the crime himself! That was his first thought. The margin of time that the medical evidence could give would be too small to upset the story that he would tell. But then the thought of his two kids came to him." Anthony stopped again. He saw that MacMorran was following him eagerly. "And he toyed with the *idea of the dream*. What was there that could falsify it? Oh, Andrew—he was *clever* and a *man* as well. Think of it. There were the gloves. He knew that his story wouldn't hold water for a second unless he could show conclusively that the murderer *hadn't* worn gloves for the strangling. What did he do?" The Inspector shook his head. "He burned the gloves. After removing the *buttons*. I looked for them everywhere. A clever man, Merivale! I must repeat my eulogy of him. Then he deliberately tore his nail and made a scratch on the dead woman's throat. Bare hands—not gloves, you see! But the position of the scratch was faulty, as I pointed out to you, because he didn't make it with his hands at work on the throat but just by the nail itself. And here I'm a little proud of myself. For a deduction that I made. Mrs. Merivale had used a skin cream that evening when she went to bed. Assheton's gloves *must* have shown traces of it. But there was none on Merivale's hands, I am told. And none on his tie after he had taken it off at the station. After he had given himself up and told you his dream story. *But he had not washed at all!* Or bathed! Don't you remember how I questioned him with regard to that? Had he used bare hands to strangle his wife they *must* have been soiled. All these things caused me to suspect that Merivale might be shielding somebody. But who could it be? And why? Which brings me to the episode of the Worthing photograph." Anthony smiled and selected another cigarette.

"Jill Merivale—you've met her, Andrew—with her acute observation of the deck-chair groove set the ball rolling with regard to that. Merivale, when I showed him the snapshot, knew what I was after, that his wife was running another man, possibly, and *lied* about it. When he realized that the signal was set at danger he said the man in the photograph was he himself and that the place was in Belgium—but he failed to convince me. There was I again, you see, with the idea that there was a lover or an intending lover in Mrs. Merivale's personal circle. Well, as you know, Merivale went to trial."

"And was acquitted."

"Yes. Thanks to his sensational and ingenious defence. The trial over, and the verdict given, he was left free."

"What happened then?"

"I think this. He was left with a conflict of warring emotions. His desire for *personal* revenge upon Assheton, as compared with the law's, and his youthful promise to his dying mother. In the end the man triumphed. The feelings of the boy were submerged. He decided to 'get Assheton.'"

MacMorran broke in with an interruption. "Just a minute. I'm a trifle in doubt. Wasn't Assheton on his guard? Didn't he know that Merivale had found the incriminating letter in the white duck suit?"

Anthony Bathurst carefully considered his reply. "No. I don't think that Assheton *did* know. At any rate he couldn't be *sure*. I think that the letter was still in his suit when he recovered it from the Catena Club wardrobe; and that he wasn't *certain* if Merivale had found it. Merivale's silence at the trial would tend to confirm this view."

"What happened to Merivale's suit? The other one?"

"That point had worried me. It was returned to him. By post. Merivale told me that this evening as well. It purported to come from the Club—where it 'had been temporarily mislaid.'"

"Merivale knew, of course?"

"Naturally. But pretended that he didn't and started his general plan of campaign. He had always been friendly with Assheton. An eminently natural position—considering their relationship."

"Wasn't that generally known?"

"Not to most people. Assheton didn't want it said that his career had been brought about by any influence other than his own acting merits. There was to be no charge of nepotism levelled against him. Get the idea?"

MacMorran nodded his acceptance. Anthony continued his story.

"Merivale spent more time, and more time still, with Assheton. Went to stay at his flat. And gradually evolved the cunning of his killing. He waited to bring him death so that no suspicion should attach to himself. If, indeed, suspicion—no possible chance of definite *proof*. When he did determine the method of murder that he would use, it was almost as ingenious as his 'dream' defence. I'll tell you what it was, Andrew, though I can't give you the entire details. Merivale refused to give away one point about it. I know the reason that prompted him. It meant the inevitable incrimination of a third party."

"I can guess some of the story. It concerned our visit to the dentist's."

"Yes. To Mr. Aubrey Lewisham. But listen. Merivale noticed that Assheton had an upper denture. And his screen work was such that Assheton used a denture powder. To hold the teeth more securely. He would use this powder two or three times a day. Merivale, when he stayed with him, watched him like a cat and noticed this habit of Assheton. After any meal, for instance, he would renew the powder. One day, when Assheton was washing, Merivale took a cast of this denture, which, from his point of view, was step number one in the plan that he had formed. Can you tell me why he wanted this, Andrew?"

"I think I can. But go on."

"He wanted this—I will call it 'substitute' denture—so that no trace of his poison should be found in Assheton's mouth when the time came for him to die. The poison that Merivale used was one of the 'curare' group but he refuses, as I said, to give me further information thereon. He has many friends in London and one of them has undoubtedly assisted him. Merivale is loyal to that friend. He took his cast to Lewisham, *in the character of Assheton*, and—well, you heard Lewisham's story—you know how he arranged delivery and the covering of the various points in the direction of which he risked discovery. Even to the slipping of the receipt into a drawer in Assheton's flat when he was staying there. Remember the details of Aubrey Lewisham's story?"

"Very well. I'm beginning to see everything. As you say—a clever fellow."

Anthony nodded. "The cleverest, I think, taking everything into consideration, that I've ever encountered. His grand opportunity came at the Carstairs banquet at the Catena Club. When Assheton left for that dinner, his denture powder had been treated with the poison. This was simple for Merivale. The powder was kept in the bathroom and taken out by Assheton whenever he went out, knowing that he would need it. Merivale *knew* that directly Assheton had finished his dinner, he would retire somewhere—almost certainly a lavatory—to use the powder on his denture. He followed Assheton to the lavatory and locked the door, having previously obtained the keys from the case in the porter's room. Assheton sprinkled the poison on his denture and died within a few moments. Merivale removed the poisoned denture and substituted the other one that, had been manufactured by Aubrey Lewisham. He had just unlocked the door for departure when he heard Hill arriving with his consignment of towels and clean soap. Merivale could only scuttle back into one of the compartments. Where he stayed until Hill went again. He used the towel that he took from Hill's supply to wrap up the poisoned denture for taking away with him, and returned the keys to the case after locking the door again. Lewisham's set of teeth, with no fixing powder to help, was ill-fitting and Dr. Batchelor was quick enough to spot the fact. When I heard Lewisham's story, I began to understand dimly what had happened and vaguely, how Assheton had died. There you are, Andrew—full score up to the fall of the last wicket."

"Which wasn't Merivale's."

"No. I think he deserved the 'break' that we gave him. Don't you agree, now that you know all?"

"Perhaps," conceded the Inspector. "Though there's the Commissioner, you know."

"We'll keep Sir Austin Kemble quiet. Don't worry about that."

"You can attend to that part of it. I can't see myself doing it."

Mr. Bathurst rose and put his hand on the Inspector's shoulder. "Andrew," he said, "we *have* done right. I feel positive of it. *Tout comprendre, c'est tout pardonner.*"

"I'll take your word for that," replied Chief Inspector MacMorran.

"I thought you would," replied Anthony Lotherington Bathurst.

THE END

Manufactured by Amazon.ca
Bolton, ON